Phoenix

Phoenix

Simon Weston & Patrick Hill

BLOOMSBURY

First published in Great Britain 1996

Bloomsbury Publishing Plc, 2 Soho Square, London W1V 6HB

Copyright © 1996 by Simon Weston and Patrick Hill

The moral right of the author has been asserted

A CIP catalogue record for this book
is available from the British Library

ISBN 0 7475 2826 8

10 9 8 7 6 5 4 3 2 1

Typeset by Hewer Text Composition Services, Edinburgh
Printed in Great Britain by Clays Ltd, St Ives plc

PROLOGUE

The bitter wind from the east chilled him to the bones. His overalls and thick coat offered little protection from the sub-zero temperatures that the icy gusts brought, and he felt the cold these days. He had reconciled himself to his old age many years before.

Without lifting his head from the monotonous task of removing decayed leaves and assorted debris from the pathways and drives of the camp, he cursed beneath his breath. The droplets which formed at the end of his nose had frozen to the grey whiskers of his unkempt moustache and his eyes watered continuously, forming streams of water that snaked down his reddened cheeks. His mind wandered back to the days when he would never have had to endure the indignity of sweeping the ground clean for hundreds of army boots to walk upon. In those days he would have been the one scoffing at the efforts of the ragged figure that swept and tidied the camp daily. He tried to lose himself in memories of the days when he, Helmut Storr, had strolled among the leafy avenues of silver birch trees that lined the roads which criss-crossed the barrack blocks. In those days he had been the one who wore the uniform – the smart grey uniform of a sergeant in the Wehrmacht.

Nowadays the uniforms of the soldiers whose boots hammered down those pathways were green, and the pimple-faced young men who shivered in the cold spoke the English of every region in Britain. Men like those fresh-faced troops had once been his enemies. Now they were his employers. He cursed again. Still, at least he had a job. So many of the British barracks today were content to use their own young soldiers, the ones they called 'squaddies', to carry out menial duties, instead of employing civilian workers.

It was still early, just 6.30 a.m., and the camp was beginning to shake itself into its usual regimented lifestyle. The old man turned the corner of Number 41 barrack block automatically, not bothering to raise his eyes from the pathways before him; trying to shake loose from the spirits of the past and concentrate on his mind-numbing task. The lines of trees were bare, leafless skeletons. Now, as he slowly brushed his way down the path that ran parallel to them, the incandescent rays of the early morning sun sharply silhouetted their ghostly outlines. But Helmut Storr ignored the beauty of this crisp, clear January daybreak, and continued to shuffle past the row of single-storey barrack room buildings built over half a century before.

He would never be certain what made him look. It might have been the shadow that was cast against the barrack wall from the brilliant sunshine. Or it may have been instinct, for through his years he had developed an instinct for death.

Helmut Storr had witnessed violent death at close quarters many times before. The facial expressions of villagers executed because they would not betray the whereabouts of Tito's partisans were still seared into his mind from decades earlier. He still awoke in a cold sweat as the ghosts of friends lost long ago on the plains of blood that had been the Russian Front walked through his memory. But this was different. Before, he had been prepared: he had steeled himself for the nauseous feelings that would invade the pit of his stomach at the sight of futile killing. This time, he could only stare wide-eyed at the sudden image of death.

Suspended from one of the lower branches of a birch tree, the body swung in the chill wind. Stiff as a shop window mannequin it dangled two feet above the frozen ground, a wooden stool overturned beneath it. As it swayed it blocked out a beam of sunlight, enabling Storr to study the victim more closely.

He was clothed only in a blue tee-shirt and grey boxer shorts, which still bore the dark spreading stain of the man's own water, that human indignity that had been involuntarily released at the time of death. There were no socks or shoes. Storr looked harder at the black skin of the body and slowly let his eyes travel upwards. They followed the legs and went along the bare arms, beyond the thin white rope around the neck and upwards to the face. The old man gasped. The image of that face would stay with him until he too was called upon to face his maker.

A thin film of frost had covered the man's cropped, curly hair. The eyes bulged almost out of their sockets, and appeared to stare back at Storr. The tongue partly protruded from the mouth, fixed there after the body had finally given up the struggle of gasping for air and resigned itself to death. To Storr, that lolling tongue seemed to be an attempt to ridicule him – the hanged man's final grotesque private joke on whoever discovered his body.

Helmut Storr had worked at the camp for over five years, yet he had never seen a black soldier amongst the hundreds of British there. But it was no surprise to him, for he spared little time to scrutinise the troops who passed through. Suddenly the sound of several pairs of heavy army boots approaching from behind broke his morbid intoxication with the sight. Storr tossed away his brush and ran towards the sound, screaming with the hysteria that seizes a man confronted by violent death.

CHAPTER ONE

His head ached now: the effects of the beer were beginning to wear off. He glanced at the grazed and bruised knuckles of his right hand and winced when a jolt of pain shot through his arm as he gently attempted to move his fingers. His hand was probably broken. Slamming and punching against a metal door like the wild man that he had been the night before would get you a broken hand every time.

Outside, the opening and slamming of other cell doors in the corridor mingled with torrents of abuse aimed at the gaolers by the inmates. The rest must have been rounded up too.

The stench of his own urine from where he had made a 'personal protest' against the wall of the cell was now beginning to engulf him, blending with the odour of stale smoke and booze that enveloped his jacket. He wanted to puke.

Alone in the white-walled cell he sat upright on the bench that was laughingly called a 'bed', glancing at the graffiti scrawled on the bare surfaces by previous occupants as he searched his mind for the previous night's events. Christ, his head was thudding with every beat of his heart. The bright single-strip electric lighting hurt his eyes.

They had been unlucky – that was the only explanation. They had run straight into the cops. By rights there should have been no one around at that time of the morning; no one to raise the alarm. They should all have got away. Instead, they had managed to get just a hundred yards before they were picked up.

A dozen thoughts jostled for position in his head. Maybe they had been betrayed! Possibly they had been overheard. Had they mentioned the plan to anyone they shouldn't have done? Had they just been fucking stupid?

Perhaps he and the others had lingered at the scene too long, transfixed by what they had done. Just one minute sooner and he would have been back at the barracks, moaning about his thick head to the rest of the lads, and bragging about how he had managed to get his hands on the breasts of that big blonde barmaid – the one the lads had always fantasised about. The boys would be queuing for their breakfasts now, and asking where 'Take Away' was. That was the worst thing about having a name like Curry – it was so bloody easy to tag on to it a nickname like 'Take Away'.

He heard the voices of the police officers outside shouting in German, but he could understand only a little of what they were saying. They were calling him and the others names – him in particular, because he was British. At least the others were their fellow countrymen. The German police were used to people like Lance Corporal Nick Curry causing them trouble, but it was usually restricted to bar room brawls at weekends and getting involved in arguments with prostitutes when pissed. This, though, was something else.

He could still recall being mesmerised at the speed with which the flames had spread. He could hear the crackle as the fingers of fire licked the dry old furniture, and the roar of the wind-rush as the flames devoured the building. He could see the sky illuminated with the dancing colours reflected from the inferno below . . . and he thought he could hear the far-off shrieks of fear and agony from within the walls of the three-storey building. The scene was everything that he had imagined and more. It was the night that he, Nick Curry, had played God.

He and the five other 'believers' had come to Lübeck as ordered. Curry knew how to follow orders – he had spent his life doing that. They had wandered suburban streets lined with middle-class villas in the city which had until recently held the dubious honour of being the nearest large West German town to the border with the East. Once sightseers had visited Lübeck to see the border for themselves. But Curry and the others had come to Lübeck driven by hatred.

They had made their way to the hostel in the port area of the old city. The six of them had been able to walk right up to the place. At 3.30 a.m. there was no need for any masks: everyone would be asleep. As a man, they had lit the lethal bottles that splashed with petrol; as one they had aimed at the open windows on the second floor. They had not known, nor had they cared, how many were inside. The hostel housed the *Asylanten Gastarbeiter*, asylum seekers and guest workers, who had flooded not only Germany but most of Europe. To Curry's mind they had already ruined Britain with their greed, taking the jobs that people like himself were being denied. Now they had to be stopped. To him, they were the cancer that had to be cut out of society.

Firemen had been forced to wait for three hours for the heat to subside before they could enter the building where fifty immigrants from Togo, Zaire and Angola had been sleeping. They had brought out the bodies of five children and seven adults. There had been panic, fear and horror. But for Curry and his comrades it was a victory.

He had never contemplated capture. None of them had. They had been told that no one cared about the hostel. It would merely be logged as another racially motivated attack, one of over three hundred recorded in Germany annually.

For Curry, it presented the opportunity of being accepted into a new 'home', surrounded by friends of a like mind. It would be a new home that he would soon need. His discharge papers had come through and he would be out of the Army within two months – all because of one small blot on his record. It had just been bad luck that he had been caught shagging another man's wife. She had wanted it, hadn't she? Simply because he had followed his human instincts and screwed the bloody wife of some fresh-faced private he was being booted out, his career prospects worse than nil and with a record stamped 'unemployable' by some wanker of an upper crust commanding officer.

His friends had rallied around. This would never have happened in the old Army, he had been told. They had introduced him to other 'associates' who had pledged to look after him. All had 'believed'.

Curry ran his hand over the stubble of his dark cropped hair and automatically felt in the pocket of his jeans for a cigarette. He should have known that they would have taken them. But the mixture of drink, lack of sleep and drama had taken its toll on his memory.

He heard the voices of the German police officers outside his cell again. He could handle them, he told himself. He felt confident. Then it would be the turn of his own people: the Redcaps and the bastards from the Special Investigation Branch would be all over him like a bad rash. He assured himself he would hold out. After all, he 'believed'.

The sound of the morning papers dropping through the letter box on to the mat along the corridor of the apartment stirred the girl from her deep, beautiful sleep. It took a few seconds for her to regain her thoughts, still clouded by recollections of the hungry lovemaking that had lasted for most of the night. She brushed her tousled blonde hair from her face and stretched her long limbs across the giant double bed.

She moved her hand to her right, but instead of the hard-muscled body of the man who had driven her wild she felt only the coldness of an empty bed. Then the aroma of freshly made coffee, wafting from the open kitchen, soothed her anxious thoughts.

Without attempting to cover her nakedness she rose from the bed and walked to the open doorway of the kitchen. Her man raised his bright blue eyes from the newspaper and smiled warmly. She instinctively returned the smile, only to see him look away, distracted by something that he had been reading. She felt momentarily awkward with her nudity, and reached for a towel to wrap around herself.

Then she tiptoed towards where he sat in sweatshirt and jeans, slouched over the kitchen table, coffee in one hand while the other was gripping the newspaper. Gently she placed herself on his right knee and kissed his forehead. The kiss was not returned. Instead he softly patted her behind.

Indignantly she turned to study the newspaper too, and saw what had been absorbing him: the picture of a sobbing coloured woman and another showing rows of bodies covered by blankets, some pathetically smaller than others, laid out against the background of a burned out building. But the man was ahead of her. Two paragraphs in the body of the story, about a burned out hostel in northern Germany, had engrossed him, while the headline: 'BRIT SOLDIER HELD IN RACIST ATTACK ON GERMAN DEATH HOSTEL' completely transfixed him.

He was convinced. It was evidence of what he had told his former bosses at the paper, weeks before, when they had rubbished him. He had believed in the story then, and he still did. It had hurt his pride at the time. No one had wanted to know – mostly because it had been brought to their attention by him, Peter Macabe. And they had wanted Macabe out of the paper – out of Fleet Street even, after nearly twenty years.

A new breed of arsehole ran the newspapers today. Macabe had grown up in a world where experience and character and loyalty had counted for something on a national newspaper. But today that breed had been replaced by a Perrier-swilling generation of accountants who would stab a 'friend' in the back as they stood shaking his hand in welcome.

To the 'new men' he was a modern-day dinosaur. He was also past forty in an industry that now loved nothing better than to burn out its journalists by the time they were twenty-five. The bosses had chosen to ignore his story, no matter what the source might be.

Macabe muttered into his coffee cup: 'I knew it. And lo, it came to pass!' He jabbed a finger at the paragraphs which told of the arrest of the soldier. 'Some bloody Brit squaddie has got himself caught doing a bit of moonlighting, it would appear!'

In an attempt to defuse her man's interest, the girl shrugged her bare shoulders with an air of indifference. She knew the emotions and frustrations that were bottled up inside him.

He disregarded her phoney display of non-interest. 'What's the odds on it being our "Barmy Brigade" after all? I bloody well knew I was right. The guys were right – pity those bloody idiots didn't think so.' He remembered his initial enthusiasm when he had first been given the tip. All the men had wanted had been a few quid for their information. It had been rumours, but they had come from the people who should know. But it had all gone to waste because those who ran the newspaper wouldn't pay up – and because they had no further use for Peter Macabe. 'Shit, I let those blokes down, didn't I?' he whispered to himself.

He squeezed the girl tightly with excitement, feeling a wave of adrenaline flood his body. It was as if a vital cog had fitted into place in a huge machine. His mind was working again, and his old juices and instinct for a story ebbed through his veins.

'Christ, I want that story!' he hissed. 'I'd love nothing better than to rub it in the noses of those buggers back at the office. Sorry – my former office!' he corrected himself. 'They wrote me off as loony. They told me so! I bring them the story and they kick me into touch. I tell you, I want this story . . . I *need* this story.' As Macabe's voice rose the tones of his north-eastern origins began to filter through his usually nondescript accent. They always did when he got excited. 'I tell you, Jan, this could prove us right. We could teach the bastards that old Pete's not washed up yet!'

It had been a long time since the girl had seen him so enthused about a story. It had been a long time since she had known him actually want to go out and start digging for a story – not after the bosses had turned their back on him. She still worked amongst those men, and she knew what they said about Peter – that he was washed up, too old, not what the newspaper business was all about. He was one of the 'old brigade' who were now too expensive to keep on staff – a guy who found his inspiration at the bottom of a bottle. She had seen his strength and self-esteem slowly leak from him. But he had always smiled for her. He thought he was hiding the pain, but she had known better.

She made her living looking through lenses and taking photographs of faces. She knew from experience when someone was faking an expression. She had seen that look in Peter's eyes. But she loved him for his efforts to appear normal when those who ran the news desk had cut his soul from him.

It was okay for her. She took pictures, and she was good at it. She was younger than him, and had a greater life expectancy in the job. She was an up-and-coming freelance who showed potential and enthusiasm. And the bosses enjoyed looking at her. She was aware of it, and used that knowledge.

She pressed Peter's face to her chest. 'For God's sake, man, listen to yourself!' she urged. 'You sound like some cub reporter on his first story. Let it go, Pete, please! You've got your goodbye cheque from the office – just enjoy it for a bit. Don't go playing Woodward and Bernstein on me now. I don't care who told you what was going on, you can't go shooting off looking under beds for a bunch of crazy nutters at the drop of a hat.'

She stopped herself. Christ, she sounded like a wife! It had been eighteen months since he had moved in with her, and she had never had a go like this before. She had thought she had understood his pain, but now she realised that she had been ignorant of it. She had coped when he had got involved with arms dealers, and with Loyalist terrorists in Ulster. She had coped with the death threats. She had coped with his drinking after he was driven out of the newspaper. Now she thought it was about to begin again.

She looked directly into his eyes. They had always been gentle eyes, but now she saw something else. There was a new life in them. She knew that if she chose the wrong words here, displayed the wrong attitude, she could lose him.

'No, Pete! *You're* not going to go off on this one,' she added firmly. She felt him pull away slightly. 'This time *we're* going to have a shot at it. If you're right, we'll have a word-and-picture package. Then we can both show them who was wrong.'

He hesitated momentarily. It was a shit gamble for her; he knew that. He was now forty-two, after enjoying twenty years at the top of his profession. Once that life had turned sour his main blessing was that he and Janine Letterman had been lovers for the last four of those years. If the bastards could have seen him now, they would have drowned in their envy. There he was with a blonde who most men would have given a month's pay to have spent the night with, bouncing on his knee and prepared to throw in everything to back her man. For the first time since he had been spurned by the new boys of the industry he had loved he felt like a man nine feet tall.

'I have to call Reijo,' he blurted incoherently. 'I'll have to – '

She placed her hand gently over his mouth. 'Oh no, you're not!' she said, grinning. 'It's Sunday morning, and God made the seventh day for resting and screwing – especially when you haven't got to get up until the pubs open. Then you can take me out and buy me a slap-up Sunday lunch so I can build up my strength again!'

As he watched her gently rise from him and walk slowly towards the doorway, exaggerating the movements of her body, he knew he would not resist. He had never been able to. But now Peter Macabe felt alive again.

It was the sort of small detail that might so easily have been overlooked. But if you were a trained professional it was second nature to examine everything. And Sergeant Ray Matthews of the Special Investigation Branch was, if nothing else, a true professional.

He glared at the face in front of him. The young figure slumped forward exhausted on to the wooden table, clutching his head in his hands. The smoke from the interrogator's half-burned cigarette that teetered on the edge of the overflowing ashtray stung the boy's eyes and spread a murky haze over the tiny grey room. The single light cast shadows of the pacing Matthews that danced around the bare walls.

Matthews had tried everything in the book. The kid was a tough, cocky little sod, that was for certain. He would have to work quickly to seize the initiative. Stick within the book, Matthews had been told. He would do that . . . but only just. Matthews had gone back to the basic tricks that had always served him well. Disorientate the subject: that was always a good move. Never let him get enough sleep, or relax. Feed the boy with over-salted food to drive him mad with thirst. Give him just a mouthful of water to ease his craving . . . and then withdraw the wonderful liquid from under his very nose and lips. Simply give him barely sufficient, just as the rule book said.

Now Matthews focused on the small tattoo just above the young man's elbow. The symbol was a black rose entwined with barbed wire. True, it was one of several, and might easily have remained hidden amongst other markings of the kind often found on the bodies of young servicemen around the world. But Matthews had picked it out. Ten years of experience in the SIB had given him an instinct.

'No more of your crap! No more about it being the result of a night on the piss!' he spat in a harsh north of England accent. 'It's bloody coincidental that all you fire-raising bastards happened to be in the same place at the same time, and all happen to have one of those sodding tattoos, isn't it?'

Only the deep breathing of his victim could be heard in the room.

Matthews erupted. 'I want the truth, you little sod, and by God you'll give it to me before you get out of here – even if I have to beat it out of you. And believe me, after this little lot I'll have no second thoughts about doing just that. Fancy ourself as a bit of a hero, do we? Think we struck a blow for our cause, do we? Some blow mate, I can tell you. I expect those back home will be pretty bloody pleased with your battle record – let's face it, it's not everyone who can do this, is it?'

Matthews opened a large manilla envelope on the bare table and took from it a handful of blown-up black and white photographs, each showing a victim from the hostel fire. He pointed to the twisted bodies of three young children, their features burned away by the flames and their pitiful skeletons charred rigid in the throes of death.

'Yeah! Some bloody hero!'

Nick Curry raised his head from his hands and stared directly back at Matthews through narrowed, reddened eyes. 'Sergeant, the next time you shit, shit a hedgehog!' he snarled. Curry smirked at the realisation that, after almost two days of intensive questioning, he could still answer his interrogator back.

It was enough to take Matthews to the limit of his endurance. The burly six foot five sergeant wiped the spittle from his thick black moustache as the blood surged into his head, ousting any semblance of self-control from his body, and he levelled a back-handed blow at Curry's head. It took him side on and knocked him spinning from his chair.

Matthews glanced at the Redcap corporal who stood by the scratched steel door of the interrogation room. 'No one saw that, did they, corporal?' he growled.

The military policeman looked straight ahead and shot an

approving wink towards the SIB sergeant who was leaning over the sprawled young soldier.

Curry could taste his own blood flooding his mouth. The blow had taken him by complete surprise and his body was gasping for air. He checked his teeth and found that one of them was now loose. On hands and knees he dragged himself to the door and clawed his way up its scratched metal surface, using it as support for his shaking body.

'You'll talk, you little bugger. You'll be only too happy to spill your guts out to me by the time I've finished with you,' Matthews whispered into Curry's ear. 'You see, after what you've done no one cares about you any more – if they ever did in the first place. And don't think you can walk away from here and start pointing to the bruises – I know how not to leave any. You're on your own, my smart-arsed young lad. So you just tell me about yourself and those other bastards. How do you know each other, how – '

Curry spun his head round to meet Matthews face on and screamed, 'I can't, you stupid sod! Can't you see? They'll know I talked. They'll all get to know. It doesn't matter what you say. They'll know I turned on them,' cried Curry.

Matthews softened his tone. 'Who'll know? What the shit are you talking about? You needn't worry about the Krauts – they'll be dealt with. If this is your first time, we might be able to help.'

'It's not just the Krauts, don't you see?' sobbed Curry. 'It's the others. They always sort out their own – just like they did with The Thief. Just like they sorted out Adebeyo.'

Matthews rapidly searched his mind. The name Adebeyo was somehow familiar. Christ! He couldn't recall, not while he was in this rage. He knew he would recall it, but he needed time.

'I need help. I can't get it here. It's got to come from outside. I can't trust anyone here – it's too close,' muttered Curry. 'For God's sake get me some help!'

Matthews recognised the fear. It was not a fear of himself, the SIB man. This was something far greater, something uncontrollable. Curry was bargaining for his life, and both men knew it.

The smell of freshly applied wax polish clung to his nostrils. Its sickly sweet smell reminded him of his childhood days – of the occasions when he would creep into the forbidden front room of his grandparents' house, the room that was polished every day by his fanatically house-proud grandmother but never lived in since the death of her beloved husband. It had been his room. After he was gone, the grief-stricken woman had made the room a shrine to his memory, restricting herself to life in the rear parlour of the tiny terraced home in the Welsh valleys. Now the memory of those distant days flashed back, bringing with it a longing for a time when life had been so innocent.

Jim Scala found himself disturbed by the silence that surrounded him, sitting alone in the wood-panelled room where portraits of military figures and heroes from long ago looked down on him. Outside, men and women chatted, laughing and shouting as they lined the bar. The occasional tap of snooker balls being struck filtered through. He had chosen to be alone, sitting on the squeaking green leather sofa with only his thoughts for company. His own thoughts were generally the only company that he had these days. His new life had taken its toll, pitching him into a world of secrets and uncertainty where he knew no one and could not share his misery. Once he had relished the company that came with soldiering in the ranks. Now he deemed himself to be one of life's loners, unable even to tell his wife of his 'new life'. That, he assumed, had been the final straw in their already crumbling relationship. But this was the life he had chosen.

The whisky stood on the table in front of him. It was not his usual drink: he was a beer man by tradition and through personal taste. But he felt that this would be an occasion on which a stronger drink might be a more suitable friend than beer. As he fumbled for the envelope buried deep in the inside pocket of his jacket he glanced around at the rows of shelves crammed with leather-bound books that, between them, must have covered the entire history of warfare and the characters who had fought it. It was a room filled with stories of momentous events that had changed history. Now the moment when his own life would be changed had arrived. After days of ignoring the long white envelope, as a helpless spendthrift attempts to ignore the mound of bills that follow a mad spree, he had hidden himself away in the Lawrence Room to face the moment of reckoning. He reached for the glass and took a swift gulp of the inviting brown liquid. The harsh smell overpowered the sickly odour of the polish as the whisky burned a route down his throat and created a warming glow that seemed to spread to his entire body.

Bracing himself, he quickly tore open the envelope and began to read the contents of the letter it contained. Everything was as he had expected. Yet, surprisingly, his hands had ceased to shake. He felt in control of himself.

The few business-like passages in the letter spelled it out. She wanted an end to it, and had eventually found the courage to do something about it. She wanted her freedom, and she wanted the children too. They hoped that the whole thing could be settled amicably with as little distress as possible to all parties, especially the children. She had claimed 'irreconcilable differences' between them. There was no family home to be fought over, since she and the kids lived in a rented bungalow on a grim little estate in Surrey. They had never possessed a home of their own. He had promised one, but somehow they had never got round to it. The Queen had always been their landlady, since she owned everything about him.

He felt angry. She was about to end the marriage that he tried to make himself believe he had fought hard to sustain. But in his heart he knew that he had attempted to believe in a lie. He had done nothing to try and keep the marriage sound. Of course it wasn't all his fault. Circumstances had killed any chance of the marriage's survival years before. His overwhelming passion for another mistress had seen to that. This divorce was probably the only inevitable thing in Jim Scala's entire life.

He took another sip from the crystal tumbler and ran his fingers over the thin scar that ran down the right side of his face. He fought desperately to recall distant images of the pretty, dark-eyed teenage girl whom he had met shortly after joining the Army. There had been love; there must have been, his thoughts insisted.

His memory opened the floodgates to a score of visions from the years before – the tender moments of their lovemaking, their laughter; sharing emotional moments as lovers do when they are about to be apart for a long time. There were recollections of tender moments when he returned from a tour of duty in foreign parts as ordered by his Army bosses. Angie had been there waiting. It was easy for him to remember the good times. She had always been there, he thought.

But he had not seen the anguish. He had not been around to see the crying, the endless nights of pain, waiting and wondering whether her man would return, or whether he was dead. No, he had never seen those. He had been too busy trying to stay alive in some far-flung outpost of the world – the burning deserts of Iraq, the steamy jungles of Central America or the dangerous street shadows of Northern Ireland.

That, after all, had been the job. That was what he was paid for, what he was good at. His lust for adventure and desire to prove himself had probably taken over his attempts to keep the relationship alive. He had insisted on trying for 'The Regiment'. He had been included among 'the best' when he found himself chosen. He was proud; he felt himself to be somebody at last. He had escaped the small-mindedness of his upbringing in the grim streets of Merthyr Tydfil. He thought Angie had understood, but had never really looked for the fear in her eyes. He supposed he had been too busy getting her between the sheets on every homecoming to notice that.

This was obviously her revenge, he insisted to himself. She was even taking Sean and Gemma, taking them from their father. The anger surged once more, so he gulped the final mouthful from his glass and then gently breathed out. Possibly the drink would make things seem clearer. Now, in his mind, he conceded that he had never really got to know his children either. In both their lives he could surely not have been around for more than a few months. His memory had played tricks on him.

Perhaps she had found some other bloke. That must be it. Some hairy-arsed little greaseball had stepped into his place. But he still felt he might have a chance. He could show her what a real man was all about. Let's face it, he thought, few men in civvy life had seen what he had seen or done what he had done.

Reality returned to his churned up brain. Angie had simply had enough. His mind told him that he could still win her back, though his heart warned him against it. His pride was hurt. She was his woman, but the reality that she would never be completely his woman ever again was now flooding his body. He threw his head back to rest on the sofa. Piece by piece his life and hopes had been chiselled away from him. The Army didn't want him – not since his injury and that cock-up in Bosnia. Angie had been there for him when he had come back. She had been there whilst he recovered from the injuries. He ran his hand over the scar again, and over the leg that still occasionally caused him pain. She had supported him when he had to face up to leaving his beloved SAS. But she had also been there when the man in the smart clothes with the plummy accent had come to visit him and make him an offer. Angie had seen the delight that Scala had shown when offered the lifeline of some murky job with the people she had assumed to be in Intelligence.

Now Scala took stock of his life, surveying his immediate world. He had rented a room at the Union Jack Club, which provided accommodation, a social setting and a meeting place for former and existing servicemen on the south bank of the Thames. To Scala, the smart club and the hospitality that it afforded were a haven. Yet he had convinced himself that this was only a temporary measure while he got himself sorted out. He had been there six weeks, since Angie had shown him the door.

Scala was still lost in thoughts when the door opened, and failed to hear the cheerful young barmaid call his name. She repeated it, hauling Scala back to the present.

'There's a telephone call for you Jim,' she said. 'It's the second time the fella's called. Sounds sort of stuck up!'

Scala grimaced. 'Just what I needed,' he sighed. 'Still, I suppose I'd better see who it is. Ta very much, Glenda.' He forced a smile and gestured to the pretty redhead to replace the drink in his glass.

He had a shrewd idea who would be calling. Few people knew of his existence, after all. Once again, Angie would have to wait.

CHAPTER TWO

The daily BA Flight 981 from Berlin had touched down at Heathrow on schedule at 8.40 a.m. The two men had travelled light, enabling them to skip the usual airport baggage reclaim formalities. The car had been waiting for them as ordered, by the exit doors to Terminal 1, and by 9 a.m. they were already en route to central London among the rush hour traffic.

The drive seemed interminable, and the older of the two men grew more irritated with every minute. Always an impatient passenger, he whistled between his teeth in an attempt to disguise his frustration and drummed his fingertips on the top of his briefcase throughout the journey.

Despite the expertise of the driver, the journey to the nondescript new office block in the heart of London's Docklands took almost ninety minutes. And now Colonel David Matherson was waiting again. He cursed Jim Scala for making him wait, although he conceded that he had given the man little warning. But Matherson considered that if one of his men was held on a retainer basis then he should expect to jump when called to do so.

Matherson's aide knew the signs. He knew that his boss would be as tense as a coiled spring until he had got this latest little exercise off the ground. Alex Carter had been selected personally by Matherson to be his aide at a time when the SAS captain had thought his career was washed up. Now he remained loyal to Matherson – the man commanded loyalty, he felt, whatever else kind of bastard he might be.

Carter attempted to calm Matherson with small talk and the offer of tea. Tea generally helped. As they waited, the two men stared out from the fifteenth floor over the toytown maze of new office blocks and waterways beneath them. It seemed an age ago that the bombers had returned, and Canary Wharf still bore the scars of that visit – a visit that had brought death and destruction. Matherson and Carter surveyed the attempts to cover the scars. To Matherson those scars were a constant reminder, if he ever needed it, of what his job was all about. He was in the front line in the war against the terrorist scum who carried out actions like this. Matherson was still a soldier at heart, and this was his battleground.

They had left early that morning, and had made good time on their journey from London to Folkestone. It had been a busy few days. Macabe had spent much of the time on the telephone, making arrangements. Janine had worked her shifts as usual, but told her bosses that she had been asked to take on another assignment. She would tell them about it when she got back. As a regular freelancer she had to seek permission for time off, but she had some time owing to her and they had agreed. The picture editor still fancied his chances, and she knew how to flirt and how to get her way. Just leave the carrot dangling long enough.

Macabe and Janine arrived at the Channel Tunnel rail terminal early. The aged dark green BMW that had been his pride and joy for more than eight years could still out-perform most of the other vehicles on the road. They stocked up on duty-free and then took their place in the queue of cars being loaded on to the train for the thirty-five-minute crossing to Calais. Despite the hassle of the journey and the early start, Macabe, watching Janine's long blonde hair blowing freely in the breeze, thought she looked stunning. The tight-fitting jeans had been expensive, but looking at the way they clung to her body he knew the money was well spent. Macabe felt good. He was embarking on a new adventure with a beautiful woman at his side. It was just like the movies.

As they waited, his mind flashed back to that meeting several months before. He had taken the call in the office and agreed to meet the men, though with reluctance. Aldershot was by no means his favourite place, and the prospect of going out there to meet a gang who claimed to be a mixture of former and existing members from 2 Para had held little appeal. The dismal smoke-stained pub that they had selected for the meeting did little to enhance his mood either.

But they had promised that he would hear something of interest, and within minutes of meeting the short toothless man who walked with a stick – the result of being in the wrong place at the wrong time on a call-out in County Armagh, he was told – Macabe had listened. His instinct told him that the man who whistled as he spoke was truthful. He spoke with too much authority and detail to be lying. The men would provide names and incidents for Macabe's story, he assured him. The Paras had served in Berlin, they had heard of the meetings, and they would tell all – if the price was right.

But the people on the news desk had scoffed and refused to cough up. They didn't want Peter Macabe. They thought he was a has-been. The story had gone away. And now the hack whom they had dubbed a washed up piss artist was out to prove them wrong.

The telephone on the desk buzzed. Carter picked it up, and heard Matherson's secretary.

'Send him in,' Carter said softly. 'He's here, sir.'

'About bloody time as well!' snapped Matherson. Then, recognising his own dark mood, he swiftly attempted to conceal it. He believed it was a sign of weakness to show that one was ruffled, and he had always thought that one could get more out of a man with a more human approach than by being abrasive. He blamed his anger and irritation on the journey and the God-awful hour at which he and Carter had been forced to set out.

The door opened to reveal his secretary, clad in her almost obligatory smart blue suit and blouse. She ushered in the tall dark man with the scar.

Scala walked into the centre of the room, each footstep sinking into the deep-pile beige carpet. He had quickly changed out of his casual clothes and now stood before Matherson and Carter in a smart blazer and grey slacks. His only concession to being a rebel had been to wear a white roll-neck jumper in place of the usual white shirt and tie. He knew that Matherson would be assessing his appearance; he always did – Matherson expected a great deal of his men.

Matherson scrutinised Scala for any trace of the limp that occasionally dogged him. On this occasion he saw none. Just as well, he thought.

'Sit!' uttered Matherson in a tone that was half commanding and half requesting, avoiding having to use Scala's name.

Scala raised his eyebrows and over-emphasised his reply. 'Thank you very much, sir!' he said quietly. It was a rare visit to the 'office' for Scala, who was normally kept at arm's length from where the decision-making was done. He presumed this would be an exception. For that reason he was quietly enjoying the air of mystery and urgency that had gripped him since receiving the telephone call.

Scala disliked Matherson. The man had used him, almost got

him killed, like a lot of other poor sods who did his dirty work. Yet Scala knew in his heart that he would go on being used by Matherson, for the man had provided him with hope and the only future that Scala could possibly expect. True, it had now cost Scala his marriage and family, and almost his life. But it had also put some purpose back into his life. The SAS had once been his sole reason for being, as he saw it. That had all gone pear-shaped in Bosnia. But this man had given him a second chance.

Matherson fumbled with the papers on his desk. 'Alex and I have just got back from Germany,' he began.

'Must have been nice for you,' remarked Scala, betraying just the slightest trace of his Welshness.

'Cut the comic crap!' hissed Matherson. 'Bloody awful journey – we've been running around like blue-arsed flies from one place to another. It seems there's a pile of shit building up that's heading straight for the fan. We've been down at the barracks in Hohne with some of our Army chaps. Don't know if you read in the newspapers about a bit of an upset that's going on at the moment . . .'

Scala shook his head. He had indeed read something, but he wanted to put Matherson through the hoop by making him explain the whole background. Let him earn his fat pension after all.

But it was Carter who picked up the briefing. 'One of our squaddies has got himself caught with a pack of bloody hooligans who burned out a hostel. Killed quite a few of our coloured brethren – a real mess. The SIB have got him now.'

Matherson broke in again. 'The bloody idiot got himself caught, which is bad enough, but then our friends in the SIB discovered it wasn't just the result of a night on the piss with a bunch of locals. Seems he may belong to an organised group of them – the Black Rose mob or something like that. Sounds a bit mad to me, I must admit – like a bunch of schoolkids getting up to naughty things, playing at being terrorists.'

Scala nodded his agreement.

'The problem is,' continued Matherson, 'that our young soldier started to blab. Wanted to talk to someone from outside, someone from London. He seemed shit scared of something or someone – wanted to do a deal.'

'And did you, sir?' Scala chipped in.

'I'll come to that later . . . So our little bird wanted to sing, and that's how we got involved.'

Matherson sat back in his chair, almost resignedly. He could have done without all this, but the powers that be had decided it was a job for Matherson's little band. On paper, his outfit did not even exist. It was only funded by sleight of hand between the Home Office and the Ministry of Defence. No one would ever acknowledge the existence of Matherson's little clean-up brigade that took care of incidents involving British servicemen, past or present. But when the shit did hit the fan, the people in power always seemed to know where to come. And now Matherson was tired. His department was at full stretch, his clean-up people operating all over the bloody place from Bosnia to Hong Kong, and now the Micks across the water were acting up again. Matherson glanced out of the window at Canary Wharf once again.

'Well, he sang well enough,' he went on. 'The problem is that what he sang about left a bad taste in a lot of people's mouths. It seems that our little bird may not be on his own. How should we put it? It would appear that there may be others of his persuasion.'

Carter broke in. 'The lad's name's Curry, serving with the Royal Kent Rangers. Been out in Germany for about three years.'

The mention of the regiment made Scala raise his eyebrows. He knew of the Rangers and their traditions; knew how highly the regiment's history was regarded by the military hierarchy. Even the pen-wielding civil servants who nested in the corridors of power within the Ministry of Defence in Whitehall would be aware of the Royal Kent Rangers.

'Fine bunch of lads,' he muttered. 'Bet our Mr Curry is a popular lad with his bosses at the minute.'

Matherson ran his hand over his slicked back fair hair, opened a thick file that lay on his desk and continued speaking without looking at Scala. 'Some of our colleagues in the other branch have also been busy.' Matherson put a distinct emphasis on the word 'other'. 'They have information that would suggest these Black Rose bandits are not your usual kind of tin-pot extremists. Not much is known about them, but what there is makes quite interesting reading.

'You see, according to our friends in Germany from the Protection of the Constitution . . .' He paused as he detected a nervous shuffle from Scala's seat. 'In layman's terms, the German equivalent of our MI5,' he explained in a schoolteacher's sardonic manner for Scala's benefit. 'They've been following our Black Rose brothers with some interest. It's known as the 'brotherhood in arms'– generally speaking they're a bunch of right-wing extremists and neo-Nazis who think Hitler had the right idea about a lot of things, particularly about our coloured friends and minorities.

They see Europe as an exclusively white club and everybody else can go to hell.

'It would appear that some of their members have been playing at soldiers as mercenaries in Croatia – something that goes back to the old days of the Ustase, the old Croatian nationalists. Christ, they even walked around in Nazi uniforms saluting each other with "*Heil Hitler*". According to our German counterparts they've now had their training and want to expand elsewhere. The trouble is, the German security bods think they're armed to the bloody teeth.'

Scala felt more and more like a schoolboy being lectured by his headmaster as Matherson spelled out the scenario that had increasingly worried his counterparts in Special Branch and MI5. He told of how the fascist groups within Britain were growing in numbers and violence. There had been a spate of highly professional yet brutal bank and security raids over the last six months, which Intelligence sources estimated had netted over £3 million. They feared the haul was destined for the coffers of the right-wing extremists, not simply in Britain but in Europe. It had come at a time when cash raised by fascist groups through drug trafficking, rock concerts and general fund-raising had also doubled. There had been a virtual civil war between rival factions as they struggled for power and supremacy. There had been beatings, and there had been at least one murder which police believed to have been related. But that had all stopped now. Agents within the various groups had reported a united front amongst those whom Scala had always dismissed as limp-minded thugs.

'What our masters are worried about is that the Black Rose brethren now want to bloom into something even more sinister, and turn their attention to targeting anyone who opposes them.' Matherson grinned, happy at his little pun. 'And if any of our fine lads in uniform are mixed up in anything like this I bloody well want to know about it!' he went on firmly.

'How the hell did a kid like Curry get himself mixed up with that lot?' Scala interrupted.

Matherson rose from his chair and walked to the window. He was a short man, but carried himself straight enough to give the illusion of being taller.

'God only knows, Jim,' he sighed. Scala was taken aback by the sudden informality of Matherson calling him by his first name. 'But there's something else that the little sod came out with. Remember a case a year or so ago, about a coloured lad serving in Germany who hanged himself?'

Before Scala could answer Matherson continued. 'A lad called Adebeyo, John Adebeyo. He was found hanged at the Allenby Barracks where the Rangers are stationed. Hell of a fuss – his parents said he was bullied and all that. Of course the MoD says it was all bollocks, but the parents kept asking for an inquiry and all that bloody stuff. The newspapers loved it all for a while, but then as far as the public was concerned it all died down. Curry now reckons there was something else – claims it wasn't suicide after all. The little bugger called it "justice". Curry reckons some of his mates had something to do with it.'

Throughout his years in the service Scala had heard various stories of racism within the ranks. The stories would not go away, but he had learned to ignore them. It was a fact of life.

'What does Curry stand to get out of telling all this?' he asked.

Carter explained. 'Well, he reckons he's been rumbled by getting caught. He doesn't feel safe any more. He'll only tell us so much, because he wants to be protected. We're getting him out of Germany. The little bastard only had a couple of months to go before he was out anyway. Caught screwing a married woman – so he's out. His prospects don't amount to very much. He wants our help – thinks the bogey men might come for him.'

Matherson had listened to enough. With a fresh air of authority that took Scala by surprise, he made great play of straightening the creases from the jacket of his grey suit and off-handedly began to brief Scala on the role he had in mind for him.

'Anyway, old lad, this is where you come in. You're going back into the ranks in Germany. Find out if there's any truth about this Black Rose connection, then report back. Basically, we can't afford the publicity, don't think the bods in the Foreign Office would be too pleased about seeing some of our brave lads mixed up in a movement that's hell-bent on kicking black arses all over the place. Let's face it, it would make a mockery of a so-called united bloody Europe, wouldn't it?'

Matherson had spoken in a matter-of-fact fashion. Having him instruct you, Scala considered like being at the receiving end of a pleasant suggestion. It had been the same on the first occasion, when Matherson had come to Hereford. There had been no blustering – not like you saw it in the movies. It had been a calm, man-to-man chat, nothing forceful. Matherson had handed Scala a lifeline when his army career had seemed to be over. He had given him the opportunity to serve his country and become involved. He would not be a full-time spook – just someone whom Matherson might call on to help out from time to time. For that, he would receive a retainer each month.

Certainly there might be dangers. But Matherson knew that, despite the SAS man's weariness, he secretly thrived on the adrenalin of action. The first job in Belfast had proved that. Once the adrenalin had started flowing, Scala could be relied upon to do anything. There had been a few other jobs and Scala had muttered his discontent, but he had always come back and it certainly wasn't for the pittance that he was being paid. Matherson knew it had cost him his family. But Matherson also knew that Scala would keep on coming back for more, that he would obey.

'You were with the Engineers weren't you, Jim?' he asked, already knowing the answer. 'Perfect!'

The freezing rain tapped incessantly against the window. It was impossible for him to see through the glass on this grim January night. Outside the temperature had plummeted to –3 degrees centigrade, but Leon Mountjoy ignored the weather and busied himself in preparation. There was a great deal that needed to be covered. This would be his chance, and he would probably not get another like it.

As he flicked through his files in the tiny, scruffy room that was his study he did not hear the gentle tap on the door. He was submerged in a history of events. The second tap was louder, and this time accompanied by the sound of his wife summoning him downstairs for the family meal. Distracted from his task he swore, but only quietly for fear of his wife hearing him. He would be there presently, he called. They should start without him.

Once again he took hold of the stack of files, handling them like a jeweller with precious stones. His life's work was here. For twenty-three of his forty-seven years this small, insignificant-looking man had been besotted by the cause. Growing up in London's East End after the Second World War, the son of a Jewish mother and a Protestant father, Leon Mountjoy had witnessed at close quarters the anti-semitism which still existed despite the end of the war fought to end Nazism. Shocked by what he had seen, he had vowed to continue the fight. For his pains he had been laughed at, ridiculed and ignored. But not for much longer. He had seen the evil at work, seen the violence, seen the threats – and he could see the danger. Now was his chance. Leon Mountjoy, small-time legal executive from a modest terraced home in North London's Muswell Hill, was about to make his mark.

It had come as a thunderbolt when the television people had said that they wanted to speak to the old campaigner, to give him the opportunity to speak about the work that he and his colleagues had been doing for years. The anti-fascist campaigners like Mountjoy, were to him, the eyes and ears that would protect society. This would be his platform.

He put the files back in order in the cabinet: the file on the infiltration of youth clubs in Scotland and the Midlands; the file on the soccer riots and on Combat 18; the file on the increase in the number of nationalist councillors on local authorities; the file which documented the campaign against a list of famous international sports personalities whose only common denominator was that they were coloured; the file on the growth of violence and international links to the Loyalist paramilitaries in Northern Ireland, and on the presence of 'exchange squads' who carried out each other's violent attacks across European frontiers. That last file was tagged *'Die Schwarze Rose'*. It was all there, and Leon Mountjoy would soon be able to expose the terrifying reality of the campaign which he had codenamed 'Phoenix'.

It was always the same. Scala woke with a start in a cold sweat, panting and trembling. It was not like anything he had known before, and it kept recurring.

Nothing in the dream had changed for the last month. Scala found himself alone, in a dark place, running down a long, endless corridor. Then the faceless figure, the flash, the pain and the darkness . . . and Scala had woken in terror each time. The nights of broken sleep were beginning to take their toll. He felt drained, as if he had run a series of marathons.

It was still early, just after 5 a.m. But Scala knew that he would not be able to return to the luxury of sleep. He switched on the bedside lamp to reveal the small, cramped room in the Union Jack Club that was his for as long as he paid his rent. Switching on the light of the adjoining bathroom, he plunged his head beneath the cold water tap in the basin in the hope of shocking himself from his terrors.

Scala stared at himself in the mirror, examining his scar closely and gingerly feeling it as a reminder of the moment when he had faced death and won. The tissue was smooth now, and the pain gone. But as he stared at the old wound Scala recalled the moment when he had been hit by shrapnel amid the storm of flames and death which he had brought down upon himself in Bosnia. He had called in the NATO aircraft that had bombed the Serb column, knowing that he was too close to escape. Lucky not to have lost his right leg, he still carried the scar of the jagged wound and still tended to walk with a slight limp. It had cost him his career in the SAS. It had cost his partner his life.

Scala's bright blue eyes were pale and drawn as he tossed back the lock of coal-black hair that tumbled on to his face. He forbade himself to allow the dreams to worry him, but to no avail. Jim Scala felt like a man losing his grip on reality.

Despite the early hour, he started to dress. He would make an early start on his trip to that grim little housing estate in Surrey to see his children. As a part-time father, it was his turn to spend the day with Sean and Gemma. He dared not speculate on when the next such opportunity might arise.

CHAPTER THREE

It felt good to be out in the clear country air once more. In cities Scala felt stifled. Possibly it was his upbringing among the claustrophobic terraced streets of Merthyr that had given him the urge for open spaces. He had never understood the reasoning.

Now he felt good. He had shaken off the terrors of the night and was enjoying the company of his children. Sean had grown since Jim had last seen him. He was now almost eight, with the same dark looks as his father. The blue eyes were piercing. Gemma, two years younger, was the image of her mother, Scala decided. Both children had been pleased to see their father – at least Angie had not attempted to turn them from him. The idea to go to the farm, to allow them to feed the animals and play in the open spaces, had been Angie's and Scala had not opposed it. It had been a success.

Now he watched the two of them in silence as they chewed their way through the traditional hamburger, fries and Coke of a day out with Dad – a day that would end all too soon. It was a scene that had been played out on a dozen occasions before. But this time, Scala could not shake off the need to show his affection to his children. He cuddled and hugged them more than at any time he could remember. He even told them how much he loved them, how much they meant to him – something that he rarely allowed himself to do. It was as though he might lose them at any moment, and never have the chance to tell them again.

His father's sudden urge to hold them was almost overpowering for Sean. It felt strange – as though something was wrong. He was still learning that Mummy and Daddy didn't want to live with each other any more. But he was used to Daddy being somewhere else. His daddy had been a soldier, and soldiers were always being sent somewhere else. Even when Daddy had stopped being a soldier he had had to go away again. That was what his daddy always did. But he still loved him, and their days together were special.

Angie was waiting for them on the doorstep when Scala took the excited children back home to the run-down bungalow that was all she could afford from the social security payment and Scala's own contributions. There was a brief kiss and a long hug for each child before Scala said goodbye to them. Angie leaned on the door frame, sending slivers of crumbling rotten white paint showering to the ground. She didn't ask him inside.

Scala felt awkward, shifting from one foot to the other. He wanted to talk to her, to plead with her once again – as he had done on so many other occasions. He had a way with women, a charm. He had always been confident that, with a cheeky smile or a winning wit, he could coax a woman to do what he wanted. Jim Scala had charmed so many into bed with that lethal combination. Most had meant nothing. But each one had been a challenge that he had to rise to.

Angie knew his power. She had fallen victim to it on so many occasions. She looked at him now, lost for words and fumbling. She stared into the Latin good looks, inherited from his parents' Italian–Welsh mixed marriage, at the scar on his face which somehow gave him more of a rakish appeal, made him more handsome. He had been her man; was still her man. He had been her lover and she knew what it was like to want him so much that it almost hurt.

But now she had to be strong. She had steeled herself for the meeting. She knew that by now he would have received the letter from her solicitor. She couldn't weaken now. God, it would be so easy. But she couldn't – not again, not after all the times before. She wanted her life back again – a fresh start and the chance to find security, love and tenderness without worrying how long it would be before her man went away again.

Scala tried to look over her shoulder. Angie knew immediately why.

'There's no one here, Jim boy!' she said with a half smile. 'And if I did have someone else, do you think I'd be stupid enough to have them here when you're bringing the kids back?'

'No, I didn't mean . . .' Scala attempted to reply, but couldn't finish. He studied Angie's fine features and pale skin. The long dark hair that was normally tied back now cascaded freely on to her shoulders. She had taken care of herself. Her figure was as trim and little as he had ever remembered, and the tight grey leggings and black tee-shirt paid tribute to the contours of her body. He wanted her back, wanted to tell her about the demons that visited him. He wanted her to tell him it would be all right. But he couldn't.

'I got the letter,' Scala muttered. 'We should talk, there's so much . . .'

Angie stood impassively watching Scala squirm and search desperately for the right words, the words that might help win her back. She shook her head.

'There's no time left for talking,' she said gravely. 'Those times have gone, Jim. There aren't any more words left.'

Rebuked, and feeling foolish, Scala hit back. 'Brilliant! "No time left . . ." I'm going away and you say there's no time for talking,' he began.

Angie gathered together the few resources that remained to her when dealing with her estranged husband. She was angry, and if he attempted to talk it out with her she feared her pent-up emotions might reveal themselves. 'That about sums it all up, Jim, doesn't it? Sums both you and me up. You're going away again and I'm here. But this time, Jim, there's a difference – I don't care. I'm tired of being both the carpet you walk all over and the welcome mat that's there when you get back. Not this time!'

The door slammed shut. Scala, hands deep in the pockets of his leather jacket, could say nothing. He stood gazing at the closed door.

'Four countries in six hours. Not bad even for an old soak of a hack like yourself.' The blond-haired giant poured more coffee for the pair of them.

Janine curled her legs beneath her body at the end of the sofa. At the other side of the open white-walled room with its scrubbed floorboards and high ceilings Macabe sat back in a leather bucket chair and took a deep draught of whisky. The journey across Europe had been fast and had tired them both.

The tall man sat down alongside Janine. He had an easy air about him, but Macabe knew Reijo Wallenius to be one of the toughest foreign correspondents that he had ever encountered. Macabe and he had first been thrown together during some of the more harrowing moments of the siege of Sarajevo. It had been back in the good old days of Macabe's career, and Reijo had been sent by his newspaper in Finland. They had shared stories and helped each other, and Macabe had saved the giant from the sniper hidden in the tower block with one of the best rugby tackles that he could ever remember having made.

'I heard about the job – I'm sorry. Any particular reason, or just the time of life?' inquired Reijo, in his heart never expecting a truthful answer.

'I'm not the first to go . . . and sure as hell I won't be the last,' shrugged Macabe with an air approaching indifference. But Wallenius knew the man well enough to know that he cared . . . he hurt. After all, he had been one of the best.

Macabe attempted to change the subject. 'So where's Helena and the kids?' Turning to Janine, he added, 'Do you know, he's got two of the most beautiful little girls that you could have imagined – hard to believe when you look at this bloody ape, isn't it!'

All three forced a laugh.

'They've gone back home, Peter. They had to go back . . . it was time . . . they couldn't stay . . . it wouldn't be right.' The truth was that Wallenius had sent his family away. For the time being he was living alone, here in the apartment in Mommsenstrasse in the centre of Berlin. 'What I didn't tell you is that I'm going back too,' he added.

Wallenius had been the Berlin correspondent for his paper for over eighteen months. But things had changed. In his deep accent, which an amused Janine suspected he might have picked up from American television programmes, he explained: 'I think I know what you want here, Peter. From what you've already told me it sounds good. But things have changed here. It hasn't been the same since the Wall came down. People are different – there's a different atmosphere. It's as though people are scared . . . they're scared of the changes that are happening. That's something that's affecting everything. The truth of the matter is that I'm scared too. Not for myself you understand – for that I don't give a shit! I'm scared for Helena and the girls.'

Macabe sat bolt upright, his attention fixed on Wallenius's words.

'I know what you want, Peter,' the big Finn continued, 'and where I can help I will. But don't expect too much.'

Macabe knew that Wallenius had spent months investigating the growth of neo-Nazi and right-wing factions, not only in Germany but throughout Europe. He also knew that he did not scare easily.

Wallenius went on, 'Once the press were safe – we were always left alone. But as I said, things have changed. There's a list of names – people in the newspapers, television. A list of people who have tried to expose the new trends, the new movements. I've seen that list . . .' He broke off to gulp down

the last of the coffee in his cup. 'Do you remember Franz Lutz?'
he asked.

Macabe remembered the enthusiastic young Associated Press
guy whom he had met on his first trip to the former Yugoslavia.
Always cracking sick jokes. Of course he remembered him.

'He's dead,' reported Wallenius. 'Killed outside Dvor in north-
western Bosnia. They found his body in no man's land. It was
said he'd been killed by a sniper. But how many snipers do you
know who use a .22 pistol and shoot someone in the back of the
neck at close range?'

Macabe winced at the thought of the laughing young man he
had come to like as they sheltered from the bullets and mortars
that had rained down on Sarajevo.

'The trouble is, Franz contacted me shortly before he died. He
was researching a story about a group of mercenaries working for
the Croats that he'd unearthed. He didn't think they gave a shit
which side they were working for. He said they walked around
freely wearing SS armbands and singing Nazi songs. The next
thing I knew, Franz was dead. Then a friend of mine who works
for television here was sent a copy of the list. He showed it to me.
Franz's name was on that list – and so is mine!'

Janine felt almost stupid asking, but she could not help herself.
'What about the police? Why don't you go to them?'

'And say what, my dear?' Wallenius attempted to dispel the
gloom of the conversation by lightening his tone. 'I go along to
the police and say, "Excuse me, I'm worried about some Nazi who
says he's going to get me"! The truth is, no one knows which side
the police themselves are on. I don't think even the politicians know
. . . Do you remember the hostel that was torched in Rostock?'

Macabe cast his mind back some years to the night the skinheads
had burned out an immigrant hostel. A Turkish family had died.

'The police had been guarding the hostel and there was no trouble
– they'd kept the skins away. Then without reason the police were
taken away – a change of orders – and the skins set fire to the
place,' explained Wallenius softly. 'I've never known a situation
where the police have been taken away from a potential trouble
spot as the crowds gathered, have you? No, Janine, I fear we're
now living in a time when we don't know who's who any longer!
The people that Peter and I are talking about have influence. There
are many now in this country who think the right wing is correct
– everyone's suffering because the country cannot cope with the
large increase in the number of immigrants, and the right has

supporters everywhere. Suddenly, we're no longer dealing with just a crazy few.'

Wallenius reached for the whisky bottle and refilled Macabe's glass and his own. 'So that, Peter, is why I've decided to return home. I've had to think of my family. I won't risk them. God knows we had a good life here, everything paid for courtesy of the paper. But something's happening – I have a gut feeling. But for me the story isn't worth the sacrifice of my family. No story is!'

Janine blurted out: 'I wish to Christ you'd hammer that into Peter's head, then.'

Macabe frowned at her but said nothing.

'But Peter,' Wallenius resumed, 'as I've said, for old times' sake I'll help you as much as I can if this story means so much. These days it's often not as difficult as it might seem to find the right people. There's a shop that deals in antiques and old militaria. Not much of a shop, but it advertises. Merely to utter the word "Nazi" here could get you thrown into prison. But it's said that if you want to buy something special – some Nazi gear or a souvenir, let's say – it can be provided. And if you want something more still – to meet people who prefer the old ways – then from what I understand from those people who talk, it's also the shop to go to.'

He picked up the telephone book and looked for the advertisement. It was called Carousel and was in the Charlottenburg district of the city.

'In a few days I'll be leaving, Peter,' said Wallenius. 'The rent for the apartment is paid up for the next two months, thanks to the foresight of my paper. You're more than welcome to use it. I owe you that at least.'

The demons had returned. Not even the drink had helped this time. God knows how much he had put away as he tried to put the image of Angie closing the door on him out of his mind.

He had just sat there and drunk, occasionally exchanging a word or two with another visitor to the club. Fortunately the girls behind the bar of the Union Jack knew Scala and made allowances when the dark mood was on him. He had charmed them, and they had shown their interest in him. Another night he might have attempted to take their interest to the limit. But not tonight. Tonight was for remembering . . . or trying to forget.

He had sat in the bar surveying the row of paintings that depicted some of the Army's greatest moments: the colourful charges of Waterloo, heroic actions from the Boer War, the taking of a machine gun nest at Ypres. Then there was the painting of the Gulf War. He had been there . . . he had hunted the Scuds that had smashed Israel. He had fought all over the world during his thirteen years of service. Then there had been Bosnia. Some had even called him a hero. And now, at the age of thirty-five, here he sat, alone, ignoring the attentions of a frisky barmaid.

What would the people back in the valleys have thought of him now? The headstrong young half-Welsh, half-Italian hero who wanted nothing else but to leave his miserable background, to escape his legacy of taking over the family's greasy-spoon caff. That was all gone now, all behind him. Jim Scala had left to begin his quest for adventure.

He had drunk his fill and thought he would sleep tonight. But the demons had returned, and as he tossed in his small bed in his small room he had seen a vision of himself lying face down in a far-off place, with no one to weep for him. As he awoke, bathed in sweat, he presumed that he had always known it would come to this – that his end would come with him lying face down in a far-off place, alone. If that was to be his fate, there was nothing he could do. He would have to learn to face his tormentor.

Further sleep was impossible. He would be leaving shortly for training at a Midlands barracks, a refresher course on what was required of a sergeant from the Engineers in a reconnaissance role. After all, Scala had begun his army life in the Royal Engineers before transferring to 9 Squadron of the Parachute Regiment in search of the adventure he craved. Matherson had told him that that would be his role when he was seconded to the RKRs. He would simply have to bring himself up to speed on present-day barracks life and extinguish any tell-tale signs of his recent civilian lifestyle. Carter had done his best to brief him on all the known aspects of the case, but Scala had wanted to take copies of the files with him. Now fully awake, he decided to banish the demons by embroiling himself in those files.

Scala opened the first folder, and the face of Private John Adebeyo stared back at him. As he read on, Scala felt he had seen hundreds of Adebeyos throughout his army life. 'Born: Clapham, South London; son of a railway worker; left school at age 16; prospects "nil"; joined Army aged 19; Initial posting: Worcestershire and Sherwood Foresters; transferred to Royal Kent Rangers on own request at age of 20.' The rest read like the sad report of a misfit soldier. He had been reported AWOL on numerous occasions; claimed he had been ostracised by colleagues and senior personnel;

claimed he was called 'nigger' and 'sambo', but failed to prove a claim that he had been subjected to assault by colleagues who had attempted to 'scrub him white' using a yard brush. Later, he had complained to senior officers after the new Armed Forces Bill became law, about racial discrimination, and more recently he had been in contact with the Commission for Racial Equality. No proof; no action. The file ended with the report of his death a year earlier: 'Verdict: suicide'.

Scala was not moved. Throughout his years in the service he had known of the racism that existed. It went with the job. God knows, there were only about a hundred blacks in the entire British Army – a force of one hundred thousand men. He had never thought of himself as racist. But what could a coloured man expect when he put himself in an environment dominated by whites? God knows, coloured workers had seized plenty of the civilian jobs that unemployed workers would have welcomed. You didn't hear *them* crying racial discrimination.

'Pissing in the wind if they think anything's going to change,' he whispered to himself. 'Just pissing in the wind.'

The bar was the same as any one of a thousand in any part of the world. The neon signs made no attempt to pretend anything else. Despite the overwhelming size of the place, with its dozens of tables and chairs, the drinkers clung three deep to the bar. Pint glasses filled with black beer were constantly lined up and the atmosphere was filled with noise and laughter.

'Bloody marvellous,' sighed Janine. 'Of all the bars in all the world you have to bring me to one that could be in the Kilburn High Road.'

Macabe took a deep swill from the glass and wiped the creamy foam from his top lip. He was in a good mood. 'My dear girl, when in doubt, and you want to find out what the local Brits are doing anywhere in the world, you should know by now that you always go to the Irish Pub. Everywhere has one. You'll get a better pint in the Irish Pub in Moscow than you do in most of the bloody pubs in London. Just trust me . . . seek and ye shall find.'

The Irish Pub was in the cellar of one of Berlin's best-known shopping areas. As Macabe predicted, it attracted hosts of expatriates who came for a feeling of 'home'.

Macabe and Janine stood alone at first, but as the number of English-speaking customers grew it was not long before they found themselves in conversation. The man in his early twenties had moved here from Manchester four years earlier. He had made the place his home, and the pretty dark-haired girl who clung to his arm was a native of what, in the bad old days, had been East Berlin. The boy was a bricklayer, North of England roots long since forgotten, seeking the better cash that German employers offered. But in the new Germany his future was uncertain. The clamp-down on imported labour would reduce the wages that he could only dream of in England. Germany was changing.

As in most places where one community exists within another larger one, so the expatriates of Berlin all knew each other. It took little effort for Macabe to be introduced to others within the group, a mixed bag of regulars to the bar. Afterwards Macabe was not certain if he had sought out the tall, lean figure in denims and greasy shoulder-length hair, or if he himself had been the one singled out. The conversation flowed around the niceties of visiting Berlin. Where were the good places to eat? What was the attitude of the Germans like? Where did the people mix? What did an expat do in Germany?

Macabe could not believe his luck: the tall, lean man had been a soldier. For fifteen long years Terry Gallagher had worn the Queen's uniform. The man from Ulster had been in the Irish Hussars, and proud of it. But all that had changed one day in 1990 when he was told he was surplus to requirements. A White Paper called *Options for Change* had paved the way. The British Army was being slashed. He and thousands of others would not be needed any more. He had thought himself a good and dutiful soldier, yet his reward was redundancy and a set of references stamped by his commanding officer with the word 'Unemployable'. The fifteen years had been scrubbed clean. At the age of thirty-seven Terry Gallagher had been forced into starting life all over again.

The softly spoken Irishman had lived in Germany for over two years, carrying out odd jobs and living off the state. 'But I tell you,' he confided to Macabe, 'I'm better off here than back home – or what I thought was home. I tell you, the state looks after me more here than it ever would back there. Jesus, it was going to take friggin' weeks and maybe months to get any benefits, 'cos I'd been given a shit-awful pay-off by the Army.' He knocked back more drink. 'So I thought to meself, fuck the lot . . .'

Years of propping up bars had given Macabe the upper hand – he was able to hold his drink while other, lesser mortals, were left stumbling over words or spewing out deeply guarded secrets as the drink loosened their tongue. Macabe was an expert who had made a living of gleaning stories from drunks at bars, and Gallagher was no match for him. Spitting beer, he stammered out more vitriol against the fat-arsed men in Whitehall suits and how they would one day regret their hasty actions in axing so many of 'Britain's finest'.

Macabe grew more interested. Were there more ex-squaddies who felt the same?

'Don't be fuckin' stupid, man!' replied Gallagher, grinning. 'There's tons of us here. Nowhere else to go. Who the fuck wants us?'

'I'd like to meet up with these guys,' Macabe blurted, almost too quickly. He tried to correct himself. 'I mean, it's a cryin' bloody shame. No one back home would credit it. I always thought we looked after our own.'

Gallagher checked himself and looked at Macabe with suspicion.

'You see, I'm a journalist,' Macabe went on. 'Only over for a few days . . . I hadn't realised the situation. It would make a great article: "The Forgotten Army" or something . . . Can you help? I'd need to get in touch with the people who can tell me what makes them tick.'

There was a bar that Macabe might be interested in. Gallagher gave him the address. Mention his name and he might meet some people, might find more of what he was looking for. The drink flowed. Macabe felt on a high. His instinct told him he was getting nearer to those who might have what he wanted.

The eyes watched him as they had watched him for the last three weeks. Every detail of his movements had been monitored and logged.

He had not known it – had never even thought about it. There was no need to worry about such things; he had never thought that he mattered that much anyhow.

This would be the treat that his thirteen-year-old had dreamed of for months. He had pestered his father to get the tickets, to take him to see his hero. Now Leon Mountjoy was delighted that he was about to make young Howard's dream come true.

The girl at the ticket office took Mountjoy's money and slipped him the envelope. It would be a good week: take Howard to see his hero play on the Wednesday, and the following day he himself would travel to Birmingham to face the television cameras. Leon checked the tickets and scurried from the ground.

He ignored everything else round about, so preoccupied was he by the thought of surprising Howard with the exciting news. The boy was at last going to see Jonah Dennison, the idol of the Premier Division, the man who had become a legend at the Highbury ground where he had thrilled the fans for the last ten years. It would be Dennison's night as well – the long-awaited testimonial. With almost childish glee Mountjoy thought of nothing but the look on Howard's face.

The eyes still followed him.

The roar of the oncoming train echoed through the tunnel and erupted on to the platform. The evening commuters jostled their way down the tightly packed stairways and escalators that took them deep into the London Underground. The battle of the Northern Line was a daily struggle to the thousands who fought it.

As the northbound train burst on to the platform, the hundreds who lined the concrete platforms within the bowels of Waterloo surged forward and the mass of bodies shoved and pushed and stabbed around him. The temperature had hovered around freezing throughout the day, but now Volker Reisz found himself sweating profusely. It would be an endless journey. The eleven stops to Highgate would seem as long as the flight from Berlin.

He stood wedged in the centre of the carriage. God, how he hated the Underground – the people, the smells. The train shuddered to the next stop and there was the usual heaving exchange of travellers. The doors closed and the carriage shuddered into life once more. He found himself thrown against the body next to him and for some reason turned.

He was close enough to smell the mixture of stale garlic and spices on the man's breath. His eyes flashed wide with horror and rage. Just six inches from his face, the man threw back his dreadlocks and beamed. He said something – a joke . . . an apology . . . but Reisz didn't hear. He felt sick and unclean, in need of a wash.

It was a full fifteen minutes before Volker Reisz could regain his composure completely. By then the carriage was considerably emptier, yet he still declined to fill one of the vacant seats. Despite the efforts of the train to shake him he stood firm, hands in the pockets of his dark green overcoat, without clutching the dangling overhead handle intended to steady standing passengers.

Reisz was a six-foot-tall hulk of a man whose muscles were honed to perfect fitness. He oozed physical power and presence. The girl saw that also. Sitting alone on the bench seat she had an unhindered view of the square-jawed Adonis with the swept-back blond hair. She liked what she saw and made no secret of her admiration. She was wearing a short skirt and boots beneath her long black coat, and as she eyed the man she displayed her long, shapely legs.

Reisz had been discreetly observing her for the last ten minutes. He knew he had power over women. It made him feel good.

At last she caught his gaze. She smiled and raised her eyes.

Reisz responded with a full glare, a look that shot fear into her heart and mind. She didn't know why. The clear, penetrating eyes seemed to look deep into her soul and strip her bare. She shuffled and, unnerved, covered her legs. Desperately seeking some other focus of attention she began to study the map of the Underground. There were others in the carriage but they were absorbed in their newspapers or thoughts, and she felt frighteningly alone.

It had been over in seconds, but it was enough. The train rattled to a halt. Without thinking, without caring, she leaped to her feet and made for the gaping doors. She prayed that the man had not followed, but dared not turn. She heard the doors close and forced herself to turn round, to see the man with the staring eyes still standing in the carriage that was now pulling away. Her heart pounding, she saw a cold sinister smile play about his mouth as he raised one hand in a farewell gesture.

Combat 18 had been bad enough: the riot at the soccer stadium in Dublin had been provoked by at least fifteen of its members. The group, which took its name from Adolf Hitler's initials – A equalling 1 and H being 8 – was now infamous. There were some who believed that Combat 18 had in fact been originated by MI5 long ago in a bid to spread internal dissent amongst the ranks of the British National Party, but that now it had become a Frankenstein's monster that was out of control. Special Branch had admitted that it was growing increasingly worried. C18 was getting stronger. It wanted a 'holy war' against immigrants – to repatriate them, to bring in segregation, to spark off a tit-for-tat racist war. That was the goal, and their numbers were spreading.

But compared with this, they were schoolboys playing a game. Leon Mountjoy knew it, and now he must warn of this new danger. He had the evidence, so it was his duty. People had put themselves at great risk to get the information. He owed it to them to make his findings known.

He placed the copies of the photographs of the burned hostel in

Lübeck into the file. He had the photographs of the burn injuries to the children, of the girl with the charred and twisted legs whose dreams of becoming a ballet star had ended in the flames on the night that Nick Curry and the other 'believers' had gone to Lübeck.

Leon Mountjoy was going to reveal the new terror that was about to be unleashed on Britain and throughout Europe. It was his pledge.

CHAPTER FOUR

The smoke from half a dozen cigarettes that wafted around the ceiling light stabbed at his eyes – those wide, wolf–like, grey, cold, staring eyes. The stench of the smoke was on him too. It would linger, and he detested that.

As ordered, they had come to the house. They were the lieutenants who would ensure that Volker Reisz's instructions filtered down to the others. Reisz sat back in his armchair and swigged beer from the bottle. The others took it as a sign to follow suit. The German was in command of this meeting; he was the one with the power.

He surveyed the group. To the unknowing, each looked very like any other man in the street: a bank clerk, a transport manager, a car salesman. Ordinary men in an ordinary world. Then there were the man from the Territorial Army and the former Royal Marine, who now ran the pub that hosted the biggest rock concert money-spinners that the movement had enjoyed in years. Now they were all studying the maps and photographs. They were professionals who knew how to carry out orders. And from this terraced house in Highgate they would take his message, and carry his orders to their own groups. They had already spent weeks rehearsing their own men – as if they needed to.

At Reisz's side sat his right-hand man. They had formed a bond – the bond that comes when men have fought side by side in battle. The clipped sentences of his speeches betrayed his South African roots. Like Reisz, Peter Coetzee had experienced many battles. As a captain in the South African Army in the 1980s he had been responsible for the clandestine units that had murdered ANC activists, carried out cross-border raids against ANC targets and participated in South Africa's surrogate wars in Angola and Mozambique. Then he had fought against transition. After the hand-over to Nelson Mandela he had become a member of the Afrikaner Freedom Front, and had toured the country inciting Afrikaners to polish their weapons for war against the ANC communists who now ruled their land.

Now Coetzee was a soldier looking to fight that same cause. The bear of a man with balding grey hair and a black military moustache had eventually found his way to the trenches in Croatia, where he had discovered like-minded friends who also believed. The opportunity was too good to miss. It was God-given opportunity – who had said that God had not been on their side? All in the room were of a like mind.

The tactics were agreed. It would need no more than twenty men to start it if they acted as a cohesive unit and followed the timetable. Reisz, Coetzee and the two best men from the other units would handle the rest.

The minibus drew to a halt by the barrier. The driver waited for the young sentry to step from the warmth of the office, check the vehicle and allow it to pass. Cursing, the soldier adjusted his peak cap to the regulation height above eye level and strode out into the freezing temperature. His heavy boots crunched into the thick snow that had been turned into ice by the bitter frost of the night before.

As they waited, Scala peered through the misted-up glass of the van and surveyed the twelve-foot high walls topped with barbed wire that formed the perimeter of the Allenby Barracks in Hohne. The scene looked bleak. The carpet of dark cloud that hung low over it imparted an air of gloom, despite the brightness of the thick snow that was banked up by the huge roadside sign which indicated that the barracks was the home of the 1st Battalion The Royal Kent Rangers.

It had been over thirteen years since Scala had been stationed in Germany as a fresh recruit with the Engineers before winning his transfer to the Parachute Battalion. Then he had served within the huge multi-storey blocks of the barracks near Paderborn. The mass of single-storey huts that stretched before him was a complete contrast.

Once again Scala was wearing the maroon beret of the Parachute Regiment, its winged cap badge replaced by the laurel wreath of the Royal Engineers. The flight from Britain to Hanover had passed quickly, but the subsequent drive to the barracks had been long and uncomfortable because the driver had been forced to take extra care on the icy roads. Only the brief conversation with the single other passenger on the bus had helped speed the time. The young soldier had been excited: it was his first day with the Rangers.

The boy had given his name as Private Christopher Jarvis and he

was following in his father's and grandfather's footsteps: they had
both served with the RKR. Looking at the young soldier dressed
in jeans, sweatshirt and leather jacket, Scala estimated him to be
no more than sixteen. Jarvis had given his age as nineteen, but his
pale, fresh complexion made him look younger.

The formalities completed, the barrier was raised. It was
beginning to snow once more, and odd flakes of white ice
floated towards the parade ground in the centre of the camp.
There were few signs of life. The occasional soldier marched
quickly, half running down the cleared roads that networked
the camp, in a desperate bid to escape the bitter conditions. A
passing officer sharply returned the salute of a lone soldier who
scurried to escape the cold by diving into the warmth of the NAAFI
block which stood at the end of the range of snow-covered sports
pitches.

Scala had trained hard at the Midlands camp. His refresher course
as a Royal Engineer had been worthwhile: the military's assessment
was that he was up to scratch. But as the bus drove towards the
concrete block huts that housed the sergeants he sighed. He had
forgotten how shit-awful an army camp could look. Turning to
the eager Jarvis he said, 'Welcome to your new home, son!' and
grinned.

It was almost dusk when Macabe found the small shop that
Wallenius had spoken of, nestling among a terrace of cheap
restaurants, food stores and bars at the base of a grey block in
the heart of Charlottenburg. He went in alone, leaving Janine in
the car further down the wide street. The old-fashioned bell sprang
into life as the door was opened. Macabe had no idea what he was
looking for or how, without being exceptionally clumsy, he would
broach the subject that was now so important to him.

From outside the shop was nondescript, bearing only the name
'Carousel' above its plate-glass window. But the interior made
even Macabe gasp. There before him, set out on tables and stands,
stretched rows of books, models, swords and assorted militaria. He
saw a small arsenal of ancient pistols, as well as uniforms that paid
homage to the glorious days of Bismarck and the Franco-Prussian
War. His eyes rapidly scoured the racks and stands, but he saw
no sign of anything that remotely suggested Nazism.

There was a shuffle of feet from behind the bookshelves. A
thin figure with rounded shoulders and a mop of grey hair was
examining him over a pair of thick wire-rimmed spectacles.

Macabe nodded, and had his greeting returned.

He stopped at the shelf that held the thinner books – manuals on weaponry old and new, and magazines, which looked oddly out of place. The latter seemed to originate in Canada or the United States. Strange, he thought, for everything else was strictly German in origin. These were English-language magazines. Some dealt with weaponry, others with medals and uniforms. As he began to thumb through the imported magazines the voice spoke in faultless English.

'Is there something in particular for which you are searching?'

Macabe was startled. 'Er, well, I'm not too sure. Just browsing really . . . How did you guess I was English?' he said weakly.

'I saw you coming,' replied the grey figure. 'Trade is quiet, you see. I saw your car. It has English number plates unless I am very mistaken.'

Macabe felt stupid and his heart had begun to pound. Some bloody investigator he had turned out to be.

'I'm particularly interested in the more recent period of history . . . I collect from, say, over the last fifty or sixty years or so.'

'And what exactly is it that you collect?' came the inquiry.

'All kinds of things really. I'm particularly keen on the war period. I understand the difficulties of trading in the surplus, but I figure if you can't find good memorabilia here then where else are you going to find it? Only America, I suppose,' he answered himself, glancing at the magazine. 'I understand they're quite enthusiastic about stuff like that over there.' Macabe waved the magazine. 'Is there more? I was told by an associate who collects that you might be able to help.'

'And who would say something like that?' the grey-haired figure pressed.

Macabe felt himself floundering. 'Er . . . Gallagher,' he said quickly. 'Terence Gallagher . . . a collector in London who makes visits here.' He cursed himself for not thinking of a better name than that of the man he had met in the bar.

'I'm afraid I do not know anyone of that name,' insisted the man. 'And as you know, we are not really allowed to trade in such items or literature. May I suggest Denmark rather than Germany? They appear much more liberal than our own state.'

Instinct took over. 'I am perfectly willing to pay handsomely,' Macabe offered. He had always believed that money was the only leveller.

He could feel the reaction. The atmosphere warmed.

'Allow me to introduce myself,' said the man, taking off his spectacles. 'Brusse, Günter Brusse at your service.'

'Peter Macabe. I'm on holiday here from London.'

'Well, Herr Macabe, since you appear to have the understanding that I can provide what you're looking for, I suggest you look further. The store is deceptive. It is a great deal bigger than you may imagine.' He gestured to the back of the building, to a flight of stairs which led to a lower floor.

Brusse had not lied. Down in the basement where the air was stuffy with the smell of old age, dust and cobwebs were more drawers and stands. This time the symbols on the rows of medals, daggers and insignia bore more sinister names that were also more familiar to Macabe: 'Waffen SS', the death's head badge of an officer of the SS Panzer Division, the ceremonial daggers of the knights of Hitler's armies. And then there were the books. And magazines.

This time he deliberately sought out the imported catalogues and magazines. He recognised the names of those too, such as *Patriot* which came from the United States. After a quick flick through the pages Macabe stopped at a section entitled 'Methods of Maintaining Personal Freedom'. He did not hear Brusse arrive behind him.

'As you suggested, Herr Macabe, some of our material does come from the other side of the Atlantic. I think you will find major suppliers over there for almost anything you want.'

Macabe had heard of such suppliers, and he had heard of the group that called itself the Patriots, a right-wing organisation in the States that had resorted to armed resistance and terror tactics to put across its message. There were other pamphlets too, some depicting the hooded 'knights' of the Ku Klux Klan standing before burning crosses, and others distributed across the border in Denmark which had found their way to their intended markets. Each advertised 'The New Front'. Some bore romanticised photographs of Hitler's more notorious comrades-in-arms such as Rudolf Hess, always a favourite, and Heinrich Himmler.

'I see you also collect the ideas, Herr Brusse,' said Macabe, glancing at the man.

'I am, as they say, a salesman,' retorted Brusse.

'But are you also a collector?' Macabe continued. 'A collector of men perhaps? Men who believed as they did!'

Brusse replaced his spectacles. 'Those days are long gone, Herr

Macabe, long gone. Only a fool would relish their return . . . wouldn't he?'

'Either a fool or someone who believes with his heart and soul,' responded the Englishman.

It was late. Macabe made a play of looking at his watch. He would return when there was more time. He would like to talk more.

'Talk, Herr Macabe, costs nothing. If you feel the need, then I will be here.'

Macabe turned to leave. As he did so, he caught sight of a photograph on a small sideboard at the rear of the store. It was a black and white picture of three men. Brusse himself was in the centre, flanked by a tall muscular figure with dark cropped hair wearing an open-necked shirt. Macabe looked closer. The mole on the man's right cheek was prominent – unduly so, Macabe thought. There was a hardness about the man, he estimated. Not so the third figure. More youthful-looking, he wore an inviting smile and, despite his casual attire, gave the impression of being used to money. The threesome, who were standing before a blurred background of a banner or sign, made an unusually odd group, thought Macabe.

A cough. Brusse was waiting to close the shop.

'Another time, perhaps,' said Macabe.

Scala thought of the spirits of an army long since past that might still linger within the walls of the block, possibly within the walls of the very quarters that he had been assigned. He tried to imagine the faces of the young men who had passed this way: smiling, laughing, anxious, frightened – the emotions that flowed through men preparing for battle. To Scala little had changed throughout the decades, perhaps the centuries. Men who were preparing to meet their fate must all have looked the same, must all have acted in the same manner as the young soldiers of today.

He unpacked his possessions and dispersed them throughout the two tiny rooms that would be his quarters. This block had been part of a transit camp, built at the height of the Nazi upsurge in the 1930s, where thousands of young Germans gathered before being deployed to their various theatres of action in the Second World War. Many would have shared the rooms that he was now making his own. The camp had been taken over by the occupying British Army at the end of the war. Overnight it became Allenby Barracks, named after the celebrated First World War general who had fought the Turks in Palestine.

Little had changed since 1945, except that today the long wooden huts that had housed Hitler's armies had been replaced by concrete and brick. The rooms were basic: a bed, a cupboard, a table and a small worn sofa with an adjoining bathroom, one of the privileges accorded to NCO. A few possessions, books and photographs, perhaps even a borrowed television, and the place would become more personalised.

The sound of heavy footsteps in the corridor alerted Scala. The knock on the half-open door was confident. Without waiting, a huge uniformed figure filled the doorway.

Scala himself stood around six feet tall. But the man in camouflage fatigues who stood before him was a full four inches taller. Scala's eyes flashed to the man's arm and focused on the chain on the leather wrist strap that denoted his rank of company sergeant major.

'Welcome to the RKR!' boomed the figure. 'The name's Mike Tavaner, CSM C Company. Told you were coming in, so I just thought I'd pop in and say hello.'

The greeting was cordial and genuine, the handshake firm. Scala introduced himself, complained about the length of journey, the cold and the need for a drink. He estimated Tavaner to be around forty, a senior soldier who had made the Army his life. Despite his massive bulk, Scala reckoned there was not an ounce of fat on him.

'Feed time in the mess is from 6 p.m. until 7 p.m. Expect to see you there. Then I'll introduce you to your compatriots and see what we can do about that thirst of yours.'

It had been many months since Scala had had to regulate himself to the habits of set eating times. Life in Civvy Street was changing him. But now there would be many things he would be forced to adjust to once again.

The homework was done. Young Howard Mountjoy had made a special effort to finish it early. His excitement was growing as he wondered what Jonah Dennison was feeling right now. Everyone who was anyone would be at the game tonight.

The stars of the soccer world had been eager to take part in the match. Dennison had proved himself to be a worthy champion and role model for thousands of youngsters everywhere. In the twelve years since he had come to Britain from Zimbabwe thousands of schoolboys had emulated his skills and his exemplary conduct both on and off the pitch. As the League's top striker he had become a multi-millionaire. His easy-going, intelligent manner and unstinting charity work had also brought him an army of fans and made him a friend of the British media. They had never considered that the colour of his skin made him different from themselves. Now the fans and the club were waiting to pay their own tribute to the soccer genius.

Howard, meanwhile, was waiting for his father. Leon Mountjoy was eager too. He wanted the night to be a special one for father and son – the kind that both would recall for years to come.

It was as though he had stepped back into history. Hardly a foot of the white walls was not covered in paintings depicting glorious achievements on the field of battle. The hall of fame recounting the regiment's numerous battle honours reminded Scala of the walls of the Union Jack Club, except that these exploits centred on just one group of men who had trodden the pages of history – the men who had served in the Royal Kent Rangers.

They ranged from the field of Blenheim, where the regiment had been raised alongside the banner of the Duke of Marlborough, through the glorious battles of the Peninsular War under Wellington to the Second World War, in which a string of daring acts of heroism had been rewarded with the shower of medals that now sparkled in neat, shining rows in the cabinets of the Sergeants' Mess. The largest of the paintings took pride of place over the immaculate mahogany bar and depicted the glorious advance of the red-coated Kent Rangers at the Battle of the Alma, which routed the Russian Army from the heights in one of the most crucial actions of the Crimea. The regiment had suffered horrendous casualties but they had pressed home the attack and shared the glory. That had meant everything.

As Scala sat back in a squeaky leather armchair his eyes rested on a smaller picture portraying the almost foolhardy action of a fallen sergeant of the RKR, killed at Monte Cassino in 1944 while attacking a German machine gun post single-handed. The sergeant's posthumous Military Medal hung in a gleaming wooden cabinet beneath. Scala silently raised his glass in a toast. 'To the glorious dead!' he found himself murmuring.

'Pretty impressive, eh?' boomed a deep voice as Tavaner strode purposefully into the room. In civilian dress, sporting casual trousers and regimental rugby shirt, the smiling Tavaner looked even bigger than Scala had first supposed. He was followed by three other men. 'Our glorious past! All decked out for anyone to see. It's like a bloody museum in here – but we like it,' he added.

Scala rose from his chair to meet the group. Introductions completed, they moved to the bar. The robust Mancunian called Colin Hasker insisted on signing for the first round of foaming German beer that oozed from the tap. Scala eyed the other two men: the softly spoken yet confident cockney Peter Hibbs and the pale man who stood by his side, an odd contrast to the rest of the group, who had given his name as Derek Scullard. Scala felt uneasy with Scullard: the man's eyes kept darting around the room and prompted a feeling of mistrust.

The toast. To Scala welcome, and then 'To the regiment'.

'It's a hell of a collection – just as well you've got someone else to clean the stuff,' Scala joked, gesturing towards the array of memorabilia that adorned the room.

'Yes, all our life is before us, immortalised in paint and silver,' answered Tavaner sombrely. 'Even the chairs we sit on have a history.' Scala perused the assortment of brown leather chairs strategically placed around the vast room. 'One of our smart lads did a deal at auction. All made for the Nazi officers who used this camp. Nearly all went to waste. Bloody good stuff, eh? These days our past is all we can look forward to, if you see what I mean. Bloody Whitehall pen-pushers have seen to that. Even your mob in the Engineers must be feeling the pinch by now.'

Scala winced, knowing he should have done more research. He wasn't certain of the latest situation on cutbacks or recruitment, wasn't 100 per cent certain of any major problems that his old outfit faced. Years ago he would have known. Shit! He should have known now. Fortunately for him more drinks came and the need for an instant response faded. The group joked and chatted and for the moment, the subject was changed.

The queues were longer than expected. Leon and Howard Mountjoy inched their way towards the turnstiles along with the thousands of other laughing, singing supporters. There was a chill in the air, but the sense of occasion and joviality amongst the fans who joked with the mounted police officers who stood guard at the gates to the ground more than countered any misgivings about the weather. Groups of youths sporting bright red and white scarves good-heartedly jostled each other. A schoolboy chewed on the remains of a giant hot dog, smearing ketchup across his face. The air was shattered by the sound of a dozen choirs of fans, all determined to sing their own anthems simultaneously.

Howard felt close to his father tonight – the closest they had been for a long time. His father's work had always seemed to preoccupy him, although the boy was unclear exactly what it was that took up so much of his attentions. But tonight was different.

Jonah Dennison laughed with his mates in the dressing rooms. It was going to be a good night for him too.

The fans slowly filled the terraces and the seated areas. It was going to be a capacity crowd. As the streets emptied and the chanting of the eager fans filled the air from within the ground the gates were locked, and all eyes strained towards the tunnel where the biggest names from the biggest soccer clubs in England would soon emerge behind Jonah Dennison. Leon Mountjoy, focusing his attention on the tunnel with the thousands of other spectators, was unaware that other eyes – cold, dead eyes – were fixed on him . . .

No one knew how it began. Dennison had shone, displaying his magnificent talents throughout. With only minutes to go before the final whistle he made one of his remarkable runs with the ball. He passed one man, avoided the tackle of another and ran on, the field opening up before him. The crowd roared their delight and approval. He had gone to the corner flag by the main stand to take the kick, no more than twenty feet from the cheering fans. Suddenly he had flinched with pain, apparently in his back, but brushed it away with his hand. On he ran, following the ball.

Then he had stopped and teetered, his eyes wild and rolling. No other player was near him when he collapsed without warning in the centre of the field. The other players, shocked and unsure of what had happened, moved forward to surround him. The crowd, all unknowing, still chanted and roared, drunk on the excitement of what they had already witnessed.

It was the signal. The lieutenants had done their work well. It had been easy – there was always someone who wanted a fight, who would react. As a man the half-dozen 'commandos' in each corner of the ground had begun to push, to jeer, to land a cosh on an unsuspecting head, to drop a smoke bomb, to spread panic.

It took just a few minutes. The 'commandos' in their 'uniforms' of shaven heads, jeans and heavy boots went about their task with clinical professionalism. The players stayed on the pitch, some still staring in confusion at the unmoving shape of Jonah Dennison, others eying minor scuffles starting up in sections of the terraces.

The fighting spread as innocent victims of the unnoticed army of thugs retaliated.

People screamed as bodies tumbled on the concrete steps of the terraces. Angry youths fought, kicked, punched and used their boots as weapons. Knives slashed and there were shrieks of sudden agony. A small girl separated from her father in the mayhem sat huddled on the steps crying in panic as hundreds ran past her to escape the terror, neither seeing nor caring, their only thought to escape. The girl was bowled sideways by the stampede, tossed like a broken doll, smashing her head against the steps which sent blood gushing from an open wound. An elderly man, head split by a blow from a wooden club, trampled her underfoot as he careered wildly into the stumbling, shouting crowd.

Scores of police officers, clad in the helmets and breastplates of riot gear, had vaulted the barriers which separated the fans from the pitch and were now fighting a hopeless running battle with anyone they could lay their hands on. Out of control, the violence spilt on to the pitch. The players ran towards the tunnel, protecting the stretcher carrying off the unconscious Jonah Dennison.

The fuse had been lit. The concrete terraces were being smashed into chunks of rubble to be used as missiles. Smoke from fires started in the seating areas filled the air. Outside the ground lines of mounted police attempted to break through the surging, panic-striken human mass.

Leon Mountjoy ran, dragging his sobbing, terror-stricken son. Clutching Howard with one hand, he punched and pushed his way to the outside with his other. The madness had transformed Mountjoy, a placid, shy person in ordinary life, into a roaring beast whose only concern was the protection of his son. The sounds of the chaos surrounding him filled his ears, and his heart rammed the side of his chest. A man lay unconscious on the ground; Mountjoy trod on the prone figure as he hauled the stumbling Howard onwards. The open gateway loomed before them.

Anxious seconds turned into agonising minutes as Mountjoy clawed a path for the two of them, beyond the overwhelming shapes of the nervous police horses. He was not certain how far he ran. The chaos and the noise of police sirens seemed to be well behind him but fear still forced him on into the maze of dark streets that surrounded the ground. Then at last Mountjoy stopped, gasping for air through his bursting lungs. He felt as though his head was about to explode. With an overwhelming sense of relief he hugged Howard to his side to stifle the boy's crying, stroking his head in reassurance.

Mountjoy's thoughts had been only on escape. He had not seen the four figures that had trailed him through the football ground and had beaten their own path through the terror-filled terraces. It had all gone according to plan, better even than they could have hoped. Mountjoy was in the open, alone apart from the sobbing brat by his side.

It was Coetzee who struck first with the rubber cosh. His gasping victim had no warning and the blow took him squarely on the back of the head, sending him hurtling to the ground in agonised shock. Howard spun on his heels to see the group of figures that were launching themselves at his father. He screamed and pleaded with them. But a kick from a heavy boot broke Mountjoy's front teeth and sent blood spurting on to the pavement. Another kick to the ribs and another. All four men were now joining in, raining blows on the shrieking figure.

Volker Reisz, half brick in hand, followed up with a blow that split Mountjoy's skull. More blood, more kicks. They cursed and called names. Howard, still shouting, could not understand them. He shouted and screamed again. But no one came. The street was deserted.

Suddenly there was silence. The four attackers simply stopped and walked away, disappearing into the cold night. Mountjoy lay spread-eagled on the frosty pavement, blood oozing from a dozen wounds, twitching involuntarily. Only the sobbing of the boy continued.

The sergeants sat back in the leather chairs that had once been used by German officers before being sent to the Front. It had been a good, light-hearted night. Their stomachs were filled with the solid food served up from the adjoining kitchen: there had been nothing fancy – no call for that.

As the beer had flowed the conversation had passed from small talk via the bawdy to the technical side of soldiering. Now they sat back in their comfortable chairs, absorbing the images on the television set in front of them. The group of six NCOs were transfixed by the scenes of the football riot back home. There had been casualties, it seemed, some serious.

Initial reports blamed the extremists of the notorious Combat 18 group for inciting the violence. There was still no news of the condition of Jonah Dennison or the cause for his collapse. The police were still investigating, said the reporter on the scene as he handed back to the studio.

To the sergeants, one skinhead looked very similar to another. Being a member of Combat 18 meant nothing. They were all thugs – thugs who needed a dose of military discipline to straighten them out.

'Just give me a few minutes behind the shed with one of those bastards and we'd soon see who was a tough guy!' hissed Scullard.

No one answered. There was no need.

Scala sat in silence. Half-watching the screen, he was also observing the reactions of the men around him.

He had never been a man to make snap decisions of people's characters. A few beers and a few laughs with a group like this did not mean that he was about to change now.

The news flash on screen interrupted his train of thought. Jonah Dennison had been pronounced dead on arrival at hospital, cause of death as yet unknown. First reports suggested that the player had suffered a massive heart attack, but the reporter insisted that these were simply unconfirmed rumours.

Tavaner, silent until now, ordered more drinks to be placed on his tab.

CHAPTER FIVE

Volker Reisz had slept well. Not even the all-night traffic outside his tiny hotel bedroom in South London had disturbed his sleep. By 8 a.m. he had risen refreshed, showered and dressed in smart black slacks and thick grey sweater to protect himself from the cold. He combed back his ruffled blond hair, ran his hand over his freshly shaven square jaw and examined himself in the cracked mirror of the small dressing table. He was pleased with his night's work. It had been well organised – but, he assured himself, whenever Volker Reisz organised anything there were no mistakes. It had always been so.

His days as captain of the student boxing and athletic team a decade before had crafted him into a born leader of men. With the blond-haired gladiator at their head, both teams had been invincible. Reisz had triumphed as a light heavyweight champion, and few had been able to maintain contact with his heels in the 400 and 200 metre events. He had powered his way to the top.

His ambition to become a teacher had subsided as the young Reisz, the son of a factory worker and a waitress who had struggled so that their son might enjoy the education that had been denied them, had discovered his natural gift for leadership and a belief in his own power. He craved adventure and more power and believing in a world in which only the strong survived, had sought to test himself to the limit.

At twenty-one he had begun to take an interest in politics. Along with others at his university he had joined the Greens, protesting at the waste and abuse of the world's natural wealth. He had risen to become a major campaigner, able to fire people with his oratory. But speeches alone did not result in action or change. Disillusionment began to infiltrate Volker Reisz's world. Germany was changing, and for him that change was not for the better. His world, the world that he had grown up in, was being changed. Some blamed the influx of foreigners. He agreed with them. Volker Reisz demanded action.

The catalyst had come in 1989 with the collapse of the Berlin Wall. The tide of human misery from the East now threatened to infect the rest of his country. Now, he decided, was the time to act. He wanted to learn the trade of killing: he would become a soldier, a special soldier fighting for his own beliefs. He had met the right people – the tall Austrian who had served with the French Foreign Legion and the short, insignificant man in the bar who had returned from the killing fields of Croatia. If Volker Reisz wanted to learn the art of death, there would be the perfect classroom.

And so in 1993, at the age of twenty-seven, Reisz had found himself fighting alongside other international paid killers near Mostar. Here he had served with other German 'believers' in the infamous Baron von Trenck Unit, which took its name from an Austrian officer who had persecuted Hungarians in the eighteenth century. For Volker Reisz and his twelve Apostles it proved an ideal training ground. All had believed in a greater Germany, wore armbands and greeted each other with salutes of '*Heil Hitler*'. They had learned the true meaning of 'ethnic cleansing' and gone about their work as their forefathers had done, probably in the same battlefields, years before.

In the trenches Reisz had met Peter Coetzee, a soldier of fortune in search of a cause. There had been an immediate bonding. Coetzee had already learned the business of killing in the terrorist bush wars of his homeland. Now he saw his people betrayed: the Afrikaners who had shaped the country for so long had no voice against the black bastards that he had fought for so long. Reisz had understood. His own country, he believed, was under the same threat.

Reisz and Coetzee and the people who believed took their hatred and their experience of death home with them, in search of a new war for their own survival. The South African and the German made a formidable partnership, and together they had found like-minded people who had pledged themselves to preserve white supremacy in Europe against what they called the 'black death'. They now had a man to lead them in that struggle. Soon, there would be others to swell their ranks. Reisz and Coetzee and the others had found their new crusade.

It had been Coetzee's expertise with the dart gun, acquired through years of silent killings of ANC terrorists, that had felled Dennison the night before. The dart, tipped with cyanide, was small but lethal. Coetzee had stood in the baying crowd by the corner post, waiting for the moment when Dennison would come. The shot had been easy – no more than 20 yards. He had seen it strike home. The black bastard had felt it and pushed it out with his hand. But it had done its work well.

No one had taken any notice of Reisz and Coetzee as they returned late to the scruffy, insignificant hotel. No one had noticed the splattering of blood on Reisz's coat where he had smashed Leon Mountjoy's head with the brick. Now Reisz glimpsed around the depressing room with its floral wallpaper and damp patch spreading from the corner. He checked his watch. He had arranged to meet Coetzee downstairs for breakfast, and he felt hungry after the exertions of the night before. Then they would meet the others, all soberly and conventionally dressed, and head for Heathrow. No one would be looking for a group of respectable businessmen. Why should they?

The plan had worked well. Dennison would no longer be a target of adulation from clean, healthy white boys. And the tiresome little Jew who had wanted to expose them would not be talking to anyone. The police would still be questioning known hooligans, perhaps those from C18. While they did, Volker Reisz and his team would be on their way home.

Howard clutched his mother's hand. He had no tears: there were none left to cry. His mother had wanted to stay alone at the bedside, but the boy had insisted. Together they sat in the small room off the ward at St Bartholomew's Hospital where Leon Mountjoy clung to life.

The tubes ran from his body. Without them, there would be no hope. The doctors had told her already of the irreparable brain damage. Eileen Mountjoy tried to come to terms with the fact that her husband would never again recognise her or their son. Anything that was locked away in his mind would remain there for ever.

As she squeezed the hand of the man she loved and had shared her life with since their schooldays, Eileen Mountjoy remembered the happy, carefree days of their courtship. She would, at least, have the past to hold on to.

She had paid little attention to the investigations that her husband had become involved in – he had always preferred his work to be a private thing. Eileen sat at the bedside, ignorant of the file in her husband's drawer marked 'Phoenix', but as she sat, others were seeking the file.

Across London, the shadows of the two intruders darted through the rooms of the Mountjoy home. To most, the raid would look like a simple robbery, carried out by opportunist thieves seeking out credit cards and jewellery. No one would notice, among the vandalised chaos of Doug Mountjoy's study, that the file tagged 'Phoenix' was missing.

The fading odour of perfume mingled with the smell of sweat as she fought against her own body to push the weights one more time. A heaving sigh erupted from her chest as she pushed upwards from her prone position to hold the two five-kilo dumb-bells above her body. The sweat had matted the curls of her dark red hair, tied back tight with an elastic band so that it lay almost flat against her scalp. Streams of perspiration meandered down her milky-skinned cheeks as she pushed her body to make one more effort.

Morning had not yet fully broken over the barracks, but Lynn Anders had been attempting to push back the boundaries of her personal fitness for the last hour. Here, by herself, she felt comfortable. There were no prying eyes, no smart-arse comments, no insult at this time of day. Lynn Anders was alone to wage her own personal battle.

She was an outsider, the only woman in the company of men, the only female sergeant who had dared to enter the male 'club'. They had said she was worse than useless, that she wasn't up to it, that there was no place for her or women like her. And she had decided to fight back: not to win the approval of her male 'comrades', but to win for her own esteem. Each time she exercised, the memories of a dozen taunts flashed through her mind. It seemed to give her more energy, more willpower. The insults, the jibes all mustered in her mind. Without thinking, the rest of her body appeared to give one more voluntary heave of the weights. Each day was the same. Each day she was getting stronger, better, fitter, nearer their equal.

It had been just over a year ago that, as a sergeant in the Royal Logistics Corps, she had been transferred to Allenby Barracks. The plump, unhappy little girl who had longed to escape the drudgery of life in the secretarial pool at Aldershot had been excited by the prospect of the posting. She had spent several afternoons brushing up on the history of the famous regiment that she was about to join. She had been told that would be a good move: the RKR were something special, so a girl should know what she was getting herself into. It was also a good opportunity to escape the attentions of the cook from the canteen who had lavished his attentions on her in the same way that he ladled his thick dark gravy over anything that resembled meat. She had wanted more than a quick screw behind the cookhouse. She had ambition, and this posting would be a good move.

It had been hard for her. They had mocked the chubby figure who over-filled her uniform. They had laughed when she had stumbled around the fitness course, unable to attain the necessary times for the battle fitness test. Each soldier in the RKR was proud of being able to run the one-and-a-half-mile course in full gear in less than ten minutes. Lynn Anders was lucky if she could make it in thirteen.

She told herself that she could win through. She had absorbed the barracking of her peers from the Sergeants' Mess. She told herself that one day she would be included into their circle. It was simply a question of time. But then there had come that unspeakable night. Since then, she had not wanted to be a part of them. But no one had listened to her, no one had wanted to know her. She had not even been allowed to leave the regiment. She was trapped. Since that night she had pledged to fight back in her own way and live in her own private world.

She was not soft and plump any longer. With her regime of exercise the fat had given way to a new firmness which showed off the curves of her beautifully rounded body, with its full hips and firm breasts. The dimensions of her new body were outlined in her pale blue leotard. A dark V of sweat now slowly spread between the crevices of her breasts as she pushed her body further.

The sound of the heavy double doors to the gym opening startled her. No one else ever came here at this hour. She stopped, dropping the weights by her side, her lungs pounding against the sides of her chest. At the squeak of soft footsteps on the shining wood floor she turned and saw the stranger.

Scala too had thought he would be alone for his daily work-out, which was the only routine of his lifestyle. Despite his injuries sustained in Bosnia, he had kept his body hard and muscular. He had made it a personal commandment that he would run a minimum of three miles each day and attempt to work out with weights, and the transfer to the new camp had provided all the facilities that he could wish for. He looked towards the jungle of heavy weightlifting equipment at the far end of the room and saw the girl alone, astride a wooden bench. She sat up to inspect the intruder who had entered her domain and looked indignant at the destruction of her privacy.

'Didn't mean to interrupt you,' he said, smiling. 'The name's Jim, Jim Scala. I just got in yesterday ... thought I'd try a bit of a work-out before breakfast ... didn't expect anyone to be here.'

The girl acknowledged him. 'Yes, I heard that we had someone new coming. I didn't realise that you'd already got here. This is really about the only time I get to exercise. The only weights I push normally are pens and a flamin' stuck drawer from the filing cabinet,' she added, grinning.

The ice was broken. Scala was interested. Did she always work out alone?

'It's better that way, isn't it?' Her mood became serious. 'After all, I wouldn't want to get in the way, would I?'

Scala detected the sourness in her voice.

He answered flippantly, stretching his body as he began his warm-up exercises against the wallbars along the side of the gym. 'Sorry, didn't mean to pry – just being sociable,' he said in an exaggerated Welsh accent.

'Forget it,' replied the girl. 'I try to – everyone else tries to forget about me.'

She stood up and Scala's eyes examined her. With her hair scraped back and her face flushed with exertion she looked plain, and the trunk of her body appeared short in comparison with the legs. But her body, he noticed with approval, was firm and perfectly rounded. She saw Scala looking at her, and immediately draped a towel around her neck and chest. He felt like a naughty boy, caught ogling the centrefold in a girlie magazine, and looked away. Then she undid the elastic band and a shock of flame-red hair tumbled over her shoulders. A new life appeared in her face, highlighting her bright green eyes and high cheekbones.

'Don't mind me,' she smiled. 'I just get a bit tetchy sometimes ... I suppose you could call it woman's trouble!' She threw her towel and other belongings into a bag and made for the door.

'Will I see you at breakfast in the mess?' Scala inquired genuinely

'I doubt it,' replied the girl. 'You'll very rarely find me there. I've designated it a sort of no go area, and if you were me you'd understand why. But I'm sure I'll see you around.'

Without turning her head to look at him she tossed her hair and headed through the heavy doors, leaving Scala to the solitude of the gym.

The smell of mass cooking flooded the room. It was just 7 a.m. but the neatly laid tables, with their trays of tea and coffee pots and toast racks, were already fully occupied. The ritual of breakfast was already being played out in the Sergeants' Mess. Relays of white-bloused young waitresses ferried supplies of hot plates piled high with eggs, bacon, sausages and beans to the tables. The sergeants could always be relied upon to possess healthy appetites, no matter what time of day or night.

Scala, showered and fresh after his work-out, looked along the table at his new counterparts, all clad in the green camouflage fatigues of everyday service, and wondered what the heroes of the past, staring down from their gilt frames on the walls, would make of their modern successors. As the waitress delivered his poached eggs on two slices of white toast with a side order of bacon, he considered that, of all the ranks in the British Army, those who bore the stripes of sergeant had probably changed the least. NCOs, and especially sergeants, had always been regarded as the backbone of the British Army.

Only one seat around the long mahogany table remained empty. Scala knew that it should be filled by Lynn Anders. It was as if the others had agreed on a code – a code which accepted the empty place. No one spoke of her.

It was a challenge that Scala could not resist. He had met the girl. True, she had puzzled him, but from the moment he had entered the mess, the inner sanctum that was the heart of the regiment, there had been no mention of her. He had to know. The mere mention of her name brought silence to the breakfast table, broken only by Scullard's considered opinion.

'She's a stupid stuck-up fat tart. Feels she's got no place with us here. She doesn't feel accepted – truth is, the silly cow can't hack it. Just a bloody secretary in a uniform. Silly cow calls herself a soldier. Bollocks! What friggin' use is a tart like that? Too bloody slow . . . too bloody fat . . . her tits get in the way!'

There was laughter at Scullard's unsubtle wisecrack, but Scala pressed on. 'But surely she can improve? She's one of us – '

Tavaner interrupted him. 'Well, that's where we tend to differ in opinion. She's no way like one of us. Basically, we have no room for the likes of her – well, not as a soldier anyway!' His face lit up in a leering grin which prompted more laughter. Scala forced a smile.

'The point is,' Tavaner continued, 'these bloody so-called career girl soldiers want everything to change for them. It can't. I sure as hell wouldn't want one next to me in a bloody trench when some bastard's trying to kill me. The rule says every man for himself

– no mention of women. So as far as Sergeant Lynn Anders is concerned, she can either get used to doing things our way and enjoy it, or sit her time out on her own.' Having dismissed his subject Tavaner drew breath and sipped his coffee.

Yet Scala's instincts told him there was more. Lynn Anders was disliked for something other than simply being a woman. There was a hidden reason for all this resentment, and he knew he must unlock the door to that secret.

Peter Macabe settled back in the apartment, pondering his next move. He read the newspapers as had been his habit for the last twenty years. It was as if they were his life's blood, his daily 'fix'.

He had read the story of the riot and the death of Dennison many times over. The police had launched a murder inquiry. But even they, according to the papers, agreed that there was little hope of finding the killer amid the chaos. They had found the dart after an inch-by-inch search of the pitch, and it had revealed traces of cyanide. But after that, the trail had gone cold. As yet, there seemed to be no motive. Dennison's blonde model girlfriend was reported to be in deep shock.

Among the interviews with casualties and statements from police officers about what the press were calling a 'night of madness and shame' there were three paragraphs on a spectator who had been found injured near the ground. He was named as Leon Mountjoy, whose teenage son had witnessed the brutal beating-up of his father by a group of crazed fans. The report ended by saying that Mr Mountjoy was critically ill in hospital, pending further brain surgery.

Macabe shrugged. 'Bastards!' he muttered. He threw down the newspaper in order to concentrate. Within minutes he and Janine had established their plan of action.

Even the six-foot-high dark brick wall that formed the perimeter of the Berlin cemetery could do little to shield the small group of huddled figures from the icy blasts that swept across the open ground. The four men who stood around the open grave were the only visitors who had braved the temperatures to gather here. They were the only ones who had cared about Jimmy Duggan in death, as had been the case in life.

The wind caught hold of the strands of wiry grey hair plastered over the balding crown of the short man who headed the group, blowing them across his ruddy face. He withdrew his hand from the depth of his pocket and attempted to replace the strands as he prepared to offer up the few words that he had been rehearsing to say over the grave of Jimmy Duggan. He spoke quietly, and the soft lilt of an Ulster accent made the few brief words appear more poignant as the four men stared down at the dark wood coffin within the grave.

'Death is a friend of ours, and he who is not ready to entertain him is not at home,' he muttered. To Paddy Hearn, the words of Francis Bacon seemed appropriate to utter over the grave of an old serviceman. Paddy had walked with death for over twenty years whilst serving with the elite of the SAS, and it seemed to him as though death had indeed become a friend.

He considered that it had come as a true friend to Jimmy Duggan in the latter stages of his life. For Jimmy had given his life to the service of his country, having spent thirty years with the Royal Air Force. Then it had been time to retire – on a pitiful pension that had not been sufficient to maintain him or his late wife, nor to reward his loyalty.

With the death of his wife twenty years earlier Jimmy Duggan had chosen, like so many others, to seek a new life with other old comrades in Germany. They had formed a unique club and in them had found a new family. But he had hidden his true depths of despair from even his oldest friends. Alone, all he had secretly craved was to join his beloved Edith. In the end, his wish had been granted. But the end had come ignominiously, in a cold icy street where the frail old man had been trying to shelter from the biting winds.

And if Jimmy Duggan had been forgotten by his service in life, his death had proved even more of an insult. For despite pleas from those around him, the Ministry of Defence had refused a grant to assist with his burial. It had fallen to Paddy Hearn and the other three standing there to prevent Jimmy Duggan from being slipped anonymously into a pauper's grave.

Paddy Hearn was short, yet still powerfully built and his air of authority commanded attention. He paid a last final tribute to the coffin, then glanced up at the others: the tall Scot Paul Campbell, the brash Yorkshireman Ronnie Newman, and the spindly shivering figure of the dour George Catton, who was delivering his own epitaphs beneath his breath in his own West Country tones. All ex-servicemen, as one they stood to attention with no need of a voice of command.

Then Hearn barked the suggestion that they had all been contemplating. 'Right, back to the bar. Let's give our wee Jimmy a wake he'd be proud of. The poor little bastard always enjoyed a good wake anyhow – pity he couldn't be here to celebrate his own. Let's show him that at least *we'll* remember Jimmy Duggan.'

Scala felt he was being thrown in at the deep end. It was the first time he had met the regimental sergeant major, but RSM Robert Kendrick had lived up to his expectations of what the men in the mess had described. He was a man who lived – and would probably die – by the book. He was regiment through and through. Scala figured that if the man would cut he would probably bleed the red, white and blue of the regimental colours. There had been the stock few words of welcome, but then it had been down to business. Scala sat intently as he listened to the plans for the exercise.

The Rangers, now classed as one of the best mobile infantry units in the British Army, trained to perfection as rapid reaction force to be used anywhere in the world, would be at the centre of the exercise. They would be facing the 'enemy' that consisted of units of the 'marching boys' of the Household Division who had taken up positions in one of the large wooded areas that spread across the ranges of Hohne. The RKR would, of course, win through. That was the expectation of the commanding officers and of Kendrick.

Providing reconnaissance for the battalion in a fully-blown Arctic-like exercise across the North German plains in mid-February was a cruel baptism, figured Scala. But he had known worse and he knew he was up to it. The RKR would have five days to prepare.

Scala left the RSM's office in the headquarters block and, as he strode along the corridor, the sound of a girl's voice caught his attention. He stopped to look into the tiny cream-walled office. There, behind a neat barricade of scratched and dented filing cabinets, he recognised the red curls of Lynn Anders as she sat grimly taking notes from a telephone conversation. It was difficult to recognise the girl before him as the one he had first seen in the gym, clad in a body-hugging leotard. Now she seemed buried in her thick regulation army sweater, khaki skirt and heavy flat-heeled shoes. Her hair was still tied back, flat against her head. As she put the handset down Scala casually strolled into the room and beamed at her. She acknowledged with a pleasant, unforced smile.

'So this is the nerve centre of operations!' he said with

feigned sarcasm. 'I wondered where you hid out. I missed you at breakfast.'

Her face hardened. 'I told you, Sergeant Scala – you'll very rarely find me near that place. Or didn't you hear me?' she snapped back.

'So where *do* you go?' Scala did his best to sound genuinely interested.

'Oh, here and there,' she confided. 'Of course I use the mess to eat sometimes, but I generally wait until there's not a crowd, so no one gets embarrassed. Or I sometimes go out into the village.'

Scala saw the opening. 'Perhaps I could join you some time?'

The girl appeared stunned by the suggestion. 'Perhaps . . . Who knows where people bump into each other?' she said resignedly. 'Don't know what the others would say, though,' she added, referring to the 'others' of the mess. 'I don't know if the "inner sanctum" would appreciate it.'

'Oh, I think we'll let me worry about that, shall we?' Scala's grin returned. 'As you say, who knows where we'll bump into one another!'

The cab sped along the six-laned Heerstrasse through the north-western suburbs of Berlin and into the jungle of grey apartment blocks that made up the estates of Spandau. The area was changing. The army barracks that had once been home to the occupying British forces had been pulled down along with the grey shadow of Spandau Prison, once famous for housing the last of the top Nazis to be held in captivity, Rudolf Hess. A community centre now stood on the site.

The place for which Macabe and Janine were heading was in the middle of a parade of shops and restaurants in a quiet street off the main thoroughfare. Poppa's Bar promised to be no different from a thousand other drinking-holes in the city. But it had been the place that the man Gallagher had spoken of while gripped by drink. He had told Macabe that here he might find what he was looking for. Janine huddled deep into the fleecy collar of her sheepskin jacket as she waited for Macabe to pay the driver.

A thick wall of smoke from a score of cigarettes met the couple as they walked into the dimly lit room. The long, highly polished bar, adorned with gleaming brass beer taps, ran the length of the nicotine-stained central wall. A thin, middle-aged man with a gaunt face and drooping walrus moustache was drying glasses behind the bar. He ignored Macabe and Janine's arrival, as did the rest of the dozen or so drinkers spread about the bar and at the scrubbed wooden tables around the edge of the room. The noise of laughter burst from the gloom of the adjoining room, where a gaggle of punters crowded around a giant pool table illuminated by one strip light.

Janine settled herself on one of the stools at the bar as Macabe ordered two beers, and quickly took stock of the situation. Her eyes rested on the man at the end of the bar, his greying hair tied behind his head in a crude ponytail. Through his thick glasses he stared back at her. Janine smiled, but the man merely turned and spoke to a man hidden from her sight, who settled back into a wheelchair to drink from his litre glass of beer. Even from where Macabe and Janine were positioned the two men's British accents could clearly be distinguished.

In the corner of the room, partly hidden by the only plant in the bar, Macabe caught sight of four men. He counted the glasses on the table and saw the empty bottle of vodka. The four were animated, and Macabe guessed that they had spent most of the afternoon at that table. His attention flicked from one man to the next, but as he rested on the last of the group his gaze was fully met. As the red-faced man with wiry grey hair plastered across his head returned his look unblinkingly Macabe felt as if he were being stripped naked, and was forced to look away.

He turned to the barman to inquire who owned the bar. Without speaking, the man looked up and nodded to the group of men seated around the table. He continued to wipe glasses as he explained in his best pidgin English. 'It is the man there – the man who looks at you! His name is Herr Hearn.'

The foursome roared with laughter. Campbell had attempted a drunken joke, something that Jimmy Duggan would have laughed at. Macabe did not hear the joke, but nevertheless pretended to smile as if he had done so.

Hearn eyed the pair. He looked over everyone who came into his bar – it was safer that way. The reason he had lived so long was that he had always been wary of strangers. Watch for the newcomer, whether it be in a pub in Armagh or a back street bar in Colombo. It was an instinct he had learned when teaching the US Special Forces back in the good old days of the Vietnam War, when friend and foe had looked indistinguishable.

He examined the girl and liked what he saw. She filled a pair of jeans well, and her stance as she sat on the stool emphasised the roundness of her buttocks. But there was something about the man. He looked shifty, as if he was taking mental note of things. Paddy Hearn felt uneasy, and he didn't like that.

He took the empty bottle and approached the newcomers at the bar. He could smell Janine's perfume and recognised it as expensive. Paddy Hearn was a man who prided himself on his appearance; always immaculate, he wore a spotless white shirt, striped tie and gold watch chain in the pocket of one of his numerous trademark coloured waistcoats. As he approached the girl, he subconsciously checked his tie.

It was as Hearn had expected. Macabe took the opportunity to speak. A plain and simple 'Hello!' that prompted a mere nod from the Irishman.

'I understand that you own the place – a good bar!' lied Macabe.

Suddenly a noise – the slamming of the door, the scrape of a chair on the wood floor as a new customer entered – took Hearn by surprise. His response was automatic, the result of too many years in the dark shadows of combat. He spun round, hands raised in aggressive stance, ready to strike. It was always the same. Janine flinched. Then, after a split second of silence, Hearn grinned.

'Don't worry your wee self,' he hissed to her. 'Just some old habits die hard, for Christ's sake! Can't be helped. Doesn't mean anything, lass.' He saw that Janine was visibly shaken. It was time to make amends. 'You'll take a drink, lassie? Both of you?'

Macabe jumped in with the first acknowledgement. Of course they would – they would love to share one with him. But only if they could return the compliment. He introduced himself and the girl.

Hearn stretched his hand out to Janine. His grip was firm and his hand hardened. 'Paddy Hearn at your service . . . They call me "Poppa" – hence the name of the bar!' The nickname, as Macabe had guessed, originated from Hearn's army days. He had always been around to look after his boys. In his twenty years with the Parachute Regiment and the SAS, his 'boys' had felt safe when they had worked with Poppa. He brought them back alive.

Macabe and Janine joined the group at the table, sharing the jokes and toasting the memory of Jimmy Duggan. Hearn and the others vented the pent-up emotions of the day: on the government that had turned its back on the likes of Jimmy Duggan, on the society that was being corrupted back home.

As Macabe listened he built up a mental picture of Poppa Hearn, the obvious leader of the group. The Ulsterman had been proud to serve, and had fought and killed around the world. At the mere mention of his former exploits, his eyes glazed over. He was lost in a world of blood and terror, the world he had lived in for the last twenty years. But the glint that also shone through the almost black eyes when such talk arose betrayed the man's love affair with the act of killing.

Hearn was a Catholic and his family had paid the price: his sister shorn of her hair by Republicans, a brother knee-capped for sharing the same blood as a dirty Brit. soldier. Paddy Hearn would die if he returned to the land of his birth: that was the price a man paid for the betrayal of joining the British Army. So two years earlier, forced into redundancy by an Army that had no further use for him, he had poured what cash he possessed into this bar. Now he lived amongst others who had served and felt no compulsion to live in a land that could not guarantee them a future despite their years of service.

The drink had flowed. Poppa's complexion grew redder. He now spat his words as the drink took greater hold. He leaned towards Macabe, challenging the journalist to meet his eyes. Poppa's eyes were fixed in the look that soldiers around the world recognised as 'the thousand yard stare'; it was the look that came as a man relived the catalogue of horrors locked in his mind. His eyes burned into Macabe and, the journalist felt, pierced deep into his soul. Macabe, unnerved, made an act of refusing to shy from the gaze.

Hearn leaned forward, as if attempting to share a secret. 'Tell me, have you ever killed anyone?' the Irishman spluttered.

Macabe could only shake his head. 'I told you, I'm a journalist – or should I say ex-journalist,' he replied, emphasising the word 'ex'.

Hearn went on, unblinking: 'Well, I bloody well have . . . I can't tell you how many men . . . I could smell them . . . they were closer to me than you are now . . . for twenty bastard years I killed like that.' Still the detached stare penetrated through Macabe. Janine felt nervous and placed her hand on Macabe's leg.

Hearn spluttered again: 'I can tell you, Peter, me boy . . . I loved it! But then what? Bye-bye, Paddy! Fuck off, Paddy! That's what I was told.'

A noise at the bar, the breaking of a glass, and Hearn shot round, once more flexing himself and raising his hands. He laughed. 'A bit twitchy tonight, eh lads?'

Janine had had enough and wanted to leave – but not before Hearn, still curious about her man, had insisted that they returned. Macabe had hoped for as much. Janine was dreading it.

CHAPTER SIX

The camp was a hive of activity. Not even the driving winds that gusted through the barrack blocks had been able to stop the preparations for the exercise. In every corner of Allenby Barracks pockets of men cowered and cursed their luck at having to work in such conditions. It was the hardest winter that even Germany, accustomed to snow and bitter weather, had seen for the last decade.

Everywhere, shivering young soldiers attempted to go about their normal duties, sneaking into hidden offices for the prospect of an impromptu brew of body-warming tea. They cursed the enthusiasm of their commanding officer for agreeing to send them out in such conditions. But that was Colonel Andrew Cochrane all over again. If it looked good on his record, that would be fine by him. Sod the fact that the squaddies would be freezing their balls off in some Kraut field while he added another few bonus points to his record sheet.

Scala was busy at work in the massive steel hangars that housed the regiment's mechanised vehicles. The sickly smell of diesel mixed with the choking fumes from a dozen exhausts. Carefully he familiarised himself with the Spartan personnel carrier that would be his in the coming exercise. He had insisted on checking the engine for himself, and ensuring that all the batteries were topped up. Wiping the oil from his hands on to the bulky green overalls, he wondered what Matherson would say if he could see him now – some spook!

Scala was amused at the antics of the young soldiers and their excuses for getting off duty and into the warmth of the NAAFI or their own barracks. He began to realise how he had missed this kind of comradeship. The boys of C Company, to whom he had been attached, were typical of the lads in so many different regiments of the British Army. Their faces were young, disguising the fact that they had become battle-hardened veterans. They had fought the unseen enemy on the streets of Northern Ireland on three tours of duty, witnessed the atrocities that neighbour could inflict on neighbour in Bosnia, and had patrolled the jungle war lines that formed the borders of Belize. And most of them were still only in their early twenties.

The acne-scarred David 'Ginger' Baker, nicknamed for his carrot-coloured hair, was a source of wonderment to Scala. The conversation was larded with a flurry of cockney cursing as the likeable young man tended the giant Warrior personnel carrier next to Scala's vehicle. Baker would be driving it during the exercise. The boy had served in the RKR for six years, had been married for eighteen months and was now facing his first divorce – all before his twenty-fourth birthday.

'Got married too young, Sarge, that was my bleedin' trouble . . . always been the same, though . . . never listened to any bleeder . . . just followed my dick. Thought I 'ad it made. Course, don't need a brick to land on my 'ead to work out that all the silly cow wanted was an 'ome in the bleedin' married quarters and an overseas posting. Seems she wanted to travel . . . Anyway, 'ere I am, she's still in the bleedin' quarters and I'm on me jack. Got to get it all sorted out . . . sooner she goes the better. Course, I gotta stay in the bleedin' Army 'cos it's the only place I'm going to get any work . . . especially after what she's goin' to take me for . . .' More curses.

Scala had seen it all before. But nowadays the soldiers that were experiencing his own ordeal of a broken marriage seemed to be getting younger . . . or was it that he was just getting older?

Baker's rantings passed the time of day. Other soldiers cursed and complained about his non-stop moaning. They joked about their latest sexual conquests and how much beer they had managed to throw down their throats on their last night out. Scala listened, hoping to pick up some slight comment about the boy Adebeyo, who had served with C Company, or about the arsonist Curry. There was none. It was as though they had never existed.

A movement in the far corner of the shed attracted Scala's attention. In the distance he could make out the shapes of two men deep in conversation. He identified the sergeant as Scullar, and when he narrowed his eyes he recognised the fresh face of the young soldier called Jarvis, the boy who had arrived on the same day as him, his eyes popping with excitement and expectation. Normally, Scala would have ignored the two. But there was an oddness about their body language – it was not that of an NCO and subordinate. It appeared intimate, almost secretive.

The two were obviously speaking quietly – almost whispering, Scala guessed. It seemed pointless amid the noise of the workshop. Then Jarvis laughed and the two men separated. Scullard's eyes darted around the workshop as he strode in his direction. As Scullard drew near he saw Scala and the two men's eyes met. Scullard looked ill at ease, searching for words.

'See you in the bar tonight. Got a bit of a celebration, so I thought I'd stand a few beers ... See you there,' he shouted without stopping.

Scala nodded his agreement. But as Scullard made his way from the giant steel hangar Scala's sixth sense, which had rescued him on so many occasions and warned him when something was wrong, was operating at full speed.

The news from America was good. The 'brothers' had been exceptionally generous on this occasion. It made Günter Brusse a happy man – for Brusse knew that *he* would be happy too.

The visit by the Americans in the heat of the previous summer had been worthwhile. It had been a promotional trip, and had been welcomed with heartfelt enthusiasm by Brusse's colleagues. The visitors had preached the cause at a dozen meetings and their presence, clad in the traditional white hoods and gowns, had helped with recruitment.

Brusse sipped his coffee in his small apartment above the shop. Books that depicted the rise of the Reich and its days of glory, and others which spelled out the dangers of the Jew and of the black, filled the shelves around him.

Certainly the news was good. The Americans were donating almost two million dollars. They had said it was an 'investment' to spread the cause; for they 'believed', as Günter Brusse 'believed', as had his father before him. It would be Brusse's task, as 'accountant', to distribute the monies. Brusse was certain that *he* would be pleased.

The gassy beer was taking its toll. Guffaws of bawdy laughter punctuated with four-letter epithets echoed around the vast mess. Peter Hibbs was in raucous mood, providing a non-stop torrent of filthy jokes and quips. Scala thought he was more like a loud, wisecracking comedian who performed in seedy clubs than a respected member of the Sergeants' Mess. Everyone was there, even the straitlaced RSM Kendricks, who propped up the beer-flooded bar with the rest of the NCOs' 'club'. Kendricks was in deep conversation with Tavaner; they appeared to inhabit a world apart.

Hasker was too busy belching to make any sensible comment and Scullard looked the worse for wear. But why shouldn't he? It wasn't every night that the man announced his engagement to Peter Hibbs's sister. God knows, the courtship had been long enough – five years. The two had met when Hibbs had insisted that Scullard accompanied him on leave to his home in Bromley. Sheila Hibbs was not one of the world's greatest beauties, but her warm heart and gentle good humour had won her Scullard's attentions.

'About bloody time too!' shrieked Hibbs. 'About bloody time you took the girl away from it all!' More drink, much of it spilt on the floor. He proposed the toast, to Derek and Sheila. They all cheered. More drink. Scala joined in the celebration, faking enjoyment.

At the rear of the mess the television flicked its images. The news reports covered the funeral of Jonah Dennison. There had been a good turn-out from the world of sport to honour the man. The soccer world was still in shock.

'Farewell to the black bastard, eh?' The hissed comment was followed by an overpowering belch. Scala turned to see Hasker swaying behind him, spitting his vitriol. 'All the bloody money in the world won't help him now, will it?' Hasker laughed. 'Should have stayed at home! ... That's where he belonged ... might still have been alive.' Hasker cleared his throat loudly, shrugged his shoulders and returned to the bar without waiting for any comment from Scala.

The celebration would continue well into the night. Scala could slip away unnoticed and return later.

Matherson took the call from Scala. It was late, and he was enjoying his brandy and Mozart alone in his flat in Barbican. It was where he always stayed from Monday to Friday, before joining his wife and family in the Hampshire countryside at weekends. He preferred to keep his two lives separate as much as possible.

Whatever the hour, however, Matherson was always available to take a call from his operatives, especially when they were in the field. Often they wanted to feel that someone was still looking after their interests back home. He owed them that at least.

Scala's call was brief. It had been an afterthought, an obvious one, and Scala cursed himself for not thinking of it before. Matherson listened quietly, then agreed. It would be difficult, but he was sure that he would be able to get to Scala's military records. They could be changed. It should be relatively easy to insert an extra item. He would see that it was done.

The mess had emptied by the time Scala returned. Hibbs had been forced to help Hasker back to his block, and Scullard had almost drunk himself into senselessness. The great room, with its silver and huge paintings, now seemed tranquil. Scala turned to leave. Then he saw the dim light and shadows that came from the lounge at the rear of the mess. There was a slight movement – a dark shadow chased across the wall.

He pulled back the curtain and saw Tavaner sitting alone in one of the huge leather chairs, morose, contemplating, staring into a half-drunk glass of brandy.

Uninvited, Scala entered. 'You all right?' He made the inquiry sound genuine.

Michael Tavaner shrugged and motioned Scala to sit. 'I get like this sometimes. Not to worry – I just like to sit and think.'

'Anything in particular?'

'In six months' time I'm out of all this, back into civvy life . . . It's my time.' He half sighed. 'Will I miss it? I've spent the last twenty-two years of my life in the Army . . . but it's my time. Fuck – it was my life! But now I have my piece of paper that says there's no more room for me.'

Scala knew the feeling: he too had been surplus to requirement. That had been after Bosnia and before Matherson and the spook section had thrown him a lifeline. But Scala had known the uncertainty.

Michael 'Mad Mick' Tavaner had been a lifer with the RKR. The Army had been good to him – but then he had also been good to the Army. The Army had given him a home when his own home in Gravesend had gone sour on him. He had grown up in the town but had seen it changed beyond recognition, flooded by immigrants and a host of minorities. There had been little prospect of finding work in the seventies. He had opted for the Army. Michael Tavaner had felt that he could no longer go home. He had never married – there had been a woman years before, but the memory was committed to painful history. His service days had been good, and he had earned the nickname of 'Mad Mick' when, after seeing four of his friends blown to bloody pieces by an IRA trap in Crossmaglen, he had exacted his own revenge on the murdering bastards who had planted the bomb. Now, at forty-four, Michael Tavaner had been told his time had come. He would, of course, receive a hand-out and a pension. But his time had come.

'It's not the same, Jim. The whole bloody Army isn't the same any more. They've cut and chopped us, and the do-gooders in suits have made bloody sure that things will never be the same again.'

Tavaner took a deep draught of his brandy. His enormous shoulders were bowed, and Scala could feel the immense man before him slowly being eaten up with hatred from within. Scala understood his depression. Tavaner felt the need to talk.

'I tell you, there was a time when we had real power. If we had a problem with a young soldier we could just take him behind a shed and lay into him to bring him into line. That's all it took. He'd never be a problem again, and we'd have some bloody good soldiers. Not now, Jim. That's all gone. Do you know our lot actually fine the boys for being late on parade? Since when did fining somebody ever produce a good soldier?'

Scala felt the gloom sitting on Tavaner like a shroud.

'And what's at home for us, Jim? I can't see ours as a land fit for heroes any more . . . no one cares . . . no jobs . . . no one wants to know. It's fine if you're a nigger boy – you can get a house, get a job, even get a grant. Anyone else gets Jack shit.'

Scala nodded. He had seen it before. Certainly the folks back home were proud of 'the lads' when they saw them on the news bulletins. It was different when it came to offering jobs. But Tavaner's use of the word 'nigger' had grabbed his attention and he seized his opportunity.

'Well, at least you've got no niggers in this regiment.' Scala made it seem like a statement.

'No place for them,' retorted Tavaner quickly, gulping back more brandy. 'Did have one, though, about a year ago. He was shit! No room for him here. Course, the bloody officers wanted to nurse him – ignore what he was. And what he actually was, was a thief. He was shown the way, though . . . We look after our own.' Tavaner breathed in deeply. 'I'm proud of my boys, Jim Scala, and I'm proud of the regiment. They've both been my life. No black sodding thief is going to tarnish either of those things.'

Clearly Tavaner looked on Scala as a confidant, a kindred spirit. He spoke as one did to an old friend. It might have been the drink, but Tavaner definitely relaxed in his company. In just a few days Tavaner had come to regard Scala as a true, professional soldier. 'Anyway, in six months' time it won't bloody matter a toss!' he sighed.

'What then?' inquired Scala.

'Let's just say I have plans,' Tavaner grunted quickly. 'Big plans. I think I've found a new kind of "family". They need me . . . and I need them. We both think the same, and their way might be the way ahead. They're going to look after me.'

Scala interrupted too soon. 'Look after you in what way? Who are you talking about?'

Tavaner rose from his chair, towering over his companion. 'Not yet, Jim Scala. Not yet.'

CHAPTER SEVEN

Wallenius's contact had been good. The Finn had told Macabe that he would be. Now, just three days after Macabe had introduced himself, he had the information that he had requested.

The information had not been difficult to obtain, if you knew where to find such things. It had arrived as promised, sent by a courier from the *Berliner Morgenpost*, the newspaper where Wallenius's man had worked. Macabe had wanted to go through the papers there and then, but Janine had insisted. She had heard that it was *the* place to go to see and be seen. Macabe had grudgingly relented.

So now the two of them were sipping their mid-morning coffee behind the huge windows of the Café Kanzler, Berlin's most famous café, on the Kurfürstendamm, the city's most elegant avenue. The brilliant sunshine of the clear day made the street look almost spring-like. But the pavement tables were empty as the men in expensive suits and chic fur-clad women opted to stay inside, away from the still bitter temperatures. Janine was gorging herself on one of the pastries that were the café's specialities. Macabe had often wondered how the girl could have a love affair with such fattening delicacies and still maintain her tight, slender figure.

He was engrossed in the photocopied papers that had been delivered. Each one added to the picture of an idealist – perfect picture of someone who 'believed'.

NAME: Günter Brusse
AGE: 58
PLACE OF BIRTH: Potsdam
MARITAL STATUS: Single
PARENTS: Father: Major Klaus Brusse, Waffen SS, killed April 1945. Mother: Eva, died September 1956. Surviving Family: None

MILITARY SERVICE: Joined German Army August 1958, released January 1962

Macabe shuffled the pages and concentrated on the details. Brusse had been just seven years old when his father had chosen to die in the woods east of Berlin with the rest of his force from the elite Waffen SS, defending his beloved city from the invading Red Army. Klaus Brusse had been a full-blown Nazi. His wife had never got over her husband's death and had longed to join him, which she finally did eleven years later.

Günter Brusse had grown to manhood with a hatred of everything to do with the communists. It had been they who had killed his father, they who had robbed his country of its dignity. Whilst serving in the Army he had been attracted to the still strong right wing and had joined a number of minor extremist groups. Then in the 1970s he had become a member of the newly formed Action Front for National Socialism (ANS) founded by Michael Kuhnen, the brilliant and charismatic leader of the emerging neo-Nazi groups throughout Germany. With their shared ideals and passions Brusse and Kuhnen had become close friends until the latter's death from AIDS in 1991. Little had been heard of Brusse since then. He had, it seemed from the records, disappeared from public gaze.

Macabe pondered the small, insignificant man who ran the shop in Charlottenburg.

He had not expected the telephone call. But when it came he acted immediately. Now, as Allenby Barracks readied itself for the planned major exercise, Tavaner prepared to make a journey. It was not essential for him to be at the camp that day: Scullard, Hasker and the others would manage the organisation. He left Hohne at lunchtime, dressed in casual slacks and sports jacket, and set off on the two-hour drive to Berlin.

The heavy-tracked vehicle was as ready as Scala could possibly have made it. He had checked his maps and equipment, and had gone over the outline of the terrain that the exercise would cover with the young soldier who would be driving the small light armoured personnel carrier ahead of the main force of the regiment. Scala was no stranger to having to rely on maps of unseen territory for his existence. He had been the eyes and ears of many a force before in his career – tracking the drug barons of Colombia, for instance, or searching out Iraqi missile sites in the desert. Christ, his leg ached!

It always did in the cold weather. It had taken all his concentration for him not to walk with a limp. But then, he was lucky still to have the bloody leg. His mind momentarily flashed back to the hill in Bosnia, from where he had called in NATO bombers on the Serb artillery below in the operation that had left him scarred and had seen his friend killed. He shrugged. He could not dwell on the past.

Other corners of his memory recalled Tavaner's morose ramblings of the night before. An instinct told him that he should see the girl, make an approach. It had to be soon – in two days they would be on exercise. The final checks completed, he made his way to the headquarters block, straightening his maroon beret before entering. He knew where to find her. A corporal was just leaving the office where she administered the daily clerical duties of the regiment.

Lynn Anders greeted him with a wide smile. It was the first time he had seen her openly do so. Her eyes sparkled, and the bright shaft of sunlight that pierced the window shone dazzlingly on her red hair.

Scala felt warm towards her. She had given him a genuine welcome. Feigning a lack of confidence with women, he spoke meekly. 'Er . . . I was just wondering . . . about the possibilities of getting together later. I had my fill of the mess last night. Scullard had a bit of a do.'

Her face dropped at the mention of Scullard's name.

'I hoped you might come out tonight, maybe have a look at the town . . . Let's face it, I've only seen the inside of the bloody camp since I've been here. Any chance you could show me? Maybe have a drink?'

The face smiled again. This time she showed all her white teeth. It had been a long time since she had enjoyed the company of a man at this barracks. No one had dared ask her. She would be delighted. But it should be kept from the rest. No one else need know.

Scala could only agree.

Janine had chosen to take just the small pocket Olympus camera. No need for heavy equipment – it would do whatever job it was required for just as well. But she was apprehensive about returning. She had taken a dislike to the man Hearn. She feared him, and yet she did not know why. She told Macabe to be careful as she drove the two of them to the bar.

She had chosen to wear a skirt – the dark green one which came down to her knees. The silk shirt ballooned into a loose fit from her waist, and she chose it purposely to disguise the outline of her breasts. Then she chose a waist-length leather jacket to cover herself.

They arrived at Poppa's early, yet the pool room and bar were already busy. There were faces that neither of them had seen during their previous visit but there was no sign of Hearn. A plain white paper tablecloth covered the scratched and cigarette-burned table that Macabe and Janine chose. She drank brandy, Macabe a large foaming beer. The camera was in the inside pocket of her coat for easy access. Macabe seemed relaxed, nodding greetings to other customers. The man with the ponytail was on his usual stool, accompanied by his wheelchair-bound associate. Janine and Macabe said little and she guessed he was assessing Brusse's records in his mind. He had told her that he was going to push Hearn tonight – to ask him openly if he had heard of serving British soldiers who might have been attracted to various extreme factions.

They had made love earlier that evening, and Janine was still enjoying the glow of the strangely tender mood that Macabe had been in. She wanted him again, and she wanted to be away from this place. It had been a mistake – an adventure for her man, but now they should leave it alone. They should be back in her London flat, drinking wine and making love. To hell with stories.

The door opened, allowing the swirling smoke to escape into the street outside. A giant of a man in slacks and with close-cut hair stood momentarily in the doorway, looking around the room. He gently twitched his greying moustache and Macabe saw the mole on the man's face.

Macabe's heart leaped. He had seen the man before, but was unable to remember where. Cursing with impatience, he fought against his own limp brain. The man moved to the bar and spoke to the barman with the walrus moustache.

Then he remembered. It was the man from the photograph – the photograph of three men in Gunter Brusse's squalid little shop.

The barman stepped into the open doorway behind the bar and returned within seconds, followed almost immediately by the ruddy-faced Hearn. Poppa and the tall man greeted each other with a shake of hands, seized two beers and moved across to an empty table. Hearn's expression was serious and his eyes darted around the room. Suddenly Hearn's gaze rested on Macabe and the girl. The journalist raised his glass in greeting. From Heard came a grimace.

The two men continued to sit there, lost in conversation, for what seemed to Macabe to be an eternity, only glancing up from the table to order more drinks. His impatience rising, Macabe could wait no longer. Leaving Janine at the table he strolled towards the two men. As he drew nearer he heard the newcomer speaking German with an English accent. Hearn and his companion halted their discussion and looked Macabe straight in the eyes, concealing their displeasure at being interrupted.

'Hello, Paddy – or may I call you Poppa? Just thought we'd call by again . . .' Macabe feigned the effect of drink on him. 'Hope you don't mind.' Quickly turning, he held out his hand to the big man with the mole on his face. 'I'm Peter Macabe, over here from London . . . do you fancy a drink?'

'No thank you,' the man snapped back. 'I'm fine . . . the name's Tavaner.'

Without waiting for an invitation Macabe sat down at the table, leaving Janine alone. He forced conversation, ignoring any possible hint that he might be unwelcome. 'Not one to gossip of course, but from appearance – short hair and all that – I'd guess that you might be an army man of sorts . . . you know, a bit like Paddy here. Would I be right? I have a passion for assessing people.'

Tavaner was caught unawares: 'As a matter of fact that's right – for the time being at least.'

Once again Macabe pushed the conversation on, not allowing the two agitated men to continue but picking up on the vitriolic remarks that Hearn had unleashed on his previous visit, about how little the state cared about the boys in the ranks.

The two men listened, letting Macabe spout.

The candlelight danced silhouettes in her red hair. Scala sat back and looked. There was no doubt about it, Lynn Anders looked beautiful tonight. The pale blue shirt complemented her colouring and the girl knew how to emphasise her eyes with just the right amount of eye shadow.

It had taken just twenty minutes for Lynn to drive herself and Scala to the nearby town of Celle. It was a place that teams of squaddies from Hohne often invaded in search of drink and local girls.

The two of them had walked through the ancient market square and past quaint old churches. Their night had begun with a drink in one of the cellar bars, but now they had moved on to the quieter surroundings of the steak restaurant. The conversation had been simple, all about home and family. Scala had given her little chance to talk about him.

She had looked across the candle-lit table at the dark, handsome man before her, with his blue eyes that shone like sapphires. His open black shirt displayed the hairs on his chest. She detected the faint Welsh tones, but could be forgiven for thinking that the man who was lavishing her with such attention could have been a well-practised Italian Romeo. She had not laughed with a man so much for a long time. She thought Scala had a natural, relaxed way with him. She felt no unease at his questioning, and as she sipped the fruity red wine she felt a warm contentment. She had spent months being wary of men, avoiding the ones who she was forced to deal with from the mess and the headquarters block.

She was not certain why she had accepted his invitation – possibly because he was new to the camp, untainted by the others, and had charm. But she suspected that she had also wanted to break out of the prison that the camp had become and which had trapped her for so long. Scala provided the catalyst for her need to talk.

The girl was twenty-eight, the only daughter of a bank manager and his wife who lived comfortably on the Surrey–Hampshire border and had held high hopes for their daughter. Her parents had frowned when she had told them of her decision to seek a career in the Army. They had thought her unsuited, but she had always proved headstrong and to their great joy had proved them wrong. Lynn Anders had thrived in the Army and risen through the ranks quickly before being posted to Aldershot, where at first she feared that her career had stagnated. Then came the posting and her hopes had risen again.

She had not spoken so much about herself in months. No one had wanted to know. She grew sad when she realised the truth.

'So why don't we see more of you in the mess? God knows it would be a refreshing change,' chanced Scala.

The girl's face straightened. 'And that, my dear Sergeant Jim Scala, is, as they say, another story,' she murmured. 'It wasn't too bad to begin with. As a child I'd always been on the . . . shall we say . . . plumpish side. I'd taken all the wisecracks and rolled with them – Christ, I got a barrage of them when I first got here. It was all good clean fun – or so I thought.' She paused. 'Now, I just find the whole bloody lot of them a crap-arsed bunch of bastards.' She felt brave at her choice of words.

Scala smiled. He guessed that it took a lot for her to swear in public.

'But there comes a time when you can't take any more. I'd had
the insults – but that wasn't it. The whole bloody lot of them
seemed to run as a "club". I was excluded. They'd go off on
secret jaunts with each other. Sometimes even some of the other
young soldiers would go with them – nothing to do with the Army,
I was told. So bloody secret. It just got worse and worse. Nobody
said what they were getting up to . . . just a little club. Christ, Jim,
I tell you they scare me sometimes.'

'So why don't you apply for another posting?' asked Scala.

'Don't think I haven't tried. But every time the request was
denied. It's always the same,' she replied. 'Things got worse last
year. We had an incident – a boy died – that seemed to affect
the whole camp. But there was still this damn secrecy. I knew the
boy. He seemed nice – he was unhappy too. I could tell . . . I know
the feeling, you see. Then he died . . . God, it was awful – and I
couldn't do anything to stop it . . .' Lost in a haze of memories
she stared down into the well of her glass.

'What do you mean you couldn't do anything to stop it? How
could you? What happened?' Scala's questions erupted, almost
startling the girl. He immediately regretted his impetuosity.

The girl needed comforting now. He poured more wine.

Scullard was the duty sergeant that night. It had fallen to him
to ensure that the camp was quiet and deal with any problems
that arose at Allenby. Many of the young soldiers ventured out
to visit the local bars, but most had returned early enough. There
had been little trouble, and Scullard had even allowed himself a
short doze in the small office reserved for the duty sergeant by the
guardroom. The picket officer had done the rounds and Scullard
now felt alone.

He heard the noise a hundred yards away, rising from the
darkness that engulfed the perimeter wall by the gate. First there
was a laugh, followed a schoolboyish giggle. Then another laugh,
this time more bawdy. Scullard saw the two and felt the rage rise
within him.

Christopher Jarvis giggled and attempted to lean on his com-
patriot. The pair collapsed. Scullard squinted and recognised the
other culprit; it was the lad Boyd, also from Charlie Company.
Scullard had not seen Jarvis and Boyd leave the camp together;
to his mind they had planned their outing as a joint venture.

Scullard marched to the barrier of the gate. He stood alone,
watching the mockery before him. The two boys were just nineteen

and both in need of drink and laughter before the major exercise. It would be their first full-scale exercise and they had mixed feelings of elation and apprehension. Seeing the waiting figure of Scullard, they greeted it with howls of laughter and derision.

''Ello Derek, me old mate,' spluttered Jarvis. 'Come to see us 'ome, have yer? That's very thoughtful. Isn't it thoughtful of Derek to welcome us home, Danny boy?'

They were at the barrier when Scullard erupted. At first they laughed, unsurely. Then the reality of the moment hit them. Scullard was on them. He could smell the drink and told the sentry to stay put in the office. He would deal with this. For a moment the two young soldiers stood frozen with fear. Then Scullard reached out and grabbed one with each hand.

'Stupid little bastards!' he snarled, spraying a shower of spittle over the faces of the two soldiers. 'What the fuck do you think you're playing at? Think you're big boys who can hold your fucking drink? I'll teach you to drink, you little bastards . . .'

Jarvis reddened in the face as a result of Scullard's iron grip on his collar.

'You!' Scullard directed to Jarvis. 'You, pretty boy . . . still wet behind the bloody ears. Think you're a big boy just 'cos you go on the piss?' He dragged Jarvis so close that their noses almost touched. In rage Scullard hissed, 'Get out of my sight . . . I'll see to you later!'

The lad tumbled backwards as Scullard let go. He saw the enraged NCO drag Boyd, protesting and offering apologies, towards the guardhouse. Jarvis ran into the night to his barrack, panting, sweating, half-sobbing.

Boyd tried to stand straight as Scullard led him to the tiny grey cell in the guardroom. Scullard still held the youth tightly, his eyes blazing with rage. He banished the sentry and kicked the heavy metal door shut behind him. Boyd offered more apologies but his assailant ignored them and caught the youth in the groin with the full force of his knee. Boyd screamed and sank to his knees as bolts of agony shot through his body.

'Another big boy, eh? Get a few pints of piss down yer and think yer a big fella!' barked Scullard. I'll not have any young bastard like you try and disgrace my regiment like this. Christ knows what any other sod might think.'

Tears welled in the youth's eyes. He tried to restrain them before they started to stream down his face.

Another kick from Scullard, and the boy cried out and rolled on the floor against the empty bucket that still smelled of the urine that it generally contained. Without warning, the night's drinking and fear took hold and the youth threw up on the concrete floor and over Scullard's boots.

'Not a word now, you pathetic little bastard,' spat Scullard. 'By the time I've finished with you you'll be pleading for my mercy and your mother!'

Jarvis lay on top of his bed, biting the pillow case and feeling his tears spreading into the cloth.

Janine saw the man first. She attempted to signal to Macabe as soon as she saw the grey-haired figure enter the bar, but he was still engrossed with Hearn and Tavaner. Finally she caught his attention. He shot a brief glance towards the man and recognised Günter Brusse immediately.

Hearn and Tavaner had dropped heavy hints that they did not want Macabe with them. They had things to discuss. Macabe had gleaned the information that the two men had known each other for over five years and had been introduced by a friend of a friend. They had discovered that they had much in common. They were two old soldiers who had seen much and expected recognition.

When Brusse spotted Macabe he seemed startled. 'A small world, Herr Macabe,' he greeted the flushed journalist.

'Indeed it is. Perhaps we share the same taste in drink,' he replied, attempting to laugh off the situation.

'And we appear to share the same company.'

Hearn and Tavaner looked apprehensive. 'You know each other?' asked Poppa.

'Only slightly,' said Macabe hurriedly. He checked his watch and shot a glance to Janine. 'It's late, gentlemen, and I think I've bored you enough. I feel it's time to leave.'

Janine had taken advantage of the distraction to take out the Olympus and had discreetly snapped the group from underneath the table with one hand. She had used the wide lens to ensure that the whole scene would be included. Without looking, she felt she must have used most of the film.

Macabe turned and signalled to her to join him. She gathered up her belongings and together they made for the door. Macabe was still smiling as he left.

As they crossed the road to the BMW Janine glanced over her shoulder and saw the three men gathered, watching, discussing the couple as they headed away. A stab of fear ran the entire length of her body.

CHAPTER EIGHT

He had kissed her a gentle goodnight. On the cheek, not on the mouth. She had wanted to feel his mouth pressed hard against her own, but it had been better this way. It had been months since a man had showered as much attention on her. Jim Scala had made her feel like a woman. There had been no groping, no clichéd compliments of the kind she had grown used to from squaddies whose only interest was to have a quick leg-over. She felt Scala had been genuine.

She was alone now in her tiny, claustrophobic room, part of the prison to which she had been confined by the others. She had fought her fight against those others. Now she had turned herself into what they might have wanted – but they would never have the opportunity. She would rather let the odious cook from Aldershot have his way than any of the others. Yet the man tonight had been different. He had not demanded anything. If he had, she wondered if she would have allowed herself to be taken. But that was not the question now.

She had been quiet on the drive back from Celle. Scullard, as duty officer, had been at the gate to check her car as they arrived. She had enjoyed the look of surprise on his face as she and Scala arrived at the barrier. The sentry had grinned. They had left her car on the car park by the Sergeants' Mess. Then came the kiss – the gentle kiss on the cheek – after which Scala had bade her goodnight and slowly walked into the darkness towards the block that housed his own room.

As the only female NCO on the camp Lynn Anders had the unique privilege of having her own room in an entirely empty block. Otherwise only guests and visitors were ever accommodated there. She had made the most of the room. Photographs of her mother and father were placed prominently on the chest of drawers. There was a hi-fi system and a television set, bought cheaply from one of the soldiers who had the right contacts, and books were scattered around. This, to her, was home.

She began to undress, to peel off the blue shirt. She felt angry, her pulse racing, but she was unsure why. As she pulled at her clothes she paced the tiny room.

The single tap at the door stopped her in her tracks. On impulse she turned off the main strip light and left the room lit by the reading lamp on the aged wooden table by her single bed. Gingerly she moved to the door, replacing the blouse around her shoulders and buttoning it. She felt a fluttering twinge of nerves in her belly and her heart pounded loudly as she slowly opened the door.

Scala stood there, offering a faint smile and clutching a half bottle of brandy. His right eyebrow, slightly raised, gave the handsome, scarred face an even more rakish appearance. He put his finger to his lips to suggest silence. She understood. No words were needed. Slowly she opened the door. Although no one else shared the block she still felt an absurd need for quietness.

She stopped buttoning her shirt. The dim, warm light of the lamp momentarily silhouetted her against the bare wall of her room and revealed the outlines of her body through the thin blue garment.

'I know it might seem like a liberty, but I took it anyway!' said Scala, grinning. 'It was a good night and I wanted to say thank you, so I hoped a nightcap might be in order,' he muttered. He made a grand act of pretending to leave if she did not approve. There was no resistance, and he used his foot to close the door behind him.

'As you may have gathered, I don't get many men visitors here,' she said, grinning. 'Haven't had the opportunity, you see . . .' She felt nervous – not of Scala, but of seeming foolish.

There was a great play of Lynn seeking out the right sort of glasses, after which Scala poured healthy-sized measures from the bottle. There was only one chair in the room: there was no space for another. Scala sat on it. Lynn, feeling uncomfortable sitting on the bed, reached across to the table to place a CD in the hi-fi system. As she leaned forward her shirt fell loose, revealing a glimpse of firm, rounded breast. She knew Scala had seen, and did nothing to cover the display. It made her vaguely aroused – an emotion she had not anticipated.

Scala reached for her hand and stroked it softly. He knew the moves; he had made them a thousand times before. None of it had mattered, except those all too brief occasions with Angie. But he knew what a woman required. He knew what was about to happen. Scala slowly reached for her and pulled her towards the chair. She offered no resistance – she too had anticipated it, hoped for it.

There was no rush; no need. Although there was no one else in the block, they still spoke only in hushed tones. Lynn placed herself across his legs, softly stroking his face and tracing the scar on his right cheek with her fingertip. Neither flinched. Moving her face towards his, she placed the side of her cheek against the scar as if attempting to share it. Then she lifted her head so that her nose touched the end of Scala's; her lips opened and she slowly moved forward to engulf his mouth with her own. Wrapping her arms around his neck, she started to rock to and fro. There was gentleness in the first kisses as she sought him out. Then, it seemed as if the floodgates of months of despair had opened and her pent-up passion was unleashed.

Scala attempted to calm her as he purposefully undid the few buttons of the shirt, and slipped it from her shoulders. She wore no bra, and as she rose from the chair she squirmed free of the dark blue trousers that she had been wearing. She stood before him, displaying the soft, milky white flesh that had been toned to firmness.

Then she stepped back to the bed and stretched back across the dark overblanket, her red hair across the white pillow. She wriggled, naked and free. Scala stood and undressed. There were no words . . . no need.

She looked at him, admiring the firmness of his muscular body. There had been no one for months. She wasn't certain if he had chosen her or she had chosen him. Now, it didn't matter. Glancing down, she saw the jagged scar that ran the length of his right leg where the shrapnel had buried itself deep as a memento of Bosnia. At first she grimaced, not knowing about the wound and shocked by its severity. Then, discarding all her worries, she pulled him down towards the bed. She was in control now. The two bodies jostled for position on the narrow bed, and Lynn won! She knelt over him, the full beauty of her body exposed in the light from the single lamp. Slowly she ran her fingers along his leg; then her tongue followed the full extent of the wound, upwards, always upwards.

Once again he was running down the dark corridors. There was a flash of steel and he saw himself lying alone in the dark. The demons had returned to haunt him. Scala awoke with a start, heaving and bathed in sweat. Lynn, snuggled beside him in the cramped bed, was jolted into shocked consciousness by his sudden movement.

Panting and disorientated, he shook his head in an attempt to free himself from the fear. It was always the same. She reached out, placed her arms around him and gently hugged him, like a mother comforting a child gripped by a nightmare. Reality slowly returned to Scala's confused mind, yet his heart still battered against his chest. Once again he had seen what he thought was the scene of his own death. Lynn held his face against her silky soft breasts, tenderly stroking him.

'Sorry!' was all that Scala could muster as he fought for breath. 'I can't shake off these bloody dreams . . . It's always the same – I'm running . . . in the dark. I've no idea where the hell it is . . . and then I just see myself lying there.'

'How long has this being going on?' she whispered.

Scala considered. 'A few weeks now . . . bloody stupid, I suppose. It'll pass . . .'

She rocked him in her arms like a baby, until she could be sure that the demons had departed.

Janine had stayed up late to develop the film in the makeshift dark room that was the bathroom of the apartment. Now she held up the final prints and proudly handed them to Macabe. She was pleased with her efforts.

Macabe looked drawn and unshaven. He had not slept, insisting on typing up the story of how the known neo-Nazi sympathiser had socialised with the British Army man he called Tavaner as well as the disaffected ex-pat. He consulted his notes once again. He was certain that the soldier had said he was with the Royal Kent Rangers, and there was something familiar about the name. Macabe searched the crevices of his tired brain; then, having no success there, dipped into the pile of notes, records and newspaper cuttings that had accrued. Their it was – the body of the story of the burning of the hostel at Lübeck. As he scanned the tattered cutting once again his heart soared when he found the paragraph he had been searching for. The soldier arrested at the scene had also belonged to the Royal Kent Rangers. Suddenly Macabe's fatigue left him.

Scullard was the first at the breakfast table. He had a healthy appetite today, and the waitress was ordered not to stint the portions. She had dutifully obeyed. The sergeant was already halfway through the mound of food on his plate when Hibbs and Hasker joined him. Scullard was wearing a satisfied grin.

'Busy night?' inquired Hibbs.

'Not really – boring as shit,' he answered blandly. 'Had one bit of drama, though. Couple of the little sods came in pissed as rats.'

Hasker showed an interest. 'Who were they?'

'The new boy Jarvis . . . and that cretin Boyd. I dealt with him, though. Put Boyd on a charge . . . I put the shits up him so much he'll never do that again.'

'What about Jarvis?' asked Hasker.

'Oh, I'll sort him out later – thought I'd leave him for a while, being new and all that. But trust me – I'll scare the hell out of him as well. I'd be surprised if he steps out of line again for a long while.'

The pain was still with him, but there was nothing to be seen. Scullard had known how to go about his work. He had also insisted that the soldier be given guard duty for the following morning. Boyd had expected retribution, and the punishment had begun without delay: had stood sentry at the barrier since 7 a.m. Even then, the events of the night before had seemed a long time ago. But he could still feel the pain of the sergeant's boot. He consoled himself with the knowledge that at least he would be out sight of Scullard when the sergeant and the company commander came on a pre-exercise inspection of kit and rooms. Here, at least, he would be out of harm's way.

Tavaner was still apprehensive. He had not liked what Brusse had told him about the man who had come to his shop and asked questions, and then appeared at the bar. They had all agreed that no risks could be taken. There was too much at stake. The plans were too far advanced to allow some nosey journalist to screw everything up now.

Now, Tavaner listened intently to the complaint of the soldier before him. The young private was angry. He had been certain that the wallet had been in his room when he had gone off for a shower. It had vanished by the time he had returned. All the boy's English money had gone, some one hundred and fifty quid, as well as the special five D–Mark piece that he had kept as a lucky charm.

Tavaner made a note and promised to investigate. He would inform RSM Kendrick too. A thief was one of the most detested forms of low life within an army company.

The news room was buzzing. It was the kind of day that editors of national newspapers dreamed of, with hot stories flooding in from all directions. By the time of the afternoon conference, when all the heads of department gathered to plan the next day's edition, they had been spoilt for choice. Two gruesome murders, a follow-up on the latest sex scandal involving a Cabinet minister, and yet another row amongst the royals were all vying for prominent positions on the front page. Even the sports desk were busy furnishing details of the forthcoming first-ever international soccer tour by a South African team. Despite all the political wranglings over the schedule, the tour was to go ahead as planned.

By mid-afternoon Paula Ryan was already running on pure adrenalin. She sat back at her desk behind the door labelled 'Assistant Editor (News)' and took a long drag on her cigarette, inhaling deeply. She had had hardly a moment to herself today, yet as she glanced into the mirror on her office wall she felt she still looked composed and glamorous in her tailored red suit. Paula Ryan believed in power dressing. She knew that soon all hell would be let loose. It was her job to ensure that the day's news stories were fully prepared and assessed ready for inclusion, and in just over an hour's time the various editors would gather for the final frenzied hours of preparing the next day's paper.

Peter Macabe had telephoned three times, and on each occasion her secretary had been instructed to fob the man off. Next time, she would take the call herself. She and Macabe went back a long way, after all. They had both started their careers in Fleet Street together. They had been friends, and there had been that crazy drunken night in a West Country hotel whilst covering the story of a young girl's abduction when they had staggered to bed in the early hours of the morning and fumbled and sweated their way through hours of awkward lovemaking that they had both regretted the following day.

And Macabe had, after all, been one of the old hacks at her wedding, when she had married the tall, handsome army captain whom she now rarely saw because of his 'observer' duties in some far-off African country. She had been saddened to hear of Macabe's downfall, the one that she had predicted years before when she had chased a high-flying position and saw him content to remain a foot soldier. She considered that she owed him the courtesy of listening to him now.

The anticipated fourth call came through. He was ringing from Berlin. The two old friends exchanged small talk, but as she chatted she rarely took her eyes from the clock above the door. Mayhem time was fast approaching.

He told her of his idea for the story – why he was in Germany. He reminded her of the fire bombing, of the people he had met in Berlin: the tall soldier in the bar, the chilling ex-SAS man and the man he knew to be a neo-Nazi. Janine had taken a photograph of them together. He told her of the disillusionment that existed within the ranks and amongst those who had served. He thought it was worth trying to put something together for the paper.

Paula Ryan half listened. She was watching the scurrying in the news room as groups of men and women wearing harassed expressions gathered around computer terminals that displayed the various stories of the day as deadline approached.

He told her he had come to her because of her links with the Army. She had always managed to get the inside track, thanks to her husband's position.

She told Macabe to 'put something together' and to 'let her have a look'. They would take it from there. Macabe would have to content himself with that for the time being. She had to go now – he should keep in touch.

As Paula Ryan involved herself in the story of the murder for the front page of tomorrow's edition, Peter Macabe and his idea were relegated to an area at the back of her memory.

Macabe had almost forgotten about the man he had met in the Irish bar. It had slipped his mind that he had given him his number. So it had come as a surprise when the man who gave his name as Gallagher contacted him that evening.

Gallagher wanted them to meet up. He had some information, he said, that Macabe might be interested in. At 10 p.m. that night Macabe should be at the S-Bahn – the overground railway – station at Alexanderplatz, at the huge square that had been the undisputed heart of pre-war Berlin, but was now reduced to a bleak memento of the Soviet rule of the eastern side of the city.

Macabe tried to conjure up the image of the former soldier who had drunk so much of the dark beer and released his venom. The mystery appealed to him: he had never been able to resist situations like this. Of course he would meet the man.

It was as Scullard had thought. The news that one of them was a thief had taken no time to spread through the men of Charlie Company. Fortunately he had been with RSM Kendrick and

Tavaner when the culprit had been unearthed. Scullard had helped with the inspection of the room while the young soldier had remained on guard duty.

Boyd had denied the whole thing of course. He had never seen the money that Scullard had found hidden in the clean pair of socks in his locker. The discovery of the five-Mark coin lucky charm had been the final proof against the terrified Boyd.

Now the word was out. Scullard had seen to that. The young soldiers of Charlie Company were as one in their anger, and could hardly be contained. Boyd was placed under investigation, and Scullard had vowed that he would rue the day that he had ever come to join the Royal Kent Rangers. Throughout the exercise he would be watching the young soldier, who had been singled out for special treatment until he could be dealt with properly afterwards. Scullard would make certain that Boyd was actually proven to be a thief. Meanwhile, it would do no harm if the other boys were told.

Scala listened to Scullard's ragings over the dinner table in the mess. Hasker and Hibbs pledged their support for any action that their colleague might take. Scala looked down the table at the group as they crammed food into their mouths, occasionally spitting chunks as they spoke. Tavaner sat at the head of the table, listening, and the newcomer was reminded of a panel of judges. The verdict was obvious. The young soldier Boyd would be pronounced guilty as charged. Scala feared what the punishment would be. But if the boy had indeed taken the money, then even he believed he deserved the sentence.

Scala took his final mouthful of the tasteless pork that had been served up. He wanted to see Lynn one more time before the exercise began in the morning. As his mind summoned up images from their frenzied lovemaking the previous night he looked at the other sergeants gathered around the table, all attempting to speak as one, and wondered how – if they had known – they would judge his actions with the woman whom they had all ridiculed.

CHAPTER NINE

A thin ceiling of mist hung over the Alexanderplatz. The dull glare from the skeletal street lamps that surrounded the huge square formed an eerie glowing perimeter where dark shadows darted through the thick, damp night air. The Fernsehturm, the giant television tower, loomed above, its 350-metre-high spire protruding through the cloak of mist like a bizarre relic from an aged sci-fi movie. Like a searchlight hunting its target, the lights from the revolving restaurant at the top of the tower shot the occasional beam over the desolate square below.

Macabe and Janine stood alone on the gloomy station platform, deserted on this miserable cold night. Macabe stamped his feet back into life, and the couple found themselves enveloped by the mist of their own breath.

From where they stood in the shadows, Macabe and Janine could hardly make out the full shape of the Fernsehturm, arguably the most noticeable landmark in the city, surrounded by grim, graffiti-ridden communist architecture and the crumbling facades of the older, multi-storey tenements. The silence was broken only by the sound of an occasional passing car and of the splashing water from the giant Neptune's Fountain which dominated the square.

Neither of them spoke as they paced the empty, dimly lit platforms. They had arrived ten minutes early and to Macabe, in his impatience, the wait seemed interminable. Janine knew better than to attempt to reason with him when he was like this. The odd train shattered the stillness as it thundered through the station.

Janine stepped back into the shadows to sit on a bench to ease the frustration of the wait. Hands thrust deep into the pockets of his black overcoat Macabe slowly wandered to the end of the platform, almost out of the sight. She could hear the soft click of his heels as he walked away from her.

She could barely make out the dark figures clustered together at the end of the platform, silhouetted against the light from an open door. They looked like a group of drunks, staggering and shouting in the miserable night. Slowly the silhouettes appeared to move towards her, and she could vaguely make out at least six of them, dancing through the dark. Although they were shouting and jeering and singing – like any group of young drunks in any city in the world – they appeared to be good-humoured. The group loitered at the end of the platform, seemingly waiting for their train.

The girl shivered, and snuggled deep within the fleece collar of her leather jacket. Macabe had turned and was heading towards her once again, while in the background the distant lights of an approaching train pierced the haze of mist. Ten o'clock had come and gone – where on earth was this man Gallagher?

Concealed in the darkness, she saw the outline of a squat man arriving on the opposite platform, spotlit by one of the station lights. He stood alone in a thick jacket as a protection against the night – but made no move, no signal to Macabe. Janine dismissed him, concentrating instead on the flashing lights of the approaching train. Its noise grew louder as the grating wheels clattered and sparked in the blackness.

The sudden movement at the end of the platform alerted her. She saw the shadows of the group move quickly, approaching her man and surrounding him. The group folded around Macabe and start to rain blows down on him. She tried to scream, but her voice was lost in the roar of the approaching train.

Janine saw Macabe stumble and roll on the platform. She had her camera on her and instinctively kept clicking as she ran towards her man down the dark platform. He was down, lost in the small crowd – she saw the feet kicking at him. The lights in the train carriages shot arms of brightness along the platform, illuminating the scene and she saw the group of drunks caught more clearly as in a strobe.

Still she clicked, the flash of her camera lost in the shafts of speeding light from the train. Then she saw her man hauled up from the ground, kicking frantically but helpless against the mob, like a fox caught in the midst of a pack of hounds. She saw Macabe hoisted high and catapulted into the darkness of the track, then caught momentarily in the light of the oncoming engine, frozen as a rabbit in the glare of car headlights.

She saw the inevitable impact but shock deprived her of any voice to scream with. Then the train had gone, the noise of its deadly onrush replaced by the sound of blood roaring in her own head. She found herself alone. Overcome by the horrific events she had just witnessed, she passed out in the darkness.

The squat figure on the far platform stepped forward from the shaft of light. Satisfied that the task had been carried out, he stroked a tuft of wiry hair over his balding head. Hearn had guessed that the man Gallagher would know how to contact the journalist from Britain. Hearn knew everything about every ex-pat in Berlin – it was his instinct and his knowledge that had enabled him to survive for so long. It had been Hearn who had decided what must be done. Hearn would identify the man for the gang. There could be no risks. It was what *he* would have expected. A job well done, which the authorities would class as an unfortunate accident or at worst the result of a vicious mugging. But, like those whom he had ordered to carry out the task, in the murkiness Hearn had not seen the girl.

It was as Scullard had hoped. Word about the presence of a thief among their number had spread throughout Charlie Company like an uncontrollable grass fire. Boyd's denial of the offence had fallen on deaf ears. The blustering Scullard had persuaded others to fall in line with his opinions on many previous occasions. No one had since spoken to Boyd, and even Jarvis had kept his distance.

The first two days of the exercise had already proved hard for the alleged thief. There had been little or no opportunity for rest: Scullard, assisted by Hibbs, had ensured that. Boyd had been allocated to each sortie, day and night, that the company had been called upon to carry out; and he had been 'volunteered' for guard duty. They had watched his every move for the signs of weakness, refusal or dissent – any suspicion of these was rewarded by more duty. The redness was already showing in his eyes, and his face was death-white with fatigue.

Two days into the exercise Boyd was on the brink of exhaustion. A ten-man team in full combat equipment had crammed into each of the nine Warrior personnel carriers, 30mm Rarden cannons pointing skywards, and formed themselves into battle groups to move the infantry sections in support of the armoured units that had already thundered across the ranges of Hohne. At speeds of over 30 mph the Warriors had followed the churned paths of the ranges, sometimes frozen hard, sometimes thick with glutinous mud. Boyd had been sitting in the bowels of one of the Warriors, shunned by everyone except Scullard. The young soldier's heavy eyes ached with lack of sleep as the vehicle roared across the open ground. But every time he momentarily nodded off, the sharp pain of Scullard's boot digging into his leg jolted the young soldier back to consciousness.

As he sat there, excluded from the chatter of the rest of the men, Boyd reflected on his 'crime'. Certainly he had been pissed; but he had known so many of the others – blokes now sharing this stinking vehicle – who had been equally so on varying occasions. And he had a clear conscience as far as the theft of the soldier's wallet was concerned.

He hoped to have seen the colonel. He would sort it for him – of that he felt confident. But each time he had requested a personal interview with the colonel the man had been 'otherwise occupied' with the exercise, or else Scullard and the other sergeants had refused him permission.

The pain in his groin from Scullard's boot was still with him, and his head whirled in exhaustion. He coughed the fumes of the giant V8 Perkins Rolls Royce engine that powered the vehicle and sat back in the claustrophobic confines of the Warrior, alone in his misery.

The morning mist that still hung over the ground, was slowly giving way to the clear conditions that had been expected. Much of the open ground before him was still frozen, the carpet of solid dark brown mud only interrupted by small pockets of unmelted snow scattered over the plain. But Scala had moved on his stomach to a position at the top of the ridge to avoid detection from searching eyes. His own tracked Spartan reconnaissance vehicle had been left two hundred yards behind, on the edge of the wooded area.

Scala's hands were red with the cold, and he blew on his fingers before gripping his binoculars to his eyes. He was some five miles ahead of the rest of the RKR column, assessing suitable routes and crossing areas and watching for surprise enemy positions. It would be his job to report any possible problem back to the column. From his position he had an excellent view of the range before him. He scoured the horizon and the edge of the thick woodland that stretched almost a mile in front of him. At first glance there was nothing. But a second more detailed examination revealed them: the 'enemy' of the Household Division had taken up position by the edge of the wood. They would have anti-tank weapons and mortars, and the unwitting Rangers would storm straight into the open killing ground in front of the trees to be annihilated by the unseen enemy. There was a frozen track that led through the open field, but Scala was positive that the soldiers of the Household Division would have set a carpet of mines there. The marshals who adjudicated the exercises would be left with little option but to declare Charlie Company officially dead.

To Scala, the exercise was like old times. The difference was that the last time he had participated in such an exercise it had been a cat-and-mouse game of survival, during those icy-cold nights in the Iraqi desert when the hunters of the SAS had sought out the Scud launchers.

His mind raced back to the nights of February 1991 when he and other SAS teams had probed their favourite hunting grounds of Wadi Amij near the small town of Ar Rutbah, the site that the troopers from Hereford had nicknamed 'Scud Alley'. When they had spotted the fourteen-vehicle Scud convoy the SAS commander had called up an air strike, and the troopers had watched as American A-10s and F-15s raked the enemy column with rockets and bombs. He could still remember how a trailer and its Scud had taken a direct hit, erupting in the air into a fireball of burning explosives and petrol. A truck had been flipped on to its side and an armoured personnel carrier riddled with holes, its occupants killed instantly as shrapnel tore through their bodies. That had been Jim Scala's war. Now he was playing at war. Today no one would die for real, and he found himself actually enjoying the tasks of the peacetime battle front.

Crawling backwards on his belly from the top of the ridge to avoid detection, Scala made his way back to the Spartan. He hauled himself on board and radioed through the enemy positions to Colonel Cochrane.

'I'm sorry, Miss Letterman. Please accept our condolences, but I fear that there is little more that we can do.' The police chief spoke in suitably grave and dignified tones. 'I can agree that the unfortunate Mr Macabe was, as you say, attacked by this group. But you have been unable to supply us with any description. The night was extremely dark, and apart from the account of the struggle I am afraid you have been able to tell us nothing that can be of help. We must suspect that the motive was robbery, and that the incident resulted in this terrible tragedy.'

Janine felt her body shaking uncontrollably. She had tried to explain that her man had been researching a story; that she believed he had died because of that story. But the overweight policeman in a crumpled suit who was going through the motions of interviewing this distraught woman remained unimpressed. It had been futile. The words of Reijo Wallenius, warning of his mistrust of the police in matters concerning the new breed of neo-Nazi, surfaced in her mind.

Macabe's mangled body had been discovered further down the track from the S-Bahn station, and she had identified it from a photograph. The explanation of his death to Macabe's grieving, uncomprehending parents in their quiet cul-de-sac in the surburbs of Newcastle-upon-Tyne had been the hardest task she had ever been forced to undertake. Thank God the embassy had helped with the arrangements for transporting his body back home.

She had loved Peter Macabe for his lust for life and his devotion to his profession. She had envied him the passion that he had shown for the job. Over recent weeks she had witnessed the resurfacing of that passion and he had died because of it.

She did not hear the last droning sentences of the police chief, sitting back smugly in his nice neat office. They had, it seemed, little interest in finding those who had killed Macabe. She pondered if their attitude would be the same if the man who had died had not been a 'foreigner'. The policeman with the beer gut and sagging jowls had offered her nothing. It would, she insisted in her own mind, be up to her to give Peter Macabe's death a meaning.

The brew was on. Ginger Baker was in charge of dishing up the steaming mugs of hot tea that were as great a gift as any freezing soldier in the field could ever wish for. The young soldiers sat round in small clusters chattering about the successes of the day. They were excited, and they had done well: Colonel Cochrane had told them so. CSM Tavaner had told them too, and they had believed.

The 'enemy' of the Household Division had been outflanked by the RKR. The message from the forward reconnaissance vehicle had saved their skins in the exercise, and given them the opportunity to consider a new tactic of taking the 'enemy' position. A good four hours after the event the young soldiers of Charlie Company were still exchanging stories about the surprised looks on the faces of the Household bastards as they stormed their position.

Despite the temperatures, the men of Charlie Company were in high spirits. They had gathered in the dense woodland that they had captured, and were enjoying what little protection from the driving winds the thin fir trees offered. But Boyd sat alone, outside the main group. Still clad in full battle equipment, he searched the faces of the others for signs of recognition. But to

the men whom he had once deemed his comrades, men such as
Taff Robert: and the scrounging lance corporal from Dover called
Skinner, he was now invisible. Boyd saw Jarvis laughing as one of
the young soldiers told how he had almost cracked open the head
of one of the Household Division men with the butt of his SA80
rifle. But there was no flicker of recognition for Boyd. And all the
time, Scullard was watching him.

He attempted to find the longed for release of sleep, but
immediately the familiar, snarling voice erupted in Boyd's ear.

'Right, you thieving little fuck! Get your arse in gear . . . there's
a guard to take, and you've got it.'

Boyd attempted to calculate how little sleep he had enjoyed in
the last three days. He could not – there had been so little. His
head was in a whirl and the trees appeared to spin before his eyes.
But there could be no argument.

The photographs revealed little. As Janine had expected, it had
been too dark to expect any great revelations on Macabe's death.
She sat alone on the polished wood floor of Wallenius's flat,
unable to prevent the tears from coming once more. Some of the
prints were still damp and sticky from the developing solutions as
she flicked through them, her heart pounding as she relived the
moments of horror. She stopped at one particular picture. The
dark photograph had captured the moment of terror as the group
had hoisted Macabe into the air. In the flash of the dim light from
the approaching train she had been able to make out the look of
terror on Macabe's face as he realised what was about to happen.
The light had also flashed up the features of one member of the
group: not clearly, but sufficient to reveal the outline of a tall man
with blond, plastered down hair who stood taller than the rest.

The men were divided into sections, with each sergeant having
responsibility for one of the groups. It also fell to the sergeants to
select the order in which the men would operate. A hot breakfast
had cheered the young soldiers of Charlie Company, and most of the
complaints at that time in the morning had been good-humoured.
They had left the relative shelter of the woodland for the open
plain once again. The final day of the exercise would see them
attempting to flush out an unseen enemy machine gun position,
as part of a live firing exercise.

The grenade pits had already been dug. A grenade would be
handed to each soldier, one at a time, the pin yanked and the lethal

high-explosive ball hurled towards the position deemed to be that of the enemy, accompanied by a warning shout of 'Grenade!' No one underestimated the danger involved in handling live grenades, but it was textbook stuff and the sergeants were in command.

The wind lashed at the young men's faces, covered in daubs of black and green camouflage cream. As the helmeted troops, identical in fatigues and laden down with webbing and ammunition pouches, stood in line awaiting their turn, Scullard was the first of the NCOs to step forward to shout the order of drill.

'Boyd!' he barked. 'Step forward . . . into the pit!'

As the remaining members of his section prepared to take cover he dutifully obeyed, took a firm grip of the ball-like grenade. He had never noticed their weight before. Now, in his fatigue, it seemed excessive and alien to his grasp. Wind and tiredness combined to flood his eyes with water. The voices of command that yelled at him seemed distant; he felt detached from the scene, as if looking down on the pit at his pathetic, exhausted figure about to hurl the lethal device at the target twenty-five yards in front of him.

He rocked and felt a faint tremble pass through his body; his head swirled. It was as if a mist had descended on him. He felt disjointed. His stomach fluttered, creased up with anxiety. From somewhere behind him he heard the command: 'Pull the pin!'

The hours of drill had turned the nineteen-year-old into a robot who dutifully obeyed without thinking. He felt the grenade in his hand, felt himself pull the pin, felt himself lob the weapon from the sandbagged pit towards the unseen enemy. It was a reflex. He was conditioned to do the right thing. But, his mind was now a fog with the unrelenting tiredness.

'Oh, Jesus fuckin' Christ . . . watch out!' yelled one of the men.

As one, the eyes of the other young soldiers focused on the lone figure in the pit. They watched in ghostly silence for what seemed like an eternity as they registered the fact that Boyd, in his exhausted and disorientated state, was still holding tight to the armed grenade and seemed to have hurled its pin instead.

As if in recognition of his fatal mistake Boyd turned to stare at the lethal ball still gripped in his right hand. Too late, he allowed the grenade to fall on to the sandy floor of the pit. He attempted to move away, but mental and physical exhaustion combined with panic froze him to the spot.

The explosive detonated, sending an eruption of smoke and flame into the cold air. The soldiers saw Boyd's twisted body hurled upwards and tossed by the side of the shattered pit. The sound of the explosion echoed across the bleak, windswept plain.

Boyd had taken the full force of the blast from below and his body had been almost cut in half. Jarvis, his all too recent drinking companion, looked at the butchered mass of rags and could not contain the upheaval in his stomach. Never before had he seen a dead man in any condition. Nothing had prepared him for his first taste of violent death.

The sound of vomiting was the only noise to be heard as the young soldiers took in the horror of the scene. It was Scullard's voice of command that returned their concentration. It was a futile gesture, he knew, but he called for the medical orderlies to attend the scene. He would make this a valuable lesson for the other young soldiers to heed. He felt no guilt, no remorse. The soldier had made a mistake. He had blundered, and had paid the price. That was all there was to it.

CHAPTER TEN

'So who the hell was he anyway?' Andrew Cochrane was in anxious mood. 'What do his family say? . . . Are we clean on this one?' There was a string of questions about the fatality that the colonel wanted answered. Red-faced, his mind racing, he shuffled the papers on his desk. He could not place the boy's name, could not conjure up an image of his face. 'Who was in charge? . . . Scullard – he's experienced enough to look after the young lads . . . the lad must have screwed up . . . must have been a bit of a dimwit. Christ, that's what the Army's feeding us these days – a bunch of no-hope dimwits for us to try and turn into professionals.' Cochrane had not smoked for almost ten years. God, he needed a cigarette now.

Tavaner and RSM Kendrick were standing before Cochrane's desk, attempting to answer the flood of questions. The battalion had returned to Allenby Barracks almost immediately after the tragedy at the grenade pit.

In reality, Cochrane felt little remorse for the young soldier. He considered what the outcome of an inquiry might be on the record of the regiment – on his own record. He could have done without this little episode. He would write the customary apologetic and sympathetic letter to Boyd's family. Perhaps, if he struck the right tone, it would suffice and they would not press for a full inquiry; no need for that, to rake up the allegations of their son being a thief . . . let him rest in piece, a tragic victim of an accident whilst on duty in the service of his country. Cochrane liked the idea of that phrase.

'What I don't want is a small army of investigators crawling all over this.' The colonel sounded firm. 'In an ideal world, I'd want it dealt with in-house. No mention of this thieving episode unless it's absolutely necessary. Don't want Whitehall thinking that the RKR are a bunch of looters. Make sure Scullard is well covered – and the rest of the boys. Talk to them, CSM, then give them a good leave.'

Tavaner knew what Cochrane was suggesting. It would fall to him to ensure that each soldier present at the exercise would tell the same story: Boyd had panicked under pressure when faced with the prospect of dealing with the live grenade, had shown no outward signs of apprehension before that moment, and had been happy without any worries. They would say how popular Boyd had been with the rest of Charlie Company, that he had had a bright future. In his enthusiasm, he had simply made a stupid error of judgement. That's what the statements from the rest of C Company would say.

There had been tears and panic. The brief, nondescript message had sent a bolt of fear through her. Sitting in her cramped office surrounded by filing cabinets, Lynn Anders had been one of the first to read the short message concerning the tragedy. There were no details of how the fatal incident had occurred, nor was the victim named.

Her mind had summoned up a scene in which she saw Scala sprawled, bloodied and mangled. She told herself that the chance was remote. But she had still cried.

And she had cried tears of relief when fuller reports reached Allenby. Her man – the man whom she barely knew, who had taken her body and loved it in a way that she had never before experienced – would return to her.

It had been quick; the girl did not enjoy lingering with punters such as him. She had not recognised him, but then so many used her talents that she could have been mistaken. He must have sought her out after a previous encounter.

The routine had been the same. She had always operated the same corner of the same street of the same area that under the communists had been a desert for girls like her. It was different now; more like people said it had been in the days before the war, when artists and intellectuals and girls of the night had all mingled in the area around the Oranienburgerstrasse. The pretty, raven-eyed girl with wild black hair that cascaded to her slim shoulders had always been one of the most sought after under both communism and, more recently, capitalism. Tonight the punter had come for her and she had led him along the dark corridor of the grey five-storey block to the small room at the rear of the video store, just as she had done a thousand times before. She was a true professional, proud of her natural skills with men. She made each one feel as if he was more than a sad punter from the street who needed the services of such a woman. Slowly she had undressed, peeling the tight leather skirt from her hips and unbuttoning the silk shirt to display her wares to the mesmerised client lying on the bed. And, as ever, unseen from the vantage point behind the mirror, the camera followed every move.

The soft blue eyes of the man who had at one time longed for nothing more than to follow his father into the family law firm observed the routine as he had done on so many other occasions. She was, after all, one of his women, and he was proud of his talent for choosing only the best to work for him. He was in the business of providing pleasure. He treated his women well, and they in turn respected him. They had not minded being watched. It was what the man with soft blue eyes liked to do; they knew that; and their initial unease had given way to the desire to offer a performance whenever possible. That was his pleasure. It was the least they could do.

He watched through the two-way mirror that stretched across an entire wall of his bright, neat office. This was the centre of his empire. It was from here that the young man with the short, well-trimmed blond beard planned his campaigns. The racks of blue videos and pornographic literature that comprised the bulk of the merchandise for sale had proved the perfect facade. It was the same with his twenty other shops in cities across Germany, which over the last five years had provided a shield for his political ambitions.

Gently he ran his hand through the stubble on his face, highlighting the natural good looks that many a Hollywood producer of the fifties would have snapped up eagerly. The beard also gave the impression of age, and added a further five years to the boyish features of the twenty-seven-year-old.

The girl had not taken long. Within fifteen minutes she was back on the street inviting fresh trade and it was time for Klaus Vogle to attend to other work. The news had been good. The friends from Canada and the United States had been particularly generous; their contributions were needed to replenish the funds that had ebbed away during the campaigns for the regional elections. But the rewards had been plentiful – many seats in many different parts of the country.

Slowly the voice was being heard, the message was being realised. They were speaking with one voice, and it was *he*, the son of the lawyer who had seen his hopes die with his business and his lost son, who was achieving it.

'I was worried!' Lynn appeared genuinely concerned for Scala's safety. It had been a long time, he felt, since any woman had really cared about him. Not even the girl in Belfast had shown any feelings after discovering his 'betrayal' of her. She had felt she was a pawn, caught up in a sinister unseen war against terrorists. That had been on his first mission for Matherson. Now he did not consider himself worthy to enjoy the true affections of a woman whom he felt he could not love back.

Scala was sitting in the room designated for the sergeant of the watch. He had seen the young soldiers from Charlie Company packed into the minibus, headed for the bars and brothels of Hamburg. Within hours they would have forgotten the shock of having seen one of their number blown to pieces two days earlier, and be lost in a world of beer and easy women. Scala envied them; the years had failed to diminish his own memories of comrades who had perished.

He had toured the camp and inspected the barriers and the guard before settling back into the dismal, bare room where Lynn's arrival had taken him by surprise. There had been no other opportunity to be alone since his return from the exercise. She wore jeans and a white sweatshirt and smelled fresh.

'Were you there . . . when Boyd died?' she wanted to know.

Scala shook his head. He had been two miles away, scouting a crossing for the vehicles.

'It must have been terrible . . . did you know the boy?'

Again Scala shook his head. He had heard Scullard talk about the little bastard that he had caught drunk and intended to punish – about the boy who had been accused of thieving from a comrade. But that was all.

Lynn and Scala chatted freely for over ten minutes, alone. The camp seemed ghostly quiet, and Scala was pleased for the company.

Lynn looked subdued. 'About the other night . . . about you and me . . . I wanted to say . . .'

Scala expected the worst. He interrupted. 'I think it's me who should apologise . . . I was the one who came to *your* room, remember . . .'

It was the girl's turn to interrupt. 'No . . . you don't understand. I don't want an apology. I came to say how wonderful it was.

You made me feel like a real woman. God knows, I haven't been allowed to feel like one here for such a bloody long time. I've been so unhappy . . . not known what to do. You've made me think . . .'

Scala was keen to hear more.

'I've got to talk to you. Not here – away from this place. I have to talk to someone, and after the other night, I felt . . .'

Scala put his finger to the girl's lips to silence her. 'Okay, we will. Trust me – we will,' he whispered.

She leaned forward and kissed him firmly on the mouth.

'You kiss like a married man, Jim Scala . . . only a married man can kiss like that.' She smiled. 'I wish I knew more about you – perhaps one day you'll tell me. There's more to you than you let me see . . . I do know that much,' she continued.

He wanted to tell her everything, to free himself of the knowledge and fears that he hid inside. He wanted to talk about Sean and Gemma; about Angie, who had once loved him enough to marry him; of how he had betrayed her too because he could not share his love for the Army and adventure; and of how he had seen sadness etched on her face when Matherson had come to the house to offer him a new life.

He wanted to confide in her, and tell her why he had been sent to spy on the inhabitants of Allenby Barracks, and of how he had found himself trapped by his love of duty because it was the only path that had offered him a future. But Scala could not say these things.

Paula Ryan stared at herself approvingly in the mirror on her office wall as she prepared for the evening conference. She was confident of appearing good, despite having had a shit day. The news pages of the tabloids would be trumpeting the nights of shame that the soccer loonies had heaped on various grounds around the country. The hacks had worked well. They had gathered a complete dossier of all the known soccer thugs and attempted to marry them to videos of the incidents, as provided by regional police forces. True to form, the political 'rentaquotes' had called for stricter controls at soccer grounds, a total ban on fans attending international matches and jail sentences for the more violent offenders.

No one knew what had started this more recent wave of violence. It had seemed to begin on the night Jonah Dennison had died, and had gone from bad to worse. It was like the bad old days of the seventies all over again.

The paper had done well to provide the coverage. Paula Ryan had received praise from the editor, too. That was why, despite the frenzy, she felt good.

She had been saddened by the few paragraphs in the *Evening Standard* that had reported how the ex-Fleet Street journalist Peter Macabe had been brutally attacked and killed in a mugging incident in Berlin. She had liked Macabe. She tried to remember why he had called her at work just days ago, but the reason remained buried among all the other hectic goings on of life at a national daily.

The battery of flashing neon lights that stretched along that infamous street in Hamburg had already enticed hordes of red-blooded male visitors keen to view the strip shows, nudity and sex acts in the clubs and bars that had given the Reeperbahn its reputation. The young visitors who had driven north from Allenby proved themselves no exception. They had arrived in the city with wads of cash stuffing their pockets, and had been only too eager to see their banknotes frittered away on round after round of drinks in a string of sleazy bars. They had toured the clubs with names that implied sexual gratification, and had seen a variety of full-breasted women perform a variety of imaginative sexual acts with a variety of partners on a variety of stages. The young soldiers had groped and fondled and negotiated fees with a string of tartily clad women of all ages and all skins, whose only aim was to relieve the fresh-faced loud-mouths of some, if not all, of their cash. The soldiers from Allenby had come to forget – to drink, to whore and so to forget about the young soldier whom they had once taken into their ranks as a friend, whom they had then turned on and accused as a thief, and who was now dead.

They had hunted together – all except the young boy whose father and grandfather had served with the men of the RKR of an earlier generation. Christopher Jarvis had felt stifled in the company of the others, unable to share the bawdy jokes, the low-life innuendo that passed between soldier and hooker. He had wanted no part in all this. Jarvis was best alone, he assured Ginger Baker and Taff Roberts and the broad-shouldered lance corporal from Dover. He would meet them later.

There had been too many other distractions of the flesh for the likes of Baker, Skinner and Roberts to concern themselves about without thinking of Jarvis's petty emotions.

Tavaner had worked late, until the goddam paperwork that

threatened to drown him in a sea of forms and reports was completed. Then he stepped from his office and walked the short distance from the headquarters block towards the Sergeants' Mess, enjoying the sharp, cold night air. The camp was still and quiet. Much as he liked being a man of action, he enjoyed moments like this. It was as though the silence washed his mind of all the day's troubles and refreshed it.

He saw the guard, in greatcoat and peaked cap, standing by the barrier on sentry duty, ready to challenge or greet any visitor to Allenby. It was the flash of the girl's white sweatshirt that caught his eye and focused his attention on the small office of the duty sergeant. He saw Lynn Anders close the door behind her and slip silently towards her own block. He saw the silhouette of the figure in the office, which he knew from the camp rota would be that of Scala.

Tavaner didn't bother to knock, but strode directly into the tiny, cramped office where Scala was sitting alone. 'Everything okay?' Tavaner asked. 'Not feeling too lonely, I hope.'

There was no smile on his lips, and Scala presumed he had seen the girl leave. 'More like a bloody train station with people dropping in all the bloody time!' Scala exaggerated the Welsh tones, in jest.

Tavaner managed a snigger. He had formed a sneaking admiration for the sergeant from the Engineers, realising that Scala was, like himself, a true professional. He had grown nearer to him; they had chatted in drink at the end of that long night in the Sergeants' Mess when Tavaner had attempted to reveal some of his own inner fears, his own disillusionment; and Scala had sympathised. Tavaner had felt he must be getting old, for he never allowed anyone the luxury of being close enough to him to share his innermost feelings. But Scala had seemed a kindred spirit. Perhaps they were two lost souls in a world that had changed beyond belief during the time that they had both been serving.

In truth, Scala had formed an admiration for Tavaner too – a healthy respect for an old war-horse who had given his life to his duty and his men . . . as Scala had done before.

'Better watch out for her,' Tavaner said gloomily, referring to Lynn Anders. 'Just a helpful hint, but I think you might find she's trouble. We've always found her difficult to get on with. A bit of a bleeding heart – a friggin' nuisance.'

Scala listened intently.

'Just got the feeling that she can't be trusted. Not one of the boys.' Tavaner went on. 'If you take my advice – '

Scala intervened. 'Nice arse, though, eh?' he said, trying to lighten the mood. He had no desire to hear of Lynn Anders' faults tonight. 'Let's just say I'd rather concentrate on that at the moment, and not her mind. But why does everyone have a downer on the girl in the first place? She got a history or something?'

Tavaner was serious. 'She's been nothing but trouble since the day she got here. Thought she could fit in, be one of the boys. Then the next thing you know, she wants us all to change, all to be nice little boys – just for her sake. But this is a man's bloody Army and God forbid that it will ever change. That's the way we run things here, and always will be the way – no room for anything else. God help us if the day ever comes when the likes of her actually start to run the bloody Army – the do-gooders, the nigger-lovers, the bleeding hearts. Thank Christ I won't be here to witness it, that's what I say!' He realised he was almost ranting, and paused. 'Suffice to say,' he went on in a softer voice, 'we don't reckon she can be trusted, that's all. Anyway . . . what I came to say was that we can always stand you a quick beer if you get pissed off over here. The offer's there.' It was a genuine offer.

As he left the small office by the barrier, Tavaner made a mental note. It would be easy to find out, easy to check. He liked Scala and assessed him to be a sympathetic ally. But he would soon discover if the man was too good to be true.

Ginger Baker was suffering. The litres of beer were resting heavily in his stomach. The smoke from the cavern decorated in grimy mauve wallpaper and mirrors and ancient red leather seats had made his eyes stream. The whooping of the punters clambering for a closer look at the antics of the two naked girls writhing across the stage was beginning to hurt his brain. He needed air and to empty his stomach.

The soldier clambered to the doorway of the club, which was guarded by a morose-looking gorilla of a dark-skinned bouncer who sat, wrapped in an oversized leather jacket, by the entrance. Baker knew he was running out of time, but the monster at the entrance saw him coming and was used to such problems. He opened the door as the youth sprawled towards him, and Baker emptied his belly in the gutter of the dark alley outside. Despite the spasm of coughing and sweating and the eruptions of his body, he decided he felt better. His head was clearer, his eyes more focused. He was ready for the next phase of the night's entertainment.

Straightening himself, Baker got ready to re-enter the dark hole that was the club, but to no avail. The oversized jacket would not let him rejoin his comrades. Baker spat the expected torrent of abuse at him, then reluctantly staggered to the end of the alley to await the others.

A door in the building opposite opened and shot a shaft of bright red light and laser beams on to the pavement as two darkened figures emerged from the noisy bar behind them. Baker studied the two men. They seemed to be supporting each other, but not as men taken by drink did; they were clutching one another, almost hugging, like long-lost lovers. The pair stepped from the shadows to be revealed in the fullness of the neon lights that illuminated the street. Baker watched. The first man was a stranger, but it was the face of the second that gripped Baker – younger, laughing, oblivious to the world. He saw the two stop, touch gently and caress each other's faces before stepping into the darkness of the side road that led away from the bustling night scene.

Baker's head cleared as he attempted to comprehend the scene. As the two men disappeared from sight he crossed the road to the bar and stealthily, as if taking part in some military exercise, worked his way around the outside of the redbrick building. Hidden from those inside, he attempted to peer through the window. It was fogged by condensation from the breath of the scores of drinkers who lined the bar or huddled at tables around the room, but Baker managed to find a small patch of clear glass. The scene was just as he had expected.

Couples were gyrating on the postage stamp dance floor to the sound of rock music played so loud that the walls vibrated. Elsewhere, through the haze of cigarette smoke, he could make out a sea of bodies pawing and lovingly embracing, chatting, half hidden by the darkness of shadows and occasionally illuminated by the battery of flashing lights. Stooping low to avoid detection from within, Baker confirmed his initial impression that in the entire, overcrowded room there was no female to be seen.

An ocean of emotion swept over Baker. He felt betrayed, revolted and duped. And because of that he felt anger, as would the others. He would never forget the face – the face of the nervous youth called Christopher Jarvis, the one who had insisted on being alone, caressing the other man's face and walking off into the darkness.

CHAPTER ELEVEN

The debate took up most of the evening: everyone wanted to have his say and voice his opinion as to what the course of action should be. But the discussions were not carried on with the usual loudness and bravado that the Sergeants' Mess was used to. The NCOs now spoke in half hushed tones away from the dinner table, breaking off each time someone unexpected arrived. It had been the only topic of conversation for the sergeants since Ginger Baker and the other members of C Company had returned from Hamburg. The men were not happy that there was a 'queer' in their ranks.

Through the usual chain of command, by word of mouth from the corporal, the sergeants had been told. Jarvis had not attempted to fight back against the jibes and whispered innuendo; he saw little option but to accept the barrage of cruel insults directed at him.

'I knew there was something odd about the little puff, right from the first time I clapped eyes on him!' Hasker snapped. 'How the hell could we get landed with a shirt-lifter?' he demanded.

'Who knows?' Scullard was quick to join in the discussion. 'But what I do know is that something's got to be done about him. The lads are against the little sod, of course – we could just let them deal with him. They're already given him the elbow – they want nothing to do with the faggot!'

Scala eased himself back in one of the large leather chairs, and wondered if the occupants of fifty years ago had held similar conversations about their men. The idea amused him for a fleeting moment, but quickly the dark mood of the gathering took over and returned his full attention to the matter in hand. As company sergeant major it was Tavaner who had convened the meeting, on the premise that the problem of suffering a 'gay' in the ranks was a company matter and should therefore be dealt with by them alone. There was no need to involve the colonel and the RSM. In any case he could not be sure how Cochrane might judge the problem. No – the problem was theirs, and theirs alone.

To Scala it seemed as though the group were sitting as judge and jury, with Jarvis's fate at their disposal. To his surprise, he believed he understood the dilemma that the company was now faced with. He had always abhorred the idea of homosexuals in the forces. Nurtured in the blinkered, tough world of working-class communities in the Welsh valleys, he had grown up with a hatred of homosexuality. Homosexuals were perverts that were never spoken of in that world. He had thought the idea repulsive and unnatural – his father had always told him so. Even as a young soldier serving at Aldershot he had taken part in the occasional local 'queer-bashing' sortie, when a small group of drunken squaddies would patrol the pubs and clubs, hunting down those whom they suspected of being 'gay'. Scala was not proud of his past activities, but he comforted himself with the knowledge that the people he had hunted were 'unnatural'.

Age and experience had done little to diminish Scala's mistrust of homosexuals. He did not regard them as a plague on the world, as did his fellow sergeants, but he was in wholehearted agreement that homosexuals should never be allowed to serve in HM Forces. He had read and heard the various political and legal wrangles that had been aired in the media, but his opinion had remained unchanged. He believed that homosexual relationships reduced the morale and effectiveness of a fighting force. He had often considered how he would react if, during the days of his SAS adventures, he had been forced to place his life in the hands of a partner whom he had known to be 'gay'.

'We could always try and transfer the little bugger to another mob,' he heard Hibbs chirp. 'Get him sent to a Jock mob – he'll like wearing bleedin' skirts!'

His intended witticism was greeted with silence. The sergeants were in no mood for humour, and Tavaner's scathing look burned deep into Hibbs. As a self-inflicted punishment, he quickly went to buy drinks for everyone from the bar.

Scala felt the need to take part in the discussion: he had been silent so far. 'Have there been complaints – you know, have the other guys complained that he's done anything or tried anything?' he demanded.

'No. But that's not the bloody point, is it?' Scullard retorted, spitting beer from his mouth. 'It's the sheer bloody disgrace of having someone like him in the RKR. We've never had one before.'

'Not that you know of, anyway,' Scala corrected him.

'We *know* we haven't had one before,' insisted Scullard. 'I know you're only an Engineer,' he went on, 'but this is a regiment with tradition. Look around you, man – the Rangers breathe tradition and history. That's why people join it. We can't have anything that puts that history in jeopardy. My vote is that we sanction the boys to have a quiet word with our Mr Jarvis one night when he's not expecting it – he'll not be wanting to stay long after that.'

'Too bloody obvious,' dismissed Tavaner. 'It would look marvellous for us if he went back to Mother and started telling the folks back home how nasty some of the boys have been to him. The last thing we want is for *them* to start kicking up a fuss.'

It took several more beers and a wealth of discussion before the group agreed on the policy – the policy that had worked before. The code of silence would be enforced against the boy, allowing the humiliation and ignominy of his situation to work on his mind. It would be enforced rigidly. No other soldier, whether private or NCO, would make any comment to Jarvis beyond an army instruction. He would be a man alone, unseen, unheard by his comrades and NCOs alike. He might as well be dead.

Scala had seen the code enforced on men who had committed a 'sin' against their own kind, and its consequences had taken its toll. Being 'invisible' to those around one had proved so great a pressure that it had often affected the man's mind. It had taken time, but it had worked. It would force a man to quit the Army for good, or at least to beg a transfer – and he remembered an almost fatal case of attempted suicide. Enforced rigidly, the code would break a man. He doubted if Jarvis would be able to endure such pressure.

The sense of loneliness was overpowering, as if a blanket of despair had enveloped him. Within days of the code being enforced Chris Jarvis was in desperation, wondering just how long he could hang on before being forced to reveal his situation to his uncomprehending family.

He now lived in dread of the moment when he would have to explain his sexual tendencies to his father – a man whose chief ambition in life had been to see his son follow himself and his father before him into the ranks of the regiment that both had served so proudly. Until this moment young Christopher had lived up to their pride. But now the shame of facing up to his son's homosexuality would be too much for his elderly father to bear, and it would plunge his already weak and ill mother into fresh depths of despair. He was their only son, an unexpected child born late in his parents' marriage. He had carried the knowledge of his homosexuality with him since his fifteenth birthday, when he had been repulsed by the offer of easy sex with an older girl at school who had freely given her favours to many others. He had known then that he was different, but had never found the courage to reveal that truth to his family. Sometimes the burden had proved so great that he had wanted to run away from their expectations. Now, if forced to confess, he knew that the family would disown him.

Jarvis lay alone on his narrow bed, listening to the CD player that had been a parting gift from his parents, but oblivious to the music being played. There had been no jibes, no cruel jokes, no questions from those whom he had once thought of as friends. There had been only silence. As the rest of Charlie Company took their meals together, shared lewd comments about girlie photographs and exaggerated stories of their sexual encounters, he had only his misery as a companion.

He had driven from his dismal flat above the shop in Charlottenburg, picking up Poppa Hearn en route. Brusse had cursed at the broken-down vehicle and the roadworks that had made their journey eastwards across the city towards the Oranienburgerstrasse appear interminable. He knew that Stein would be in a bad mood too – he had gathered as much from the brief telephone conversation that had ordered him to the meeting.

As far back as he could remember, Brusse had always responded without hesitation when Stein had called. It had always been so, since the days when the two men had been the eyes and ears and the main supporters of Michael Kuhnen, the man with vision whom the 42,000-strong hard-core neo-Nazis within Germany saw as their new Messiah.

At first Brusse had been envious of Stein, the former lieutenant in the Bundeswehr who had served alongside Kuhnen during their military service. As the new Messiah had set about organising his reign of terror and violence in a bid to win political influence, Brusse had watched jealously as Stein had made himself invaluable to the man who idolised Adolf Hitler. The two had become inseparable, and it had been only a matter of time before Stein was cultivated by the old guard Nazis who dominated the right-wing factions.

Now it was Stein who had been handed the mantle of the new Messiah. Brusse, like so many others, had found himself mesmerised by the ambitions of the ruthless but charming young man from the comfortable middle-class background who wanted to change the face of Europe. The march of Klaus Stein's vision was already underway, and Günter Brusse was prepared to give up his life for a glimpse of its success.

Brusse pointed his ancient Mercedes down the Strasse des 17 Juni, where forty years earlier the people of Berlin had protested against their Russian oppressors. He drove through the open parkland of the Tiergarten and between the towering columns of the Brandenburg Gate, now the colossal symbol of a united Germany. After a few minutes of negotiating the network of streets they arrived at the Oranienburgerstrasse, which in the 1920s, before the rise of Hitler, had been the heart of the old Jewish quarter. Now, following the ravages of war and the sterility of the Russian occupation, the area was regaining its old vibrancy. Once again Jewish restaurants were in business, rubbing shoulders with bustling new cafés, art galleries and bars. To Hearn, the centre of Jewish renaissance seemed a distinctly odd place to meet the man who, like his predecessors of the thirties, despised everything Jewish; but, like Brusse, he knew better than to ask questions.

The bright sunshine of the day was turning to dusk as Brusse and Hearn made their way to the rendezvous. The cafés were already full of the students and scholars who haunted the area, debating matters over which they held no control. Provocatively dressed prostitutes, faces vividly painted and drowned in cheap perfume, had emerged to ply their wares. Hearn roughly dismissed the advances of one middle-aged hooker who approached the pair as they searched for the café, sending her flying and shouting a barrage of abuse.

Brusse was the first to spot the café. It stood directly opposite the magnificent black and gold-leaf dome of the Neue Synagoge, the biggest synagogue in Germany, gutted during anti-Semitic riots and later destroyed by Allied bombing, but now restored. Like the others, the café was filled to capacity. The smell of roasting coffee mingled with the aromas of cigars and cigarettes and the heavier smell of cooking. The din from a hundred voices was almost deafening. The crash of a tray made Hearn jump in nervous anticipation, hands raised.

Despite the crowd Brusse had no problems. The man with the neatly trimmed stubble and pale complexion was where he had said he would be, in the far corner of the room. Stein met Brusse's gaze. Brusse also recognised his companions. The deep staring eyes of the blond-haired man on Stein's right were already locked unblinkingly on him. The other man, who had a dark moustache, was engrossed in the challenge of ordering more drinks from a flustered passing waitress.

It was like a reunion of old friends, yet it went unnoticed in this crowded place. Poppa Hearn was the first to congratulate the pair on the success of their recent mission. It had been a double success: the rich nigger Dennison would no longer exert his influences over adoring white youngsters again, and the weasel Mountjoy would never again pose a threat. Volker Reisz was quick to accept the congratulations of the old soldier he respected, while Coetzee smiled with false modesty as he gulped down a fresh glass of frothy beer.

Hearn's harsh Irish tones were tinged with obvious admiration. 'A job fuckin' well done! My old mob couldn't have done any bleedin' better. There you go – in and out before the cops know anything about yer. It'll make the bastards sit up and look, I can tell yer! They won't know what's hit 'em.'

Reisz nodded his agreement, a grin snaking its way across his mouth. He stroked his slicked-down blond hair and sipped the coffee before him. It had been Stein who had sought out Reisz as a willing recruit. He had been promised greatness, but the reality was that Reisz had a passion for his work. He classed what he did, what he was good at, as a necessity. And he had found in Stein, and in those others who believed that Adolf Hitler's regime had opened the door to building a new civilisation, a paradise on earth, the path to a new destiny for the country he loved.

It was Stein who brought an end to the mutual back-slapping. He was in no mood for humour and the usually soft pale eyes now blazed with fury. He had received disturbing news. The man whom he had for years deemed a traitor and an insult to the German nation was daring to challenge the new movement. The man who was idolised by millions, not only in Germany but throughout the world, was about to place his toe in the muddy world of politics.

The others were instantly aware of the person Stein was talking about. The whole world knew of him. The legendary Rainer Fassbeck, it seemed, was no longer content with the admiration of millions through his exploits on the tennis court. Now the three times champion of Wimbledon and winner of a string of other international titles was about to announce his intention of throwing himself into the political arena at the next regional elections.

A silence fell on the table. The five men seemed stunned by what Stein had just told them. Fassbeck had spoken against the growth of right-wing violence before, and had been subjected to threats himself, because he had a beautiful coloured wife. The marriage of the world's tennis number one and a glamorous Brazilian supermodel had made headlines around the globe, and in the succeeding four years they had played the perfect couple. But behind the scenes they had suffered the cuts and jibes of those who believed that 'foreigners' would prove the downfall of the new Germany, and that he in his privileged position had betrayed the cause by taking an outsider as a bride. For a while the couple had exiled themselves in Monte Carlo, but Fassbeck had felt uneasy at being driven from his homeland by threats.

'It would appear that the man is no longer content to be merely a sporting hero,' explained Stein in a low but attention-holding voice. 'According to what I hear – and what I hear is usually correct – the traitor has made himself a pawn of the Social Democrats, who would seek to humiliate us publicly. He believes himself to have a following. He is going to campaign in the Baden-Württemberg region against us – against all that we have sought to achieve.'

The others grunted their disgust. They knew the significance of Baden-Württemberg. It was a fascist stronghold where for years an escalating campaign of terror and violence had been visited on foreigners and refugees there. It had been decreed so by Stein, who had assured his followers that it was proof that a multicultural society does not work. Their support had grown. Now Fassbeck was daring to challenge him.

'I have decided that Herr Fassbeck will be beaten – and not at the polls,' said Stein. He was grinning, but his expression was one of menace. 'I am certain he will see himself as a symbol of resistance to our movement, and I have no need to tell you that we cannot tolerate any sabotage of our plans at this precise moment.'

Once again there was a grunt, this time of agreement.

Stein continued. 'Gentlemen, we know our goal. Within a very short time we will be in a position to make the whole world aware of the power of our movement – of our march, of our rebirth. The rise of our power from the ashes of that of generations before – like the great bird rising from the ashes of the fire. When that happens, the world will truly hold its breath. Until that time we cannot allow any undesirable propaganda from a person such as Herr Fassbeck. He must not be given a platform, if you take my meaning.'

The heads nodded once more.

'I am sorry, Volker, but this is no job for your fine group.'

Reisz raised his head in amazement. It was the role that he had expected to fulfil. Nevertheless he held back his argument as Stein went on.

'We cannot afford, at this time, to initiate any action against us from the security services.' Stein was aware of the amount of criticism that had already been directed towards the joint security agencies of the Bundesverfassungsschutz and the Federal Criminal Office, the Bundeskriminalamt, to cope with the growing threat of the fascist movements within Germany. 'Therefore, Poppa, I feel we must call on the services of our other colleagues.'

Hearn could not conceal the look of delight that spread across his face at the prospect of using the talents of those he had been responsible for seeking out and recruiting to the movement.

'There will be outrage, of course, and people will inevitably point fingers at us. But it must be seen that our hands are clean. There can be no trace to us, no link. And who would suspect?'

Reisz now grinned in admiration. The plan was agreed. The arrangements would be made.

'Tell me about your wife. What was she like?' begged Lynn. 'I know it sounds bizarre, but I would somehow like to have a picture of her in my mind . . . I'd like to know what my rival looks like.'

Scala shuffled on the stool. For the last forty-five minutes he and Lynn had been the only customers in the run-down bar in the centre of the main street in Hohne. He had wanted to be away from the prying eyes of any passing off-duty soldier, and the Bürgerstube bar was hardly the place that most squaddies would relish visiting. The aged dragon-faced woman who served the beer was not renowned for offering a warm welcome to any member of Her Majesty's Forces. She had been so ever since the death of the childhood sweetheart, who had been taken from her by the bastard British during the bloody battle for Caen over a half a century before.

Lynn's question caught Scala by surprise as he attempted to discover more about her, and about that fateful night over a year ago when the coloured boy had died.

'There's nothing to describe, really,' he murmured quietly. 'She was just a simple little girl who loved the idea of being married to a soldier – until a soldier's life got too much to cope with. She was dark . . . and slim . . .' Scala found himself conjuring up with fond remembrance every minute detail of the woman who had loved him for so long. But the image of her standing on the dismal doorstep in that grim housing estate, and closing the door in his face would bring him pain for ever.

He gathered his composure. 'There's nothing really to tell. I suppose, like most soldiers and their wives, we got married too young and regretted it after.'

Scala wanted to know more about the girl. She had softened to him. He wondered if, had he not married Angie, he might have met and loved a girl like Lynn Anders. It would have been easy to have done so. Now he was aware of her misery. Every request for her transfer over the last year had been refused. Each time she had been fobbed off with a different reason. Now she was trusting him; she needed him, the outsider who brought release from her pain.

He had shown signs of unease when she had raised the question of his wife. It was a subject to remain taboo, Lynn decided.

CHAPTER TWELVE

The fist slammed hard on the table. He was angry. It had been the fifth time in succession that Hasker had lost the hand. He was over £70 down and of all those playing he could least afford such losses. The divorce settlement three years earlier from the wife who had refused to compete with the 'mistress' that was the Army had seen to that.

The game had begun in a friendly way. But whenever the sergeants played poker, and beer flowed and money was won and lost, the game took on a more sinister tone. They were all friends, but those who chose to take part were well aware that friendships took second place to the game. Hasker had known, and had taken his chance. But even he in moments of sobriety would concede that he was no poker player: he should never have played the game. He lacked the necessary cool temperament and blank facial expression; instead, his face was an open window.

It was late, almost midnight. The game had been played for hours, and it was Company Sergeant Major Tavaner who that night had enjoyed the company of Lady Luck and amassed almost £200, most of it Hasker's. The group had gathered under the subdued lighting of the rear room of the Sergeants' Mess, which on these nights could provide an atmosphere of high drama. There were six of them: Tavaner, Hasker, Hibbs, Scala and two other sergeants recruited from the motor pool to make up a suitable number. Only Scullard was missing: he had hissed and privately protested when drawing the rota as duty sergeant that night. Allenby Barracks had been quiet, with many of the occupants spending the evening at local bars. Scullard had certainly witnessed most of C Company heading for the distant lights of the main street of the garrison town. Only one light shone dimly from the barrack room blocks that housed C Company. It came from the room of the tormented Chris Jarvis.

Scala could never remember a time when he had enjoyed playing cards. Even a family game of snap with Sean and Gemma had been a chore – he had always been too impulsive. His mind wandered to Lynn – to what she was doing . . . what she was wearing . . . the warmth of her body. As Hasker cried out again in anguish at losing more money Scala returned to reality.

A brighter light interrupted the gloom as the curtain that separated the room from the main mess was quietly parted. A dark figure whom Scala did not recognise came into the room and knelt by Tavaner's side. At an appropriate moment the figure leaned forward and whispered in his ear. Even in the dim light of the card table and through the haze of cigarette smoke that swirled around it Scala could see the CSM's neck muscles tighten in anxiety; his eyes blazed an anger that Scala had not witnessed before. There was another whisper on either side, to Hasker and Hibbs. The room was thick with apprehension.

As one Tavaner, Hasker and Hibbs rose from the table and dived through the dark curtain that led to the outside door. No words were uttered. Scala's eyes were locked on Tavaner as he strode purposefully from the room and into the night air. He wore only a thin tee-shirt and jeans, but seemed not to notice the sub-zero temperatures outside the building.

Scala jumped to his feet, scattering cards and money across the green baize of the table as he followed the three into the darkness. Adrenalin was pumping through his body. His instincts told him of danger.

He could see the silhouettes of the three sergeants outlined against the whiteness of the snow as they marched toward the barrack block that housed C Company. His feet slipped on the thin covering of ice that had formed on the cleared pathways that led to each of the buildings as he tried to catch them up, and his eyes watered in the cold.

At the third block, from where the single dull light seeped through the curtain at the window, Scala saw the three men disappear through the doorway. He was running now. Once into the darkness of the corridor of the block he heard the commotion. There were many voices – how many he could not tell, but all of them were excited and baying. He went towards the sounds. In the beam of light that shot from the doorway into the darkness he saw the three men push and jostle their way through the crowd that had gathered outside the door. He heard the shouts and sneering, then there was silence as the three entered Jarvis's room.

Scala saw the shadows of men darting in the ghostly shaft of light that emanated from the room and illuminated the occasional face within the pack of men.

Scala reached the entrance a split second after the three sergeants. At first he saw nothing – just the mass of young soldiers, some in army fatigues, others in casual civilian clothing, who fought to squeeze into the small room. His view was obscured by the giant form of Tavaner's body; then, as Scala forced his way through the crowd, he heard the sound of hysterical sobbing. As the crowd jostled for a better view Scala's eyes rested on the source of the cries. He focused on the trembling figure of Jarvis, kneeling naked on the floor of his room before Tavaner.

His pale white body, pathetically scrawny in this crowd of hard, muscular soldiers, was shaking uncontrollably. Tears snaked down the boy's face as fear grew within him. He shook his head in disbelief and panic. Scala's eyes sprang to the corner of the room as a slight movement attracted his gaze. His heart leaped as he stared into the wild eyes of another figure, clothed only in a pair of shorts. The eyes of Derek Scullard spat defiance at Scala as the sergeant sat curled on Jarvis's bed.

The look of dismay on Tavaner's face was now replaced by one of fury and rage. His neck muscles twitched uncontrollably as he fought to retain control of that rage. The veteran sergeants Hasker and Hibbs could find no words to utter. The only sounds that echoed around the room were the feeble mutterings of Jarvis.

'Oh, God forgive me . . . have pity!' he pleaded to the sea of faces surrounding him. 'I couldn't help it . . . he made me . . . I had no choice!'

He was caught by a kick from the mob which sent him sprawling, smashing his nose against the concrete floor. Tavaner, now in control of his emotions, held his arms up to warn the crowd of red-faced men against more violence.

Jarvis's uncontrolled tears now mingled with a stream of blood that gushed from his nose and dribbled over his lips. He spat the blood from his mouth and pleaded at Tavaner's feet. 'Please! You must believe me . . . I couldn't help it . . . he said he'd crucify me if I didn't do what he wanted . . .'

Hibbs raised his foot as if to kick the hysterical youth, but Tavaner restrained him.

Scullard said nothing, defying the unbelieving looks shot in his direction from fifty stunned faces pressing into the room or crowding in the corridor eager to get a glimpse. Scullard, the sergeant who ruled with a rod of iron; Scullard, the bully who tormented the young soldiers of C Company; Scullard, the man who had boasted of his killing prowess, of his heroism against the terrorists who fought from the shadows in the streets of Belfast, had been caught in a love clinch with Jarvis by a drunken squaddie who had returned early from the bars of Hohne intent on hurling abuse at the faggot of C Company. Disgusted at the discovery, the drunk had raised the alarm to the rest of the block. It had been Baker's idea to call for Tavaner. Tavaner would know what to do in a situation such as this. He always did. Without him to control this situation, there would be mayhem.

Scullard knew there was nothing to be said to the pack of men. He fixed his gaze on the disbelieving stare of Hibbs – the man who had been his trusted friend and companion for years, whose sister he had screwed and to whom he was now engaged to be married. The rage and sense of betrayal that gripped Hibbs's contorted face were obvious to every man there.

Still the boy snivelled, crawling on the floor.

Tavaner took control, calming the situation. 'Get this little piece of shite out of my view.' He fired the command blindly into the mob. 'Take him to the sheds – we'll talk to him in a little while. And for Christ's sake shut the little bastard up ... don't want him squealing and waking every bugger up. Get him out of my sight!'

It was Taff Roberts who took the towel from the nearby sink and wrapped it around Jarvis's mouth to block the screams. The blood from the bleeding nose spread across the white cloth as the naked boy was dragged from the room and into the darkness of the corridor.

'Okay, lads, clear the room. That's all for tonight ... leave this to us,' commanded Tavaner. The room cleared in seconds, leaving Tavaner, Hasker, Hibbs and Scala alone in the room with the snarling Scullard.

'I haven't got to explain anything to you!' shouted Scullard. 'The boy's a faggot and he got what he wanted ... he would never complain ...'

'Just shut the fuck up, you dirty little pervert bastard!' muttered Tavaner. 'I don't want to hear about you ... I've seen enough ... Screwing the arse off a young puff in his room leaves you with no case. I feel sick to the stomach to think you've been with us for so long, and you've fucking well betrayed us like this. How long have you ... and he ... when did you know?' Tavaner fought for the right words.

Resignedly Scullard revealed how he had first met Jarvis. It had been at the regiment's depot near Chatham, when the boy had arrived as a raw recruit. It had been at the time when Scullard was on a new course, and had gone to see Hibbs's sister . . . and when they had decided to become engaged.

He spoke of how he had fought for years to suppress the feelings of mixed sexuality that had tortured him. Certainly he had liked women, but there had also been a place in his heart and mind for love with another male. There had been other relationships – brief encounters which had always been easy to conceal from the others. The fresh, innocent-faced boy Jarvis had been different. Scullard had wanted to make him his own. It had not been difficult to make the connection and discover the boy's own sexual preferences. Jarvis had welcomed the attention. The boy had been willing to encourage Scullard's advances; Scullard had promised him special treatment.

Hibbs could hear no more. He sprang forward and drove a wild punch directly into Scullard's face, catching the unsuspecting sergeant beneath the left eye and sending him reeling backwards, smashing his head against the wall of the tiny room.

Now it was Hibbs's turn to be hysterical. 'You bastard!' he yelled repeatedly. 'All the fucking time you were screwing my sister you were shagging with that little faggot . . . I'll kill you . . . that's what I'll do . . .' Hasker held Hibbs as both Tavaner and Scala attempted to restrain the wild figure.

'Trust me. I'll deal with this . . . I know how you feel, but this has to be handled properly,' spat Tavaner.

Scullard relaxed his mood, sensing a feeling of protection from Tavaner. The CSM paced the floor, thinking long and hard.

'What about Boyd? Were you behind that? You were, you little bastard, weren't you? You got bloody jealous . . . you couldn't take him being around your little shag, could you? You piled all the shit on him, so the kid didn't know what was happening. By Christ, man, you as good as killed him yourself – just through some petty bloody jealousy amongst queers!' Tavaner was raging now as he realised the full scope of the events unfolding before his eyes. 'You're finished, you little shit. You realise that? You're dead! But I'll not have you taint the rest of us by your actions. You have been one of us, worked alongside us – you know the people that we work with . . .'

Scala pricked up his ears. Too late, Tavaner realised that he had spoken wildly; he had been loose-tongued in the heat of the moment, but the damage was done. Scala had already seen too much. Tavaner would deal with him later.

Tavaner knew that the scandal would spread like the plague throughout the camp within hours. He wanted the man away from the place . . . they could not risk any kind of public inquiry. No one could be certain what a man like Scullard might reveal to save his own skin. They could no longer trust him. Scullard was aware of all that, too.

'I want you out of here. Now, tonight. Get the fuck away from Allenby – go AWOL, get away from the regiment. It can be arranged,' blurted Tavaner.

Scullard was breathing more easily now. He was finished as a sergeant in the Rangers. He knew it. Yet out of loyalty to his betrayed comrades he would not subject them to an open investigation, which would smear the reputation of the unit that he had served and loved.

As Scullard quickly dressed and ran out of the room towards his own block, Hibbs was still shaking with rage.

'Don't worry, mate! You'll get your chance to have your pound of flesh,' whispered Tavaner to him.

The white carpet of snow that lay across Allenby Barracks gave it a luminous appearance as Scala followed Tavaner along the darkened paths towards the motor sheds where the gathering would be. Composure now returned, Tavaner had thought quickly. Whether he welcomed the idea or not, Scala would have to be included in the plan; he had seen too much. As they walked quickly and silently through the camp Tavaner mulled over the consequences of confiding in him. He had already studied the man's record and he felt him to be sympathetic.

Hasker and Hibbs followed more slowly, the latter still fighting to comprehend the nightmare scene that he had just witnessed. His mind was racing. What could he say to his sister? How could he explain the man's betrayal?

The shape of the huge motor shed loomed before the group, rising out of the white ground. Scala saw a chink of white light escaping from the base of the rolling door and as they grew nearer he could make out a low hum of voices from within. Like a stalking animal instinctively protecting itself from discovery, Tavaner glanced around to ensure that no one had accidentally witnessed them arriving at the shed. The temperature was well below freezing, yet the sweat of rage shimmered across his forehead.

The four of them sneaked through the side door of the shed, into the dusty rays of the dim light emitted by a single lamp suspended from the turret of one of the Warriors that were parked in a neat row. The air hung heavy with the sickening odour of diesel and oil.

There was silence from the excited group that waited inside as Tavaner and the others approached. Some twenty men had formed a human cordon around the lone figure of Jarvis, clothed only in thin boxer shorts and standing between two parked Warriors. Scala recognised most of the faces and was surprised to discover among them Baker, Roberts and the lance corporal from Dover, David Skinner, as well as the mild-mannered Kevin Rogers and the acne-scarred Clive Turner. He had never considered them the kind of men who would form a lynch mob.

Jarvis was still sobbing but was now a little more under control. Yet he was still shaking with fear and shame and the numbing cold. His hair was matted with blood and sweat, and he pushed the heavy strands from his eyes as the group of sergeants approached him. The towel had been removed from his mouth and the terrified youth attempted to speak, wiping away crusts of congealed blood from his top lip.

'The prisoner will speak only when he's spoken to!' boomed Hasker.

Scala noted the word 'prisoner' and feared the next moves in the black drama that was being played out. There was still silence from the ranks of men lined up on either side of Jarvis. The lamp cast a giant dark shadow of him on to the huge metal door of the shed.

Hasker's voice boomed out again in the expanses of the shed. 'The prisoner will remain standing at all time to answer his guilt!'

Jarvis blurted, 'What guilt? I told you – he made me do it.'

'Silence!' blasted the voice.

The mob shuffled with impatience and anticipation of the impending drama.

'Private Christopher Jarvis, you have been brought before us to answer these serious charges.'

'What charges?' squealed Jarvis.

Three aged scratched wooden chairs were brought for Tavaner, Hasker and Hibbs, who, it appeared to Scala, had elected themselves to sit as judges in this mock court. He stood behind them, staring directly into Jarvis's darting eyes. The boy's body was now turning blue with cold.

Tavaner now took over the proceedings. 'Private Jarvis, you stand before us accused of being a dirty, perverted faggot. How do you plead to the charge?' he uttered in a deep, low voice.

The boy spluttered. There were more tears; his head was whirling with terror and cold. 'I've told you . . . he made me . . .'

The boy was not allowed to finish. It was Skinner who stepped forward, clutching a full bottle of what Scala saw was whisky.

'Wrong answer, boy!' Tavaner nodded to Skinner.

The bottle was raised and thrust into Jarvis's spluttering mouth. He gulped the burning liquid deep into his throat. His body rebelled and he spluttered out the alcohol, sending a spray across the room over the lines of soldiers.

'Do you agree that your disgusting actions have brought the Royal Kent Rangers into disrepute?'

Jarvis attempted to babble. The bottle was rammed into his mouth again and held as he gulped more fire. His body heaved. Fear gripped him and the dark stain of his own urine spread across his shorts, bringing hoots of derision from the mob. The hysterical tears returned as he realised his own wretched humiliation.

It was Roberts who struck the first blow with an icy cold wet towel flicked across the boy's back. Others followed. Some were aimed at his groin, and sharp pains convulsed his shivering body.

'Do you agree that you have betrayed your comrades?'

Once more the bottle, half empty now, was thrust deep. Jarvis hoped he would pass out – it would be a dark but merciful release from the pain, the humiliation and the cold. A dozen more questions that required no answer were fired at the crumpled figure, now red from the blows rained down on him by the jeering soldiers eager to inflict pain. Unable to focus on the faces of his tormentors he sank to his knees, his stomach heaving against the litre of whisky that had been poured into it.

Scala steeled himself to stay to the end. He considered whether he would intervene if the punishment continued, but before he had found the answer Tavaner signalled an end to the proceedings. The sergeants would leave the room. Lance Corporal Skinner was assigned to carry out the rest of the 'duties'. Scala assumed the boy's torture was complete as he followed Tavaner and the rest of the group from the scene. Yet he was aware of the stripped figure being dragged away behind him, he knew not where. The pack were still baying.

He was panting. The events of the last hour were whirling in his mind: the anguish of discovery, the fear of retribution from those whom he had once counted as friends, and the shame which he knew the scandal would bring to him. Scullard packed in a frenzy, throwing just a small number of belongings into a canvas holdall. He picked up the photograph of the smiling girl whom he had dared to call his fiancée. He knew he could no longer live the lie that had been his life, and put the picture back on the shelf. Then he quickly changed out of his army regulation fatigues and threw on a comfortable tracksuit. His heart was heavy at the realisation that he would never again wear the uniform that had been his pride for so many years.

He found it difficult to control his breathing, and heard himself wheezing with tension and the dramas of the night. Then he heard another sound: heavy footsteps echoing along the corridor towards his room. As if rocked by an explosion the door was flung open and the menacing outline of Hibbs stood there. Scullard saw the rage deep within his eyes and the red glow of outrage that pulsed through his face. The lust for revenge – for his sister, and for the betrayal of a friendship – flooded his entire being. Behind the looming figure was Hasker, peering over Hibbs's shoulder.

Scullard briefly attempted a defiant sneering grin. Then the two figures smashed into him before he could ready himself. The force sent him sprawling across the room and over the sofa, banging his head against the concrete floor with a sickening thud. The pain surged through his head as he gasped to regain his breath. Then Hibbs drove a series of gut-wrenching kicks directly into the shrieking man's groin. Yet Scullard refused to retaliate.

'Fight, you cock-sucking bastard!' screeched Hibbs. 'Fight me like the man I once thought you were. I'm going to beat the living crap out of you for everything you've done . . . for the lives you've wrecked. And by the time I'm finished with you, no other little faggot boy will want to look in your direction.'

Still Scullard refused to defend himself. It was as if he felt a need to be punished for his disloyalty. One blow took his front teeth, and he could feel the salty taste of his own blood gushing into his mouth. It spurted bright red over Hibbs's dark green fatigues as the blows continued. Scullard's body was engulfed by pain as his two attackers snatched him like a child's toy from the floor and pinned him against the wall, repeatedly crashing his skull against the rough plaster and scattering the few items of furniture around the room.

Scullard's agony seemed to have lasted for hours before the other two men burst into the room and dragged away his attackers. Scala took Hasker in a rear headlock while Tavaner grasped Hibbs. It took a superhuman effort from both of them to restrain their two enraged colleagues as Scullard crumpled to the floor in a writhing heap. Suddenly the room filled with other excited figures who, alerted by the sound of the fight, helped Scala and Tavaner. Hibbs and Hasker were hauled from the barrack block into the night, leaving Scullard spitting blood.

Tavaner acted quickly. It had taken just one short telephone conversation with Poppa Hearn to find an instant answer to the situation. Scullard must be hidden, it was decided. He could not be allowed just to disappear on his own. It was Hearn who selected the squalid bedsit in the crumbling grey block in the heart of the Kreuzberg district of western Berlin that would enable Scullard to evade the military police who would soon be out hunting for him. Few would search for an army deserter in a working-class district of immigrants and low life, where only those bent on crime walked the streets alone after dark.

   Alone in Scullard's room, it was Tavaner who outlined the plan to the still bruised and bleeding sergeant. His left eye had all but closed, and crusts of blood were still forming at his mouth. An hour later, as a heavy snow shower descended on the camp, no one saw Scullard, still racked with the pain of his beating and clutching the holdall crammed with his few meagre belongings, sneak from the barracks in the direction of the station. He would begin the ninety-minute rail journey from Hohne to Berlin a full two hours before the camp awoke. And once there he would simply vanish.

CHAPTER THIRTEEN

The chill wind had brought a fresh dusting of snow that left a powdery veneer on the ground. A stiff silence hung over the patchwork of roads, paths, open ground and blocks of buildings that made up Allenby Barracks. The girl buried herself deep in her thick coat as she gingerly made her way to the cookhouse, where she would begin the daily chore of serving up mounds of bacon, sausages, beans and eggs to the hundreds of shivering men. She coughed to clear her lungs in the sharp air as she stepped along the slippery path, past the rows of blocks where the young soldiers were housed. She wondered if her parents would be suffering such a bad winter back home in Hartlepool.

Her daily route took her along the perimeter path round the vast playing fields that stretched from the camp buildings towards the woodland on the far edge of the base. The winds had levelled the snow that had settled some two feet deep on the fields, and turned it into a smooth cloak. It was all far removed from the shouting and smells of her kitchen workplace. She took a deep breath as if to soak in the serene and peaceful landscape.

At first she was not sure what it was. It seemed to be a twisted tree branch protruding from beneath the snow, and she dismissed it from her thoughts. But there was something about it . . . She looked again – and now there was no doubt. The fingers of the hand that pushed up through the surface of the snow were gnarled like a claw. Only one hand and an arm – a grey-white colour that stood out against the snowy brightness.

The girl narrowed her eyes to look more closely. She made out an outline – an outline of what she took to be a head, a nose, barely visible under the sheet of snow. Then she forced herself to distinguish the rest of the corpse that lay part buried in the field that had been the scene of many a game of soccer and rugby and cricket. She felt a scream rise within her, yet in her panic could not hear its deafening echo resounding through the rows of barrack blocks.

Steeling herself, she edged her way on to the field towards the still, stiff body. In the background, voices started to shout. Christopher Jarvis's half-open eyes stared sightless at the sky, yet gripped by an almost peaceful expression, the mouth open to expose the teeth in a macabre smile.

Jim Scala had slept little as he tossed and turned and clawed at the rough grey blanket that covered his small, cramped bed. He had lain awake, listening to the sound of his heart thumping against his chest after witnessing the events of a few hours earlier. No matter how hard he tried, he still saw the boy's face and its anguish at the tirade of abuse and insults heaped on the terrified youngster in that dark, cold workshop by the men who had once been his comrades. Scala did not know what had become of the boy and cursed himself for leaving him. Yet to interfere would have alerted the rest of them to Scala's real purpose at the camp. Finally he fell into that limbo of half sleep which left the mind still churning while only the eyes bowed to physical tiredness.

It seemed to Scala that he had enjoyed that limbo for only a few fleeting moments when he heard the frantic tapping on his door. At first he thought it was merely the product of his churning mind; then reality won through. The banging grew louder. Still dazed, he staggered up and snatched open the door.

Even in the gloom he could make out the girl's tears. Her eyes were wild with anxiety and red with crying. Without waiting for an invitation she surged past Scala and into the room, ignoring his nakedness. Rapidly closing the door, he reached for a towel and wrapped it round his waist. Lynn Anders sat on the end of his bed, and held her head in her hands, sobbing uncontrollably. As soon as she had heard the news she had thrown on a tracksuit and sneakers and had instinctively headed for the haven of Scala's room.

'What is it, for God's sake? Lynn, for Christ's sake tell me what's happened!' begged Scala as he knelt beside her, holding her hand in an effort to comfort her.

'It's happening again . . . it's happened again . . . I can't believe it . . . I know it's happened again,' she blurted.

'What the hell are you talking about? What's happened again? For Christ's sake, woman, make sense.'

'It's *them* . . . they've done it! I know it . . . and it's all my fault,' she cried, burying her head in her hands once more. 'I should have stopped it. . . . Oh, God forgive me, I should have stopped it . . .'

'Stop *what?*'

'You don't understand . . . he's dead!'

'Who the bloody hell's dead?'

'Jarvis – Chris Jarvis is dead! They found his body this morning, in the snow . . . and *they* did it . . . I know it . . . *they* were responsible!'

There was a second of silence as the news sank into Scala's befuddled mind. Could the girl be right? He had left him but a few hours before, and he had still been alive then. It was, he tried to convince himself, inconceivable that even that mob had done anything further to the boy after the end of the so-called 'court'.

He sounded feeble. 'What happened?'

'I don't know for certain . . . they found his body in the snow . . . naked. They reckon he got drunk and fell asleep or something . . . But I've heard talk about Jarvis being caught with another bloke . . . the whole camp's talking about nothing else. They're calling Jarvis a queer who got caught.'

Scala listened intently. 'What do you expect me to do about it?' he asked her. 'And what do you mean when you say it's your fault? And who are "they".' There were a host of questions he wanted answered.

Lynn composed herself for a moment. *They* are the people who run this bloody camp . . . *they* are the ones who have blood on their hands . . . *they* are the ones who threatened me to make me keep my mouth shut . . . *they* are your sick friends in the Sergeants' Mess. I just know they're behind Jarvis's death. Oh, Christ forgive me – I wish I'd done something before instead of being a shit scared woman! If they knew about Jarvis, they wouldn't tolerate it – they couldn't abide having a queer in *their* camp, in *their* regiment, in *their* company. They'd kill first – just like before . . .'

Scala's mind was racing, not least because of the feelings of shame and disgust at himself that were building within him. He was also afraid of being discovered by some unthinking private who might knock blindly on his door and hear or see Lynn. 'Now's not the time. Meet me later . . . tonight . . . and tell me then. But for God's sake speak to no one about this until then.' He spoke gently now, rocking the girl to and fro. 'Just a little while longer, that's all I ask. Tell me tonight!'

The dirty black Opel saloon sped along Route 2 through the flat, featureless landscape that led to Berlin. It had been Skinner who had volunteered for the two-hour drive to keep the rendezvous.

Huddled over the wheel, he cursed as passing lorries sent waves of dirty spray lashing on to his windscreen while Roberts snored contentedly in the passenger seat.

It had been Tavaner who had chosen them. He knew their experience and their commitment. They were among the best that he had. And, like him, they believed. He had instructed them to leave Allenby early, before the shit started to fly about the 'gay boy'. What Tavaner and the others had in mind for them to do was far more important than worrying about some dead little queer, he told them.

The girl was one of his most beautiful and experienced, and she worked his body with an expertise gained from almost ten years of working the streets and clubs. She writhed across the mauve silk sheet that covered the king-sized bed in the centre of the dimly lit room, revealing every inch of her body. It was a good body, long and lithe. She looked after it well, and she prided herself on knowing what a man wanted.

It was her room, paid for by the man who reclined naked on the bed with her. He always came to her at moments like this, to the small apartment at the end of the Potsdamerstrasse. She was his favourite, and he owned her. She would tend to his needs. Yet it was always the same.

Tossing her long straight black hair down her back to display her firm breasts, the girl had gone to work on him in the way she always did. As before she had plied him with oils and their aromas filled the air, mingling with the girl's own secret smells. She had teased his body with her mouth. She had played with him. But as she gathered herself up, cat-like, to straddle him, hoping to feel his body deep within her own, it was also as before. She had wanted to please, but there was never any response to her expert manipulations. Always Klaus Stein remained limp and immovable. She had apologised, feeling humiliated. But Klaus Stein had remained calm with the girl, knowing that she could not share the blame. All the expertise in the world would do nothing to help him. It had always been so.

The girl sighed with frustration and effort, which prompted a smile from Stein. He patted her bare behind, and leaned forward to kiss her left nipple gently in appreciation. Once more he would content himself with the role of voyeur. It had been so from his boyhood.

At first he had felt shame and humiliation. But over the years those feelings had subsided, supplanted by hatred of his pathetic family – the family that had, he believed, forsaken their birthright. His grandfather had had a vast share-holding in the chemical production empire of IG Farben, and had amassed a great fortune at the time when the company had been manufacturing the deadly Zyklon B gas that had been used to exterminate those millions of filthy Jews in the death camps of the Nazis. But that had been long ago, before the arrival of the Russian invaders who had occupied half the country and driven his family westwards; before his grandfather had committed suicide with the shame of his poverty; and before the father that he despised had bowed to fate and become a lowly lawyer instead of challenging for his birthright. Now Klaus Stein was committed to his own destiny. He would prove himself a man in many other ways than the bedroom.

The naked girl was writhing once again in a final desperate attempt to bring life to Stein's limp manhood. But this time he dismissed her efforts impatiently, his gaze fixed instead on the small television screen that continuously blazed, volumeless, from the corner of the apartment. What he saw made Klaus Stein's body surge with anger: his eyes bulged with rage and his nostrils flared. The girl knew the signs and hastily escaped into the bathroom.

Stein leaped off the bed and turned up the volume. He was transfixed by the sight of two men embracing in mutual admiration and friendship. The image of Rainer Fassbeck, the traitor who had taken that Brazilian bitch as a wife, was vivid in his recollections. He thought he could even make out the black whore's image behind Fassbeck at the glittering gala that had been held the night before.

And there was Fassbeck, the 'traitor', laughing and shaking hands and openly hugging the tall, handsome idol in his smart black evening clothes. That man had been a legend to millions – but that had been before the years and a broken leg had ended the playing career of Michael Kinze, the legendary striker who had taken Germany to the triumphs of soccer's World Cup finals on no fewer than three occasions. That was before Kinze had, it seemed to Stein, also turned his back on his followers by accepting an offer worth millions to manage the scum that was the South African team.

Kinze had returned to his homeland in triumph. The African Nations' Cup was already South Africa's, and the side's first international tour was almost halfway through. It had made no difference to the outside world that over two-thirds of Kinze's players were drawn from the slums of the South African townships. Kinze's legend lived on, the public adulation with Fassbeck proved it, and Stein's rage burned deep.

Scala arrived early. He had wanted to be alone to wrestle with his own thoughts throughout the day, but that had proved impossible because there had been too much to do – the repercussions of the events of the day resembled nothing he had ever experienced. All the NCOs had been interviewed individually by Colonel Cochrane. All had pleaded their ignorance of the affair – even Scala had stared boldly back into Cochrane's eyes and denied his knowledge of Jarvis's torment.

Only one sergeant had been absent. At first Scullard was merely thought to be off the base for a short while. But Tavaner had warned the others of how talk of his involvement with Jarvis would grow. The rumour factory would be in full swing by midday; stories, some of them wild, would take over the camp by late afternoon. The only good thing was that Scullard was nowhere to be found to talk about the stories openly. The likes of Cochrane could be handled; better for the others to accept, reluctantly of course, the hideous reports that Jarvis and Scullard had been lovers. It was sickening, but it would explain Scullard's absence. That's what Tavaner had told them.

The belief that, shamed by his actions, Jarvis had taken his own life – either deliberately or accidentally through drink – was encouraged by the sergeants. They believed it to be true, therefore the rest of the camp would follow suit.

Scala had been pleased to leave the camp behind. He ordered a taxi and took it to the remote bar on the outskirts of the vast surrounding forests that Lynn had suggested. He wanted to be alone with his thoughts and his drinking before facing her. The events of the last twenty-four hours danced in and out of his brain. He felt like shit: fatigue, lack of sleep and his own guilt were all taking their toll.

He told himself that he could have saved the boy. He knew it was true. But what would Matherson have said? Fuck Matherson! It would be Scala who would have to live with the image of the boy's face in the middle of the night, probably for the rest of his life. Matherson, and before him his SAS commanders, had always instilled the need to concentrate on the 'bigger picture' of events rather than the minor points. Was saving Jarvis's life a 'minor point'? Scala agonised.

Deep in his heart, Scala toyed with the thought that he had turned his back on the young soldier in need because of his own rejection of homosexuals – the stance that his father and the unbending, ignorant lifestyle of the valleys had instilled in him. There was no room for 'queers' in the Army – he knew that in his own mind. But intolerance should not result in murder – of that he was certain.

He was questioning his own ethics now. He would kill an enemy without consideration if ordered to do so. But he had never consciously turned his back on a comrade in need. His belief lay in serving his country and his comrades without hesitation. It was also the belief that had wrecked his marriage . . .

He had believed in his own principles. But he wondered if he had become a victim of his own prejudices too. He had never faced up to the fact that he too might have been a racist . . . he had never had to. But now for the first time he assessed his own beliefs. It was true – he did not accept that a coloured man might have a role to play in British society. Blacks had no place in the Army. That was a white man's world and always had been, and he heard himself saying that it always should be. Once again he felt it was the insular upbringing of the valleys, where in his childhood hardly a single coloured person walked, that had subconsciously instilled these beliefs into him. But would he kill a man simply because of the colour of his skin? The question flashed through his mind and he feared his own answer.

Alone with his worrying thoughts, he took solace in drink. Within ten minutes of arriving at the quiet bar, empty except for the pretty teenage blonde barmaid, he had drained two litres of the heavy beer. 'Like piss!' he judged in his mind. Now he chased the gassy stuff with the almost obligatory glass of harsh German schnapps that burned his throat as he threw it back.

His mind raced back to a hillside in Bosnia, and to the image of the bloody mass that had been his friend, killed by the same bombs that Scala had called down on the massed Serbian artillery which he, Jim Scala, had decided should be destroyed. Then, he had wondered if he had played God with his friend's life. Now, with the image of Christopher Jarvis haunting his mind, he wondered if he had played God again.

Poppa Hearn had been expecting the two men all day, and he was impatient because they were late. But the slamming of the door to the bar took him by surprise. He whirled round as usual to confront the invisible attacker, but saw only Skinner and Roberts. He had seen them before, and knew that Tavaner had chosen well. They would carry out the mission without any doubts or hesitation. He knew that they believed.

Scala saw the silver Golf GTI that was the pride of Lynn Anders pull up outside exactly on time. Getting there an hour early had given him the opportunity to take stock of his emotions and feel the warmth of the drink deep within him, yet he still felt like shit. He forced a smile to his lips to greet the girl as she entered the bar.

She walked straight, cautiously surveying her surroundings, her long legs emerging from a tight knee-length grey skirt below a bright sweater. Her hair was tied back and she wore little make-up, which highlighted the brightness of her eyes against the pale skin. She sat at a distant corner table and ordered a large glass of wine.

'Did anyone see you leave the camp?' she asked Scala in a voice that was no more than a whisper.

'Only the poor sod who had the misfortune to be on guard duty. I took a taxi . . . How has it been for you?' He realised the stupidity of the question even before it had left his lips, and shrugged with embarrassment. 'So tell me . . . what were you talking about this morning? About this all being your fault . . . about it all happening again . . . as if it were your fault!' he insisted quickly. 'Were you there? Did you see what happened to Jarvis?'

'No, of course I bloody well didn't,' she snapped back. 'I meant it another way. It seemed like history was repeating itself, that's all. And those bastards are behind it . . . I've heard the stories about Jarvis and that bullying bastard Scullard. God knows how the poor kid got mixed up with a swine like that! I can imagine what must have happened . . .'

Scala feigned ignorance.

'I can see that the kid must have gone through some kind of kangaroo court – hosted by those bastards, I bet – just like the other guy,' she went on.

'What other guy?'

Lynn took a large swig from her glass and gestured to the barmaid to bring her another. Her eyes began to mist as she set in motion the recollections that were locked deep in her mind.

'It was just over a year ago,' she began. 'We had a coloured soldier sent to the camp. His name was Adebeyo. God, did they give him a bad time. He was the first black that had ever been sent to the RKR. To say that he didn't fit in – or wasn't allowed to fit in

– was an understatement. Wherever he went he was called "nigger" and "coon". He was always in fights with the other guys, always in trouble. Cochrane was next to useless about it. God knows, the lad tried to complain. But Cochrane, typical of bloody officers, didn't want to know. He didn't want a racist allegation on his own record or on the record of his precious bloody regiment, I guess.'

She gulped more wine before continuing. 'Anyway, things got a bit out of hand. Adebeyo was threatening everyone with the Comission for Racial Equality and all that crap. Of course, it wasn't allowed. The sergeants saw to that. In fact they were encouraging the other soldiers to make his life hell. They were as bad, you see, always picking on him during training and exercises. I often saw the lad in tears after they'd finished with him.'

A tear toppled from her own eye and snaked down her cheek. 'Anyway, one night I'd been in the mess – oh yes, I was tolerated in the mess then, you see. It was late, and I left alone. I started to walk back to my room, and then I heard it – it was like a pack of mad dogs on the rampage. I stopped, and saw it was coming from the block further down the path, where Adebeyo's room was. It was horrible . . .'

Scala saw the picture vividly in front of his eyes as the girl spoke. It had been as he had imagined. Fired with hatred and encouragement from the sergeants, the young soldiers had discovered Private John Adebeyo to be a thief – piece of jewellery and a wallet had been discovered in his drawer during a random search. The young soldiers had gathered for blood – the blood of a black thief. The sergeants had presided over his judgement, and the sentence had been left to the members of the 'jury' of howling wolves that were the men of C Company.

Certainly Adebeyo had screamed his innocence. Scala could hear his screams of protest as the mob had been whipped into a fury, as they dragged him shouting and screaming and crying for his mother, into that cold, remote section of the camp. Scala saw the useless struggles as the terrified young black boy had the rope placed around his neck and looped over the tree. He saw the boy's eyes bulging in panic and terror as the other soldiers had heaved on the rope to raise his body slowly from the ground, his shoeless feet kicking in the freezing night air. Then his sobs and choking gasps had fallen silent. Scala had seen it all. The picture was as clear in his mind as a photograph . . .

'The only problem,' continued Lynn in a shaking voice, 'was that I saw the whole thing. I wanted to scream, to try and stop them, but nothing would come. I just froze in horror. I couldn't believe this was happening . . . I saw him hanging there . . . his eyes seemed to stare right at me . . . I couldn't help it any longer . . . I screamed at the top of my voice. They heard me, but it was too late. The boy had stopped kicking.

'I saw the sergeants you see,' she went on. 'I saw Scullard put the rope round his neck . . . but I couldn't do anything. I saw Hibbs and Hasker – they were all bloody well there, organising it like a Sunday school outing.' Lynn was crying openly now. Scala took her hand and gripped it tightly.

'It was Tavaner who saw me first . . . heard me scream . . . Company Sergeant Major Mick Tavaner – the bastard!' she spat. 'He took me, dragged me away, took me into the Sergeants' Mess. The others came too . . . they were wild. I was terrified – oh Christ was I petrified . . .'

Scala could feel anger rising within him at the thought of the three manhandling the girl.

'Tavaner spoke quietly to me, but he scared me to death,' Lynn continued. 'He warned me what might happen if I said anything . . . how they would do anything to protect the honour of the regiment. He said no one cared about a little nigger thief and that I should forget what I had seen – it would be better for everyone. He said I should watch out for myself . . . because things could happen to nice little girls who spoke out against their male comrades and who took the side of thieving black bastards like Adebeyo. I was terrified . . . the trouble is, I knew he was right . . . You see, Jim, no one cared . . . I knew that then, and I know it now . . . I tried to transfer, but I was always blocked . . . I was a prisoner.

'Since then I've hardly set foot in the mess. No one's spoken about Adebeyo. I've never forgotten about it, but all these things today with Jarvis and Scullard brought it all back. Oh God, I wish I'd had the guts to speak out. But I didn't . . .'

Scala reached over the table, drew the girl's head towards him and softly kissed her forehead. He stroked the tied back red hair as she wept again at the horror of that night. There would never be any comfort for the girl. Of that Scala was certain.

CHAPTER FOURTEEN

In sleep the girl had murmured peacefully like a child. The dreadful recollections of the black soldier's death had faded in the gentle lovemaking that had followed.

Scala thought that the girl's retelling of the events of that night had freed her soul, like a confession to a priest. He had been totally absorbed by the story that Lynn Anders had wanted to air for so long. Then he had comforted her, soothing away the tears. His own demons of sleep had been forgotten as they had taken a small, simple room in a nearby hotel. The girl had needed love that night, and Scala was the man whom she had chosen to unburden her own nightmares to. He had not chosen to let her down.

It was still dark when Scala awoke from the short sleep that he had allowed himself. Lynn was still asleep. In the light of the single bedside lamp that had burned throughout the night he studied her bare, blemishless shoulders and tranquil face. Her hair wildly covered the white pillow of the double bed that filled the room, and he gave a silent smile as he wondered how her bank manager father in the comfortable house in its middle-class surroundings would react if he could see his daughter at this moment.

Hearing the truth about Adebeyo's death had made Scala re-evaluate his own prejudices. As the graphic events of that night were related to him, he had concluded that no matter what the extent of his own intolerance might be, he could never allow himself to be willingly taken over by the blood lust of a racist mob. No man should die because of another's bigotry, he conceded. He had learned something about himself. He knew he would fight such bigotry.

The girl had trusted in him, he knew that. He could not allow himself to let her down, and he knew her life would be at risk should he rashly reveal her story to Matherson. He knew too that there would be others who would allow the girl to be sacrificed to the 'bigger picture' of events. Scala assessed that the girl's testimony, although dangerous for herself, was vital. Yet he felt also that Lynn Anders had suffered enough, tortured by her own silence.

They would return to Allenby by the time full daylight had spread itself over the camp. They should, he thought, return undiscovered. He silently rose from the bed and quickly slipped into his jeans and denim shirt – the one, he remembered, that had been bought by Angie two years before. She had loved him then, he thought.

In bare feet he tiptoed from the room and crept down the stairs into the stillness of the darkened reception area. He saw the battery of telephones on the far wall and headed for them. As he moved he saw the slumbering figure of the aged night porter dozing in an armchair, partly hidden in the shadows of the far corner of the room. But his gentle wheezing convinced Scala that the man was unlikely to wake and so, slowly and deliberately, he began to dial. On Matherson's insistence he had memorised the number – a freephone number that would put Scala in contact with his controller at any time of day or night. Scala could barely make out the time on his watch. He hoped that Matherson would share his sense of urgency at this unearthly hour.

With one eye fixed on the sleeping porter, Scala waited for the call to go through. The image of the normally immaculate Matherson being startled by the ringing bedside phone amused him. Scala thought of the man's immediate panic and his tousled hair falling over his face, and afforded himself a wry smile.

The telephone at the end of the line burst into life and Scala counted the number of rings before it was answered. 'Hello, sir. Scala. I have a sitrep, sir. Can't wait, sir, sorry,' he said quickly. The porter slept on as Scala began to unfold his report on the current situation to his silent boss. 'We have another man dead, sir. Almost a hundred per cent certain of those responsible . . . I estimate that many members of the company are involved. Organised, I believe, by the NCOs. One of those NCOs is now missing.'

In staccato terminology, Scala painted a concise but complete picture of the situation for Matherson and answered the occasional brief question. 'Require help, sir. We have a witness . . . A female, sir . . . Will require protection. I can't provide. Will need extricating soonest, sir. Personally unable . . . could compromise my position, sir . . . Needs more investigation . . . Will do, sir.'

The discussion over, Scala tiptoed once again past the porter, who almost woke himself with a loud snort, and returned to the sleeping girl.

*   *   *

'It's really quite simple. The boy simply couldn't live with his own shame – suppose you could call him a tortured soul.' Lieutenant Colonel Andrew Cochrane assumed an air of self-confidence in his assessment of Private Christopher Jarvis's unfortunate death. 'I've known of such things before. It would seem apparent from our investigations that the lad lost his head . . . God knows what goes on in the minds of . . . of . . . of . . .' Cochrane became flustered as he searched for the correct word.

'Gays . . . queers . . . faggots . . . homos . . . take your pick!' the man sitting opposite interrupted curtly.

'I was about to say, "in the minds of people such as a young lad like this", actually,' retorted Cochrane with a renewed aura of self-confidence. 'Let's face it . . . I suppose it's like in any, er, normal relationship. A lover's tiff can lead to all kinds of things. It would seem that Jarvis became confused and started drinking . . . and for one reason or another found himself drunk and outside . . . he'd obviously been wandering around a while . . . the drink must have muddled his mind, and before anyone could do anything it was too late. The poor lad succumbed to the cold.'

The bulky figure of the man opposite remained unmoved. There was no sign of any appreciation of the colonel's summing up of the events leading up to Jarvis's death. Cochrane shuffled nervously behind his desk as the grim-faced man in civilian clothes pondered.

'Did anyone in the company have any idea that the boy was homosexual? Did he give any clues?' came the question.

Cochrane snapped back immediately, 'Of course not! Like every regiment in the British Army, we are wholly aware of the regulations and of the problems that can arise from any breach of them. We take the greatest steps – '

'I understand that one of your NCOs is missing,' the civilian broke in. 'A Sergeant Scullard. Is there any likelihood that the events could be linked?'

The suggestion appeared too much even for Cochrane to contemplate. 'Absolutely not! I take personal insult at the idea that one of my most senior NCOs could be – '

But the interrogator showed no interest in the rebuttal and pressed on with the questioning, ignoring the colonel's red-faced protestations. Sergeant Ray Matthews of the Special Investigation Branch loved to see men like Cochrane suffering the pains of such indignity. He was well aware that, despite bearing the lowly rank of sergeant, his SIB status gave him overall command of any situation

which originated from an incident such as this. He recognised
the frustrations that such outrankings caused senior officers, and
derived additional pleasure from Cochrane's obvious discomfort.

'With respect, sir,' Matthews stressed, 'I don't believe that there
is ever any such thing as an open-and-shut case when a young
soldier's death is involved. It's my job to investigate all possibilities,
and that's exactly what I'm here to do in this case. Of course, I shall
expect your full cooperation and that of all your men. After all,
given that the Royal Kent Rangers have suffered an unfortunate
number of incidents involving young soldiers over the last year or
so I would have thought that a man such as yourself, who places
great importance on the reputation of the regiment, would wish
to ensure that its record is not tainted by half truths or downright
mischievous stories.'

Mathews was enjoying himself. He had waited for this moment
for months, ever since those whom he described as 'cloak-and-
dagger merchants' had stepped in to rob him of the prize of the
little arsonist shit Nick Curry. Matthews could still feel the bitter
taste of defeat when the soldier caught at the scene of the fire
bombing had been taken from him. Now he was determined to
enjoy his second opportunity to investigate the ranks from where
Nick Curry had sprung.

Cochrane felt little option but to nod his agreement.

'But let me also assure you, sir, that if I find any trace of
irregularities I shall not have the slightest bloody hesitation in
bringing the full weight of the law to bear on those responsible
– without any regard for whatever reputations may be involved.
I trust I make myself understood.'

Once again, the begrudging nod of agreement followed.

No one saw them leave the bar that morning. They looked innocent
enough, blending with the other passers by in the busy street. But
still the two men in leather jackets and jeans peered long and hard
into the crowds to avoid any risk of recognition before stepping
towards the car that they had left parked overnight.

They were travelling light: each had just a small overnight bag.
But they left with more than they had arrived with. The lance
corporal from Dover was also carrying a small leather shoulder
bag, which he held by the small handle. Roberts, the Welshman,
clutched a large brown envelope as he fumbled for the keys to
the Opel.

The drinkers in the bar the night before had not seen anything odd in the way that Hearn had concentrated his attentions on the two soldiers. Everyone was aware that the army man enjoyed the company of fellow combatants, and Skinner and Roberts had always been particular favourites of his. The group had spent the evening engrossed in each other's company. And to the unsuspecting eye, there was nothing strange about the fact that the two men had stayed the night at the bar. Now Hearn, standing by the window of his upstairs room, was the only person to observe the two figures climbing into the car and heading off towards the centre of Berlin. His eyes narrowed in anticipation, he too scoured the street for any sign of the unusual.

Sleep was impossible. The stabbing pain from his groin was relentless and his left eye had all but closed. The taste of his own blood still was in his mouth, and the savage pain from the raw nerve ends where his front teeth had once been jolted his entire body. Derek Scullard lay still, wretched in his misery, as he pleaded for sleep to overcome his pain. But it would not come.

The dampness from the stained bed seeped into his clothing, and the smell of decay and age infested the air in the squalid room to which he had been directed. He had done as ordered by Tavaner and gone straight to the crumbling apartment block in Kreuzberg after his train arrived at the main terminal at the Zoo Station. No one had noticed his shattered figure creep into the building and up the three flights of stairs to the dismal apartment. As arranged, the door was open, and there had been no physical contact with another soul.

Less than twenty-four hours before, he had been a respected senior sergeant in one of the most famous regiments in the British Army. A life had been planned for him. He was to be married. He had been a follower as well, and he had been assured that his loyalty and service would be rewarded within the new order. Now all that was gone.

He had been reduced to this sad mass because he had been unable to control his own base instincts. He glanced at the cracked mirror on the door of the broken-down wardrobe that was the only other piece of furniture within the foul room, and for the first time caught sight of his battered and bruised face. The sight in itself seemed to prompt more pain. He was unable to recognise his features from the face that he had shaved the day before.

Outside, the air slowly filled with the noise of everyday life among the immigrant community. Scullard could faintly distinguish the shouts from the Turkish market at the end of the street, and he was certain that he could hear the laughter and chatter of African voices filtering from the dingy café opposite. His own pain was still too great even to contemplate obtaining any food – much less eating it. But he had been told that that would be organised too. He would wait.

The man carried his suffering with dignity and in silence, refusing to allow the pain within to show itself. He walked slowly from the headquarters block of Allenby Barracks with only his grief as a companion. Once he had been proud and straight, but despair had turned his face as grey as the hair on his head, and his body seemed bent and broken as if carrying a burden.

She watched the man as he made his way along the paths to the barrack block. She wanted to hold him, to offer support, to share in his grief and to lift the blanket of hopelessness that was draped about him. But Sergeant Lynn Anders knew that she could do nothing for the man. He had come to take his son home to share the last journey that the pair would ever make together.

Once the man had served proudly with the Royal Kent Rangers. He had been even prouder when his son had told him that he wanted to follow suit. The man had fought with the Rangers against the North Koreans over forty years before. He had been prepared to die in battle for the honour of the regiment that he loved, and he had been able to console himself with the knowledge that, although many of his comrades had died in battle, it had been part of a heroic struggle for freedom. But there would be no such consolation this time. His son had been taken from him meaninglessly, apparently through an ignominious drinking accident. There would be no glory for this father's son.

Lynn Anders did not know if the man had been told the full circumstances of his son's tragic death. She hoped he had not, and that Colonel Cochrane had shown compassion.

Scala entered Lynn's office without her seeing him. He saw the tears welling in her bright eyes and realized that her face was fixed on the shambling figure outside. 'Didn't mean to interrupt,' Scala whispered softly, startling her. 'I thought I'd come and see how you were.'

Fighting back her distress, she busied herself shuffling unimportant papers on her desk in an attempt to hide the tears. 'I wanted to take the old man and just hold him for a little while . . . I wanted to tell him that everything would be okay. But I can't . . . and it's not going to be all right, is it, Jim?'

He wanted to offer words of comfort, but he knew that nothing he could say would help.

'How can you tell an old man like that that his son died because his supposed comrades thought he was queer . . . a queer who should be punished because they didn't know how to cope with him . . . that he died because he was gay, and that his only crime was that he didn't like screwing women?' Lynn flopped into the chair behind her desk, head in hands. 'I've got to do something, Jim. I've got to make those bastards who think they're God pay. I'm going to tell everything I know. I've made up my mind.'

Scala rushed over and grabbed her hand. 'No, Lynn, that's not the way. At the moment it's too risky. You must keep silent!' he insisted firmly.

'But I thought you understood, Jim. I didn't think you were like the others. I thought you would want me to tell.'

'There's more than one way to skin a cat. You must wait just a little while longer. There are a great many things going on that need to be sorted out . . . just trust me about this.'

The girl looked into Scala's face. 'What are you talking about? What things going on? Surely two men being killed is enough of a situation, isn't it?' A veil of suspicion covered her face as she studied the scarred man before her. 'Who are you, Jim Scala? Or should I say *what* are you?'

'I'm exactly who and what I told you I am – no more than that!' he brazened. 'I just think that after what you told me last night you should be careful. If what you said is true – and I believe you – then you're dealing with some pretty dangerous people. I think you should exercise control, that's all,' he reassured her. 'Just don't do anything hasty . . . anything that you might regret. That's all I ask.'

Lynn sat in silence, and Scala was uncertain whether he had convinced her.

The huge blue eyes of the small girl blazed wide as she anticipated the excitement of the coming day. She wriggled constantly on the stool at her dressing table, making it impossible for the dark-skinned woman to brush the child's shock of blonde curls.

'For goodness sake, Anneliese, will you please be still if only for a moment, just until I've finished your hair!' she sighed in frustration. 'Otherwise you will never be ready, and what will all your friends say when they see your hair is in such a state?'

The big eyes looked back at her mother from the mirror with an innocence that defied all attempts to remonstrate with her.

The woman hugged her child lovingly, understanding the girl's excitement. 'There, you're finished,' she said. 'Now stand over there and let me look at you.'

The child obeyed, gingerly picking her way through the dolls and assorted toys that scattered the vast pink bedroom, haughtily holding a pose identical to that which her mother had struck on a hundred catwalks in her previous life. The statuesque woman with the silky dark skin and long sleek black hair eyed her daughter proudly. Marjo Fassbeck smiled approvingly and conceded that the little girl had inherited the best of both parents: the poise, elegance and fine complexion of her Brazilian mother, combined with the perfect blue eyes and corn-coloured hair of her famous German father. The child standing before her in a frothy white silk dress would indeed be the star of her own party. A child should always be allowed to have special memories of its fifth birthday, she thought. Today would indeed be special for Anneliese.

The two men sat before him as he marched into the stark office that had been made available for the investigation. Scala acknowledged the company sergeant major but waited for the introduction to the second man, who was dressed in civilian clothes. Scala reached up to remove the maroon beret from his head and folded it neatly before standing at ease.

'Sit down, please, Sergeant Scala!' invited the second man. 'My name is Sergeant Matthews. I'm from the Special Investigation Branch. I expect you understand what I'm doing here.'

Scala nodded.

Matthews held a single file of papers on the desk before him, and appeared to be searching through them as he spoke. 'The business regarding Private Jarvis is, I think you'll agree, very distasteful, so I think it would be in all our interests, as well as that of the Army, to have the whole thing cleared up as soon as possible.' Without waiting for agreement he continued. 'Sergeant Scala, can you tell me where you were on the night of the tragedy?'

Scala flashed a glance towards Tavaner, present to supervise the proceedings, but was rewarded with only a blank stare.

'I was playing cards in the Sergeants' Mess with a group of others. CSM Tavaner was also present – '

'Yes, I am aware that there was a card school going on. I meant afterwards.'

Scala flushed with anger at the interruption. 'As I was saying, I was playing cards in the mess. We played until late. Then I returned to my room.'

'With anyone?' Matthews spat back.

'I don't know what you mean. I went to my room alone.' He wondered if there had been talk around the camp – if he and Lynn had been unwittingly indiscreet and their affair had been discovered.

'I remained in my room *alone*,' he emphasised.

Matthews appeared irritated at Scala's tone. 'Did you know the boy Jarvis, Sergeant Scala?'

'No, I can't say I actually knew him. I've only been here for a few weeks. We arrived together, but apart from that I've been too busy settling in. And then we had the exercise.'

'The exercise in which a friend of Jarvis's died, you mean? Is that the one?' Matthews had fire in his eyes now.

Scala nodded.

'Do you think that Boyd was queer as well?' the policeman went on relentlessly. 'Obviously you'd heard that Jarvis was a fairy.'

'As I explained, I haven't been here all that long. I could hazard a guess.'

'How do you think the rest of the men took to the fact that one of them was a nancy boy, then? Don't think they'd have liked it, would they?'

The questions rained down on Scala. He answered them as blandly as possible: he thought it better that way. He wanted to limit any sign of his own involvement in the affair, yet he could feel his own anger at the apparent hostility of the bloody policeman opposite. He fought to retain his composure. And still the questions kept coming.

What of Scullard? Had Scala liked Scullard? Did he know of his apparent homosexuality? Any ideas where the man might be now? What was Scala's attitude to faggots in the ranks? Did he approve of coloured soldiers in the Army?

'Haven't really got any feelings about them at all,' he answered boldly. 'But I don't see what this has to do with Private Jarvis's death.'

Matthews was studying the file in front of him. Scala glanced once more towards Tavaner, as if for support, but the CSM remained impassive. Scala thought he was putting on one of his poker-face expressions to hide his emotions.

'It may have everything to do with what has been going on in the camp,' Matthews retorted, examining one of the documents in detail. 'I have a copy of your Army record, Sergeant Scala. It would appear that you have no love of blacks. Let me see ... ah yes! ... in 1988, whilst stationed at Aldershot, I see you were disciplined for taking part in a fight ... admittedly outside the camp ... but you and some others were involved in a fracas with some coloured civilians, were you not? A broken glass was involved ... nasty business, eh?'

Scala appeared angry. 'I was provoked ... that was made clear at the time. The Paki had been asking for trouble – pawing the woman that I was with.'

'I see it cost you a chance of promotion. Could have gone up for warrant officer, couldn't you?' the policeman went on. 'Cost you dearly, eh? Maybe that's why you were caught shouting abuse and inciting trouble that time in Brixton. That could have been very nasty – stupid of you to get yourself noticed causing trouble. I think under the circumstances the police were very tolerant.'

Scala remained silent.

'You really don't seem to have much time for our coloured brethren, do you, Sergeant Scala? What other prejudices do you have? How about our gay friends? What do you feel about them? What was your reaction to the bum boy Jarvis? I think you didn't like the idea.' Matthews was shouting now, apparently unable to keep his temper. 'I'll tell you something, Sergeant Scala, I can't stomach bigots like you. I think you're nothing but bloody troublemakers – '

Tavaner exploded. 'That's enough, Sergeant Matthews! This is not some bleedin' inquisition – and there will be no harassment of the men in my company in this way. I suggest you restrict yourself to the incident that you're here to investigate, not look back into history!'

Matthews' rage began to dissolve and he attempted to compose himself. 'I'll just say this, Sergeant Scala. I've known men like you before. I've hunted them ... sometimes out of the Army ... so just because you're in the Army doesn't mean you can hide. If I find there's a case to answer here, and that something happened to Private Jarvis at the hands of people like yourself, I'll come down on you – by Christ, I'll be down on you. Now that's all. Get the hell out of here.'

Scala could hear his own blood surging in his ears as his anger rose. He looked at Tavaner, who signalled with his eyes for Scala to leave the room. Replacing the maroon beret on his head, he stormed out of the door and down the corridor of the drab office block. Then he could no longer restrain the smirk on his face, pleased that Matherson had acted promptly. The false insertion on Scala's record had been a hurried last-minute decision, but one which Scala was convinced would now bring a reaction.

They were lost in the warren of streets in that part of Berlin. The map had been near to useless since most of the area was being redeveloped. The place had changed dramatically since the maps had been charted. For almost half an hour the black Opel saloon had been a familiar sight in the area, for to the two men each street had appeared identical to the next. They were near, they knew as much; they could almost sense it. Their frustration was beginning to mount.

Skinner saw the police car in the driving mirror. It seemed to be following them. 'Shit! That's all we friggin' well need – a bastard copper on our tail!' he hissed.

Roberts felt his face flush. 'Pull over, man! Let him get by.'

The Opel came to a slow and deliberate stop at the side of one of the identical streets. The green and white BMW drew up behind and a tall police officer in a green uniform stepped out and headed towards the Opel.

A still flushed-looking Roberts wound down the window and waved his tourist map in the man's face. '*Sprechen Sie Englisch?*' he inquired. '*Wo ist . . .?*' He pointed forlornly to the map and attempted to demonstrate that he required directions.

The policeman beamed. Another lost British tourist! The officer did not speak English, but in what seemed an agonisingly drawn out charade he gestured the correct route for the two men to take.

Then the BMW disappeared from sight, leaving Roberts and Skinner gently gasping with relief. All they had to do now was to follow the instructions.

'A word, please, Jim, if I may?' Tavaner seemed mildly official. Scala, still giving the appearance of anger at his treatment at the hands of the SIB man, took a long hard gulp of the cold lager and followed Tavaner to a corner of the mess where no one could overhear.

'That business this afternoon was a bit of a bugger, eh?'

smiled Tavaner. 'I think that geezer Matthews has a rat up his arse.'

Scala could only nod in agreement.

'But it's given me the opportunity that I've been wanting to take for some time,' continued Tavaner.

Scala sat up and gave the man his full attention.

'I can't say that what I heard this afternoon about your bit of trouble came as any surprise to me. I knew, you see . . . I'll be honest with you about that. I'd suspected as much anyway. After all, you were with us that night when we sorted the little sod out.' Tavaner appeared quite matter-of-fact as he went on. 'I've been waiting for the right time to approach you about something you might be interested in . . . a kind of proposition if you like . . .'

'What kind of proposition?'

'Not too fast now! "One small step" and all that crap. But I have a suspicion you might be interested. I wasn't certain until the other night and all that stuff with Jarvis – but you were there, and whether you like it or not you're in the shit with the rest of us. But *we* help each other.'

'Who's *we*?' demanded Scala.

'Let's just say that *they* are people who believe in the same thing that I do, and a lot of the lads here . . . There are some people I'd like you to come and meet. Let's say the weekend, shall we? Interested?'

Scala's heart leaped as he gulped down his remaining beer.

She felt like a schoolgirl whose secret love had been discovered for the first time. Alone with her accuser, in the bare office that smelled of staleness, she felt trapped like an animal in a cage.

'But how did you know? We've been very discreet.'

'Listen, love, there's no such thing as being discreet on an army camp, is there?' Matthews smirked. 'There's bound to be talk, there's always someone to see you. It's okay – it's no real sin if you want to go screwing around with one of your comrades-in-arms.'

Fury rose within her. 'You make it sound dirty! What the hell has it got to do with you anyway? It's none of your business if Sergeant Scala and myself enjoy a . . . enjoy . . .'

'An "affair" is the word you're searching for, I think,' snarled the policeman. 'Let's say that you two are an "item", shall we? But tell me, Sergeant Anders, what do you know about your man?'

She listened, ashen-faced, as Matthews read from the file on

Sergeant Jim Scala. She had felt that she had known her man. They had loved together, he had understood her, taken time with her; he had been gentle and caring. She had felt that she could love her man. What she was listening to now was the description of someone else.

The log on the fire collapsed, sending a shower of sparks floating up into the dark chimney. Rainer Fassbeck placed more wood on the glowing embers to rekindle the flames that brought a warm cheer to the elegant living room with its expensive trappings, the reward of his years at the top of his profession in the sport that had been good to him.

Fassbeck enjoyed his home. He had been one of the first to move into the eighteenth-century houses in the fashionable Köpenick district in the south-eastern suburbs of Berlin. The area had felt a breath of change since many of the crumbling houses that had made up the area had been lovingly restored, and now a new affluence permeated it. It had been the perfect place for the former jet-setter to settle down with his beautiful wife and daughter and start a new phase of his life.

Suddenly his attention was drawn to the sound of hurried footsteps approaching from the hall as Anneliese stormed into the room. He looked on her with the admiration and love that a father saves for a precious once-in-a-lifetime moment with his daughter. Marjo had not exaggerated, he thought. In her fresh white party dress the small girl *did* look like an 'angel'. He hugged her tightly. This was going to be a special day for his girl.

But she was impatient to see the gifts that had been arriving throughout the morning from people around the globe who had fallen under her spell, and Fassbeck could restrain the child no longer. She bounced out of the room, out of the hallway and down the long curved driveway that led to the postbox by the massive iron gates that divided the Fassbeck home from the rest of the world.

His body had finally given in to the sleep that he had craved most of that day. Ignoring the tumult from the gabbling crowds outside, Derek Scullard felt safe at last.

He did not hear the slight creak of the bare floorboards as the footsteps cautiously ascended the decaying stairs towards the first-floor room. The shadows of the two figures entered the room first, through the unlocked door. Scullard had not been expecting visitors. There was no sound as the men crept into the shabby room. The crumpled figure turned in his sleep as the intruders divided, one to each side of the damp single bed.

Instinct woke him. The sense of danger that becomes second nature to a professional whose life has involved killing alerted his body. Too late. His good eye, the one unaffected by the beating he had taken the previous day, bulged as a sense of fear gripped him.

He vaguely saw a hand reach out for his head whilst another came down hard on his shoulder, pinning him to the bed. For a fleeting second he thought he saw a gleam of light reflected off polished metal. Scullard struggled, but in his own weakened condition he was no match for the figure that gripped him. He gasped for breath and attempted to rally a scream, but nothing came out. He saw the flash of the knife as the second man jerked it down and across in a swift slicing movement. He felt no pain as he saw the fountain of blood shoot from his neck – only a warm wetness as it flooded his clothes. Panic gripped him and again he tried to scream, but again there was no sound. Then he felt his whole body shake and enter convulsion. During a lifetime of soldiering Derek Scullard had wondered how he would face death. Now, as if in slow motion, he saw himself witnessing it.

The angelic blue eyes widened with delight. It was as she had hoped. A small pile of birthday cards lay at the bottom of the postbox and there was a present too, brightly wrapped in multicoloured paper and tied with a big pink bow.

In her impatience, the path back to the house seemed to have grown longer. The blonde child broke into a run, dishevelling her crisp white dress. The smile of joy revealed two rows of tiny gleaming white teeth as she strode into the luxurious living room. Her father stood there rocking with laughter at the side of her fussing, beautiful, dark-skinned mother.

Rainer Fassbeck took the pile of envelopes from the child, leaving her with the colourful package. Her fingers tore at the ribbon and paper as Marjo searched for clues to the identity of the sender. But Anneliese was impatient and did not care who had sent it. She continued to tear until she had managed to remove the sheet of paper around the bare cardboard box that she now held tightly in her small hands. She could wait no longer. In her excitement, she needed no permission to open it. She lifted the lid.

The wall of flame that erupted engulfed the entire living room and hallway, bursting through the windows and sending showers of razor-sharp glass cascading over a 100-yard radius. The explosion that ripped through the house lasted just a second, to be followed by a still silence.

The two figures in the dirty black Opel heard the explosion as they drove away through the maze of streets in the old town as they had been directed by the helpful policeman. The mission had been accomplished.

The grey, wolf-like eyes watched with satisfaction as the last shiver of life departed from Derek Scullard's body. The corpse lay there, arms outstretched rigidly in death, his one clear eye wide open and wearing an expression of disbelief.

Calmly Volker Reisz smoothed down the blond hair plastered close to his scalp. He and Peter Coetzee looked at each other. There was no need for words.

As quietly as they had entered, the pair disappeared into the gloom of the crumbling apartment block where Derek Scullard's body would remain undiscovered for weeks, perhaps months, the victim of a crazed immigrant seeking money.

Violent death had visited twice that day. An innocent young life had been snuffed out along with that of her loving parents, while a man's wretched torment had been ended by those he had believed in. Few would believe that the two tragedies had any connection.

CHAPTER FIFTEEN

She let the steaming water creep into every crevice of her body as she stood beneath the shower. The jets of water that rained down on her were almost scalding. But it was as she had wanted.

Lynn Anders was trying to cleanse herself. She had felt dirty and used and soiled for the last three days, ever since the angry sergeant from the Special Investigation Branch had told her those stories about the man with whom she had shared her bed; the man whom she had permitted to know more about the intricacies of her body than any man before.

For a full five minutes she stood beneath the shower in the women's locker room after her morning workouts. Each morning since Matthews had spoken to her he had punished herself with a hard routine in the gym. She wanted to believe that the words he had spoken had been false, but the army record of the man she had made love to and trusted had supported what he had said. It was clear that Jim Scala was not the free-minded, humane person she had thought, but a racist bigot. Lynn Anders felt angry at her own naïvety and her weak female emotions.

She had not allowed herself to see or speak to Scala since the meeting with Matthews. He had tried to see her, but she had always found an excuse to resist. For apart from her feelings of stupidity and remorse, she was now fearful for her safety. She had told Scala the nightmare story of Adebeyo's death and made threats to expose the 'inner sanctum'. Now she believed that her man might well be part of the evil syndicate. No amount of steaming water could erase her feelings of doubt and fear.

Winter had at last relaxed its grip on Allenby Barracks. The thick snow that had been a permanent feature of the camp for the last two months had given way to wet mounds of filthy slush that were now piled high throughout the camp.

With the milder weather, the mundane tasks of daily life at an army barracks had also returned. The continuous round of tidying the camp and sprucing of equipment was combined with the endless preparation that went on to ensure that the battalion could move at an instant's notice to any far-flung trouble spot. There was wild talk that it was being posted to Bosnia in the coming weeks for duty with NATO'S Implementation Force (IFOR). But the wild talk could never be confirmed. With the departure of the snow, the men of C Company had spent two days on the firing ranges refreshing their skills. The noise and excitement of weapons practice had provided welcome relief to the monotony of inaction.

A cloak of silence had descended over the Barracks on the matter of Derek Scullard. There had been no news of the missing sergeant, still listed as AWOL. The camp, normally rife with rumour on any variety of subject, was gripped by a curious silence, the like of which the man from SIB had never experienced before. At each step his investigation was confronted by a wall of non-communication and indifference. It was as if the boy Jarvis had never been a member of the Royal Kent Rangers, or that his passing was a myth.

Frustration was building within Matthews. He had focused much of his attention on the Engineers sergeant who wore the maroon beret. The man was trouble, of that Matthews was confident. Scala too was sure that his every move was being scrutinised by the policeman. It would be a pleasant relief to join Tavaner and other members of C Company for their visit to Berlin over the coming weekend. There, at least, he could escape the accusing eyes of the man who had taken an instant dislike to him.

There was a lot to do. Günter Brusse sometimes wondered if the others actually realised how much was involved in preparing for these visits. It had seemed as though everything had been left to him. He had had to close the shop for a day to work on the arrangements in the privacy of his apartment. It would be a monumental achievement if everything was ready before he had to leave for the airport. He had not even watched the television coverage of the funeral of the Fassbeck family, for which thousands had lined the streets to pay a final tribute to the murdered sporting hero and his family. It had been that other traitor Kinze who had led the mourners and carried the tiny coffin of the five-year-old child.

So much importance had been placed on this visit, and Stein had shown such exuberance at its possible long-term results, that

Brusse felt he was standing on the brim of a great moment in history.

The minibus that belonged to the Royal Kent Rangers picked its way through the neat rows of comfortable apartment blocks and parks that made up the suburbs of Berlin to the west of Charlottenburg. The two-hour journey had passed quickly as the occupants chatted and joked amongst themselves.

Scala and Tavaner had sat together at the front, listening to the banter from the young soldiers. Scala understood the younger group to regard their company sergeant major with a reverence beyond the respect due to him as their immediate commanding officer. It struck Scala that they looked on him more as some kind of 'saviour'. Together, he judged, Tavaner and this selection of his young soldiers made a formidable adversary. They were a tightly bonded unit, prepared to die for each other, he guessed. In his way, Scala admired Tavaner for winning the affection of his men in such a manner.

The plans for the trip had already been laid. The members of the group would be free to go their own ways, but would meet up later. Tavaner and Scala left the bus together, allowing it to travel on and drop the younger men in the city centre. Tavaner had wanted to be alone with Scala, and at first it seemed to Scala that they were strolling aimlessly past well-kept gardens of well-kept houses in a well-kept street. It was not until they reached the slight rise at the end of the street that Scala realised their destination, as a vast construction loomed before them.

The colossal Olympiastadion held Scala in awe at first. He had seen photographs and newsreel pictures before, but had never had the opportunity of seeing it for himself. The towering sides of the monument that Hitler had built for the Olympic Games of 1936, and where he had made many of his rallying speeches to the German masses, stopped him momentarily in his tracks. Tavaner suggested that before anything else, the two men should take the lift to the top of the Glockenturm, the belltower, which afforded a spectacular view of the whole stadium. He did not exaggerate. Scala's imagination was racing.

As the two men slowly explored the vast symbol of the years of Nazi domination conversation between them was comfortable. Yet Scala knew that soon the light-hearted small talk would take on a more sinister tone.

*   *   *

Alex Carter fastened his seat belt in preparation for landing, glancing out of the window at the view of Berlin. It had been a hell of a rush that had left him cursing, but he had managed to catch the plane by the skin of his teeth. Christ, how he hated Matherson for his sense of the dramatic, he thought. Everything had to be done at the bloody gallop. The flight would be arriving on time. Despite the initial frenzy he felt relaxed as he mentally went through Matherson's final instructions once more. He peered down at the city, wondering where the hell in that teeming mass Scala had buried himself.

Carter had always liked Scala. It had been he who had first suggested Scala's recruitment to Matherson after hearing of the SAS man's problems in Bosnia. Carter thought he would have done the same thing as Scala – called in the planes and destroyed the bloody Serbs who had been playing merry hell with the peacekeepers. It had been a pity that there had been a diplomatic outcry because of the carnage; otherwise, he considered, Scala might well have been hailed as a hero. In his days based at Hereford Carter too had always acted on impulse. But he was only too aware that the British Army could always be relied upon to put the blame squarely on some other poor bastard's shoulders once the shit had hit the fan.

'Where are you, Jimmy boy?' he muttered in his slight Glaswegian accent as the aircraft made its final descent through the clouds. 'I know you're down there somewhere, but where the bloody hell are you? Just come to Daddy, Jim, my boy. Come to Daddy!'

As Alex Carter pondered, confined in his standard economy class seat, the man four rows ahead sipped the last drops of his champagne and stretched out in the comparative luxury of business class. He had always insisted on travelling in style, and the Hollywood studios of the fifties and sixties had been quick to please their brightest up-and-coming star.

Today, however, few people recognised the man who had once been the ridiculously handsome hero of a score of westerns and action movies. Now, like his movies before him, Guy Rockwell had faded into history. In his heyday, as one of the big box office attractions, he had captured the hearts of a generation of young female fans with his smiling blue eyes, high cheekbones and mop of coal-black hair. But now the thin-faced American with grey, balding hair could travel unhindered anywhere in the world without the discomfort of being identified. He preferred it so. Years of living as a recluse in the mountains of California had left him with a love of solitude.

The Hollywood years had long since passed for Guy Rockwell. He preferred that too. He had branded the money men who ran the studios as Zionists who were destroying the whole fabric of the America that he believed in. It had been Guy Rockwell's sworn duty to combat that decay. It had cost him his career. But he had found a new goal now, funding his own extremist group, which he had proudly named The Pioneers, as a private army to strike at those who threatened the wellbeing and very fibre of his country. He had called for an armed struggle to make America a better place for Americans, and a holy war against those who would pull it down. He had promised violence, and that had followed, with a series of bank robberies staged across the United States and violent attacks on those who openly dared to speak against the movement.

Guy Rockwell stared down at the view of Berlin. Like the pioneer heroes of his old western movies, he was heading to a promised land.

'It's difficult to think that this is where it all began.' Mike Tavaner was in reflective mood as he looked out over the sunken terraces and giant pillars of the Olympiastadion. He narrowed his eyes to make out the platform where Adolf Hitler had once stood with the dream that the world would see the divine truth of his super race – only to see that dream shattered by a single black American athlete who dominated the Olympic Games that Hitler had hoped would spotlight the might of his new nation.

Now Tavaner and Scala were standing beneath the roll of honour of those who had competed in those far-off games. Scala read the names on the plaque: '100m Lauf Owens USA . . . 200m Lauf Owens USA . . . 400m Lauf Williams USA . . .' The list of sprint champions was dominated by the name of the black legend 'Jesse Owens', the man who had shamed Hitler's supermen.

A sudden chill wind made their eyes run, and the two men dug their hands deep into the pockets of the bulky ski-jackets that both were wearing.

'Have you ever thought that maybe the old feller had some reasonable ideas after all?' asked Tavaner in a quiet voice.

'I thought we were supposed to be on the other side – you know, the good guys,' retorted Scala.

'Certainly, but don't you sometimes feel that we've made a

real balls-up of our lives and our society since then? For God's
sake, just look at the two of us. We're supposed to be two
highly regarded and motivated professionals – but who looks
after us when we're no further use to the system? Certainly not
the arseholes in Whitehall.'

Scala realised that Tavaner was now speaking from his gut. He
was in no mood for jesting.

'Look at Germany, for Christ's sake!' continued Tavaner. 'After
the war we were supposed to be the victors, and supposedly to the
victors go the spoils. Well, you tell me what bloody spoils we can
look forward to.'

Scala had heard the arguments before, from the unemployed
who filled the pubs back in the valleys. He let Tavaner talk on.

'In a few weeks' time I'm out of all this lot . . . out of the Army
. . . and I'm not certain what I've got to look forward to.' He leaned
against the stone wall that contained the roll of honour. Jim, I love
my country . . . I loved it when I joined the Army, and I still love
it now. But it's not the same country . . .'

Scala interrupted. 'Christ, have you thought about a career in
politics when you get out of the Army?' he joked.

'In a way, Jim, yes. But not quite in the way that you mean.'

Günter Brusse's eyes searched the crowd for the man he was to
meet. He found it difficult to understand how someone who had
once been so famous could now appear so anonymous. Brusse was
waiting as arranged in the centre of the airport concourse as the
crowd of new arrivals began to trickle through Immigration. He
studied each face as it passed by. Finally he settled on the man
with thin, balding hair who was last in the file of passengers who
had arrived from Heathrow. The face was familiar, and Brusse
envisaged how the man would have looked on the movie posters
outside a thousand cinemas thirty years before. Now the smiling
blue eyes that had captivated so many women were shielded by
thick, black-rimmed spectacles. But the man had a presence, of
that Brusse was certain.

Scala listened hard, oblivious to the background noise of the
bustling restaurant. The sudden cold snap had given both Tavaner
and him a healthy appetite. Tavaner continued to speak as he
guzzled his hearty meal of the traditional German soup called
Leberknödelsuppe, hardly stopping to chew the mouthfuls of
spicy dumplings, ox liver and onions. Scala could smell the

garlic in it from where he sat. He had settled for the mixture of potato, leeks, parsnips and bacon known as *Kartoffelsuppe*, and each thick spoonful sat heavily in his stomach.

Tavener was halfway through the story of his life. 'I tell you, there was nothing for me back in Gravesend. There was no future. Oh, it was fine if you were a Paki or a black – the do-gooders on the council saw that they were all right. They got a bloody job. But the likes of me had no chance. I decided my best bet was to join the Army,' he explained. 'To my surprise, I found I liked it. And the Army liked me – liked what I had to offer them. I'd have gladly died for my country then, I tell you . . . died for the Rangers too – the RKR was my home. But bit by bloody bit they've chiselled away . . . more bloody paper shit . . . more "Don't do this" and "Do that". A man can't even think nowadays.

'I started to notice things, you see. I suppose it really started back in the early eighties, after we'd been in Northern Ireland. We had an incident – nearly all got the bloody chop. The Provo bastards had set up an ambush down in Armagh, near to Crossmaglen. We were driving straight into it, you see. Fortunately one of the boys in the vehicle in front spotted something . . . saw something wasn't quite right, and shouted out. We stopped dead while he went forward to take a look. He ended up taking a bastard bullet – the Provos fired a few shots and pissed off as usual, leaving our lad squealing like a stuck pig. The bullet wasn't that serious – only got him in the leg, although it could have been nasty. Bloody hero, that kid, I tell you . . . he saved our bleedin' lives. Sure enough, he came back to duty with us after a spell in hospital, but he was never quite the same. He'd lost his spirit, and wanted out of the Army.'

Tavaner took a gulp from a litre glass of beer to wash down the hot, spicy soup before going on. 'I took an interest in the kid – helped to get his papers signed so he could get out. Do you know what, Jim, my lad? The shithead who was our CO at the time only stamped the boy's papers as "Unemployable". I ask you – the kid had been a bloody hero! So now he's in civvy street with a reference that says he's no fucking good to work. That did for him. Couldn't get a fucking job anywhere, not even as a bleeding roadsweeper, just because some prat takes it upon himself to play frigging God! Last I heard, the lad became a pisshead, got himself divorced and all the rest of the shite that goes with it. So I started to look at things a bit different then. I saw it was happening all over the bloody place. They were cutting back our bleeding Army and our soldiers had nowhere to go afterwards.'

Scala had finished his meal and was listening intently. He too had experienced what could happen to a man once the Army and society had turned their back on him.

'I started studying a lot of the lads that were being chucked out after "Options for Change" got them the chop. They had nothing – sure, they got a bit of money to go out with, but most of them were hardly more than kids and just pissed it all up against the wall and then wondered where the next lot was coming from. The only problem was, there *was* no more. They were stuffed. Meanwhile, they could look around and see their black brothers getting hand-outs all over the place.'

Scala had heard the complaint on so many occasions. He had always felt sympathy for those whom he had called the 'forgotten ones'.

'It made me question the system, Jim, I can tell you. I wanted to do something to put it right. Then, about two years ago while we were stationed here, I met some people. They were Brits, and a lot of them were ex-military. They were as pissed off as I was about how they were treated. They'd set up a life of their own over here. At first I'd never seen such a sorry bunch in all my life, I can tell you. But I got to know them more . . . and they introduced me to some other people . . . people with ideas . . . who want to change things . . . and they're people I can understand. Jesus, we didn't fight the Jerries to find ourselves wiping the arses of every other lazy bloody no-good immigrant in the world, did we?'

Tavaner was whipped up now. It was the most animated that Scala had seen the giant of a man all day.

'Anyway, these people made me understand what the hell was going on in our country, and all over the bloody place. They want to change things too . . . they don't want to see us giving any more away! They realised that we were going to have to fight for our own rights. All they wanted was to have the blackies sent home – and to do that they had to deal from a position of strength. It started off as a bit of a lark to begin with, I suppose – you know, weekend outings and all that. No harm – just showing a few people around guns and the like. One day they asked me to help, and, to my surprise I jumped at the chance. They wanted men who were experienced in the military. At first they wanted to be trained, then I got more involved. It wasn't difficult to whip up interest from some of the other lads at the RKR, the ones I trusted, the ones who felt the same as me. Let's face it, we all felt that we were going to be shat on at any time.'

Scala intervened: 'And in the time-honoured fashion of keeping a careful eye on the recruits, you were able to spot which of the new lads would be suitable material for your ideas.'

'Don't get me wrong, Jim,' insisted Tavaner. 'I never once ordered anyone to join in . . . as you said, in the "time-honoured way". I was able to persuade some of the guys about what these people were saying – not that most of them needed any persuasion. But I never ordered anyone to join!'

Scala knew how the sergeants would operate. It would be the same as in any army unit anywhere in the world. The trained eyes would always pick a man with potential out of any new group: a man with initiative and the ability to instil confidence in those under him, who would follow him – sometimes to the death. The chosen man would then be groomed by his senior for possible promotion and given the opportunity to put his initiative to work. He had seen it too back home in the valleys, where the technique was used by union officials eager to recruit more followers. Tavaner had used it to choose those who were likely to be influenced into following him.

'I suppose having a black guy come to the regiment didn't do much for your image with your new friends!' said Scala, grinning.

Tavaner was adamant: 'No room for a git like that – it was simple. Anyway, if the truth be known, the sod was a thief! As I said, Jim, we know how to look after our own. Let's face it . . . you've seen that.'

The image of the last time he had set eyes on Christopher Jarvis flashed into his mind. 'Yes, I've noticed,' he responded.

'The thing is, Jim, our friends have plans – big plans. With that little shit Scullard buggering things up for me, I'm a senior man down. I'm looking for a replacement. I gather from your record that you might be of a similar mind too, so I'm going out on a limb here and offering you the chance to come in with us. Say "Yes" and you'll be well looked after, say "No" and I know you won't say anything of this – I know I can put you in the frame with us on the Jarvis caper.'

CHAPTER SIXTEEN

Scala knew the look. He had seen the look of a man on the edge of insanity a score of times before. The man opposite had the look.

'Here's the fella I told you about!' Tavaner broke the deadlock of silence that had existed between Scala and Hearn as they faced each other, each man examining the other. 'Paddy Hearn, meet Jim Scala.'

Hearn reached for Scala's outstretched hand in welcome, and squeezed. Scala was unsure if the man was deliberately using excessive force as a way of warning a stranger of his power, or if the grip was his usual one.

Unblinking, Hearn stared directly into Scala's eyes, challenging him to look away. It was the sudden shriek of unexpected cheering that eventually broke that challenge, startling Hearn. Releasing Scala's hand he spun round towards the sudden noise, hands instinctively forming themselves into fists. But he quickly recovered his composure. Straightening the jacket of his blue suit he gestured for Scala and Tavaner to join him at the table by the end of the bar, away from the pandemonium of the crowded saloon, and signalled the barman to fetch them some drinks.

Hearn was bothered. He prided himself on his ability never to forget a face. That gift had helped keep him alive in many a shadowy conflict. There was something about Scala's face that tickled the depths of his memory. Yet the completed image would not return. He had a feeling about the man who sat at the table with him. He knew the kind of man that Jim Scala was.

Scala was certain. The pair had never met. But when Scala had first joined the SAS all those years ago Hearn had been a near legend to its younger members. He had boasted of his extended years of service, of how he had trained the shit-awful Yanks in Vietnam and of how the Sultan of Oman had personally honoured the flame-haired Irishman who had led near-suicidal missions against the communist fanatics of the Liberation of the Occupied Arabian

Gulf that had attempted to take over his country. Hearn's chosen weapon had always been the knife. The death-defying exploits of Poppa Hearn had become part of the legend of Hereford.

The three men drank from the three glasses of schnapps that the barman brought. Hearn downed his in one. Scala deliberately chose to sip his. He would not rise to Hearn's unspoken challenge.

'The regiment or the Paras?' Hearn finally spoke.

'Paras!' Scala replied. 'Good years, too!'

'Killed anyone?' asked Hearn, as he made no secret of studying the scar that ran down Scala's right cheek.

Scala noticed and subconsciously ran his finger down his face, tracing the outline of the jagged scar. 'What do you think?' he answered.

'So how did ye get that?' Hearn pointed accusingly to the scarred tissue.

'Some bloody Mick didn't like the beret I was wearing when we were out in Derry one time.' Scala saw Hearn stiffen at the mention of the derogatory nickname 'Mick'. 'Didn't see him standing in the alleyway at first. Threw a bloody bottle, which I ended up head-butting. Still, we got the bastard . . .'

'You'll understand that I'm from there.'

'Can't mistake that bloody accent,' said Scala, grinning.

Hearn called for a refill. 'Aye, the family's still there. Me brother's going to be a virtual cripple all his life cos some bastard Provo knee-capped him twice, as well as his arms. Me sister was tarred in the street . . . and all cos I chose to join the British Army to defend the bastards. Now I can't go home. I'm a dead man if I go back there, I know that. Memories die hard over there.'

'Have you killed?' Scala attempted to ask innocently.

The glazed stare returned, to delve deep into Scala's innermost being. The memories of each kill seemed to Scala to be flashing before Hearn's eyes as he relived each terrible yet wonderful moment.

'And what do you think, Mr Scala?' Hearn returned the question. 'Yes, Mr Scala, I've killed.' Again he swallowed his drink at one gulp. 'Yes, I've played God for my country. And I was good at it – one of the best. Over twenty years with the SAS. They didn't want me to go – it was the rules that said I had to go. The men at the Ministry didn't want me to be God any more, Mr Scala. And so I'm here . . . with a lot more like me, a lot more poor bastards who had the pleasure of being shat upon by the men who sent us to kill.'

Tavaner saw his opportunity. 'Jim has had his fall-out with those people too,' he interjected. 'He took exception to having to take second place from the black bastards. Cost him his future – no more promotion for Sergeant Scala.'

It was as though Hearn had discovered a kindred spirit. His mood lightened and the ghosts of his victims lifted momentarily.

'I think Jim would be good for us. He should be introduced,' Tavaner whispered to Hearn. 'We could do with a man like him. He's up for it . . .'

Hearn pondered.

The girl wanted to cry. She bit her lip to stem the yelp of pain that she wanted to unleash as she lay spread-eagled on the bed. He was not like the other punters. Those she could handle, if necessary, by walking away. But this man, she had been told, was 'special'; she must endure.

She was one of Stein's favourites. He had looked after her well for the last year, since she had been introduced by one of the other girls. He had liked the fairness of her skin and the unruly mop of blonde curls that she refused to tie back from her face.

She had not known the identity of the man she was to meet tonight. There would be no exchange of money. This one was 'personal'. There was no need for her to be told; she was instructed simply to arrive at the room in Oranienburg where he would be staying. She looked good; she knew so.

At first the man had appeared to be a gentleman. He had watched closely as she had stripped to her skimpy silk underwear. There had been champagne, but there was no conversation. Then he had taken her, ripping her remaining underwear harshly from her body, making her cry out with the sudden pain; he had forced her to the bed; he had turned her, he had ridden her and he had held her hair tight, pulling backwards as he groaned with pleasure. Then, when spent, he had slapped her, and refused to allow her to leave, until he was once more ready.

The girl was bruised, and each time she felt the thrusting pain deep inside. But she had been instructed to endure.

Klaus Stein was watching the sadistic scene on his close-circuit screen. He sat transfixed at the girl's obvious pain and terror. He found it distasteful, and his stomach churned each time as he watched the man in the room drive himself on to the girl and use her. But Stein would not react – could not react. He wondered if Guy Rockwell had always treated women so. Possibly women had been such a cheap commodity during his golden era in Hollywood that he had known no different. Now Stein watched powerlessly as the distasteful scene unfolded before him, constrained by the knowledge that it was the funds from Guy Rockwell and the scores like him across America that were the life blood of his own organisation. For the moment, at least, Klaus Stein could do nothing . . . except watch.

It was his role; and, from the look of things, Scala considered that the man was expert. So Scala let out a congratulatory whistle as he surveyed the stocks on display within the cellar, deep beneath Poppa's Bar. What he saw made the numerous hidden arsenals of the Provos that he had helped to bust pale into insignificance.

'It's like a bloody Aladdin's Cave!' he sighed in admiration as he stepped deeper into the dark room, shadowed by Hearn and Tavaner. 'A bloody Aladdin's Cave of death, that's what it is!'

Before him stretched racks of weapons ranging from brand-new AK-74 assault rifles – the second generation of classic Soviet-made AK-47s that were now standard issue to most Russian troops – to dozens of 9mm Heckler & Koch MP5 sub-machine guns, manufactured in Germany but now the favoured weapon of Britain's SAS forces. In between, a vast array of weaponry from an American-made .50 Barrett sniper rifle to a mini-arsenal of the deadly RPG7 rocket grenade launchers filled the wooden racks. Boxes of grenades were piled up to the ceiling, as were trays of knives and blades of all descriptions.

'You've enough stuff here to start a bloody war!' muttered Scala.

'Let's hope it doesn't come to that, Jim,' laughed Tavaner. 'But you only get what you want if you have the power to back it up with, as I said earlier. A lot of this stuff came across the borders from Bosnia and Croatia, but I have to say that our friends in the States have been very generous too.'

Scala turned, surprised.

'Oh, yes! We have friends – and not always in low places' Tavaner went on. 'Fortunately we have ways of importing materials from the States. We have a network of shops, you see. The Yanks have a ready supply of militaria, and they love to flood our friends over here with it. So how better to send over the bits for weapons than to send it with all that stuff? Paddy here looks after it all, and distributes it when necessary. All done on a very proper basis – just like the Army, eh?' Tavaner explained. 'It's fallen to myself and one or two others to show our friends how to put these toys to the best use. I tell you, it scares the shit out of the coppers over here.'

Scala had stopped, his attention caught by boxes of putty-like blocks wrapped in cellophane, which he knew from deadly experience to be Semtex, the favoured Czechoslovakian-made explosive of the IRA.

Hearn saw Scala's line of sight. 'Ah, yes! See, it's not just the Provos who can get to play with this lot. Came in quite handy the other day, though. That nigger-lover Fassbeck got a surprise present he wasn't expecting!'

Scala recalled the images – the photographs of the dead family, the picture of the child's coffin being laid to rest. He wanted to strike out, to see the blood of the men who had created that horror. But he knew he must fight back his anger.

Tavaner continued, with a sense of pride in his voice: 'So you see, Jim, we have the power. We have places like this all over Germany . . . all over Europe . . . even back home. And what's more, they're getting organised. But let's hope that people see the light, eh?'

The door to the crowded bar opened, unleashing a fog of smoke that billowed out into the dark street. Through the haze, the girl saw the two men leave and head towards her. She sat in the ancient BMW, hidden by the shadows cast by the street lights, and followed the pair with her eyes. She recognised the taller of the two men; but the slighter one, who she thought laboured his right leg somewhat, was a stranger.

She watched as their shadows danced in and out of the doorways of the row of shops on this cold wet night, and saw them hail a passing taxicab. The BMW's engine fired first time, and she pulled in behind the cab as it made its way down the dual carriageway and into the heart of Berlin. The girl positioned her camera with the extended lens by her side on the passenger seat. Tossing back her long blonde hair, she felt a surge of anticipation. She understood the rush of excitement for she had seen her man enjoy it a hundred times before. But he would never have the opportunity to know such feelings again, so now Janine Letterman was hoping to finish Peter Macabe's final story for him.

Alex Carter checked his message list at the hotel reception. There was still no word from Scala. He would have Matherson breathing down his neck tomorrow, he knew that. But he could not move without word from the man on the ground. He considered that, if patience truly was a virtue, then he, Alex Carter, was a suitable case for sainthood. But Scala was trying even his patience.

He ordered a large malt whisky from the hotel bar and rehearsed the speech that he would use to fob off the outraged Matherson. Once again it would be Alex Carter who would bear the brunt of his boss's wrath as he provided a plausible excuse for the wayward Scala.

'You bloody owe me one, Jim boy!' he sighed in exasperation.

She was a temptress. She knew her attractions to men and she milked them. But tonight she had a larger than usual audience, and she was playing harder at her nightly game.

The throbbing music could be heard three streets away. The tiny dance floor was hers, and so was the audience. The other girls who used the club were used to her antics by now, and just ignored them: the louder the music became, the more frenetically she gyrated on the dance floor. The ample breasts swayed freely under the loose-fitting shirt, and the minuscule black leather skirt inched forever higher up her thighs. The air was filled with the sound of male voices clamouring for more.

The taxi came to a halt outside the bar that was one of dozens that nestled off the countless side streets that led from the Kurfürstendamm, the smartest street in Berlin. It was the kind of place where Tavaner and Scala had expected to find the hard-drinking remnants of C Company. Tavaner fancied he could distinguish Baker's yells even as he paid off the cab.

The bar was a sweating, heaving throng of humanity – mostly men looking for loose women and the occasional woman looking for the easy pick-up. The girls who hunted in packs were obvious, in their thick, gaudy make-up and outfits that left little to the male imagination. The air was heavy with the stink of beer, cigarettes and cheap perfume. It was, as Scala expected, the perfect place to find his soldiers.

The cheer of welcome that erupted as they stepped into the bar told them they had hit the right place. C Company had formed a kind of beach-head to the bar, preventing the other customers from encroaching on their territory. It also happened to be the most opportune spot from which to study the girl's provocative movements.

Tavaner reached the bar first and was handed a litre of heavy beer which he tackled with vigour. Scala laughed aloud as he studied the antics of the full-bodied girl on the dance floor. It was so the world over: the soldiers were happy as long as they were occupied with beer and obvious women. He presumed it would always be so, thank God.

The bar was in uproar as every man vied for the attention of the girl. They yielded and bayed and shouted lewd invitations and reached out sweaty, grasping hands at she cavorted wildly to the thumping music that flooded the room.

But the baby-faced one, the freckle-skinned youngster who had been taken under Taff Roberts's wing, sat motionless. While all the hands had been reaching out to grope, and filthy taunts had been echoing around him, the gentle-faced boy had remained speechless, partly through drink and partly in awe of the girl's physical talents. And it was he whom the girl spotted. She had chosen him. She inched nearer to him, thrusting her hips and bosom wildly in the direction of his bulging eyes. The shrieks of derision from his comrades deafened the transfixed youth and brought the beach-head to near hysteria.

It was an insult. The men in the far corner, swarthy Turkish youths who regularly inhabited the bar, muttered angrily among themselves. They had ruled here until the pimple-faced British squaddies had arrived. Another night, and the girl would have distributed her favours in their direction. Her choice of the pink adolescent boy was the final insult. Enrouraged by his yelping seconds, he summoned enough courage to reach out. She was offering her breast to him to touch because he was British, and pissed, and had more money.

They came as a wave, overpowering the shocked, drunken British squaddies and knocking most of them to the ground. As the stunned soldiers gathered their senses the girl was manhandled to the far end of the bar where the Turkish gang held sway.

'Oh, fuck!' Scala saw the escalation brewing, and looked to Tavaner for support to prevent the imminent battle. But Tavaner, glass in hand, had the grin of the devil etched on his face.

'On them, my lads! Don't let the dark-skinned fuckers get away with it!' he bellowed at the figures staggering groggily to their feet.

As a man they rose. Some reached for glasses, some for bottles. The thump of the music was drowned out by screams and the overturning of stools and tables as the rest of the drinkers attempted to flee the impending mayhem.

In ghostly silence, the line of British soldiers strode across the
dance floor where seconds before the girl had freely cavorted,
towards the corner where the group of Turkish youths jabbered
and pawed at her. At first the Turks attempted to ignore the
oncoming British. After all, the girl was theirs; they had paid for
her favours on other nights. The first bottle to fly caught one of
the Turkish youths on the temple, sending blood gushing down
his stubbled face. It was the signal: the battle was on.

Scala saw Ginger Baker freely pummelling the one who he
thought was the leader of the group as he lay prone on the floor.
One of the dark-skinned youths held Roberts by the arms as his
partner drove punch upon punch into the Welshman's belly. With
a wicked, sadistic grin Skinner prepared to drive a jagged broken
bottle-neck into the face of the terrified youth he held against the
wall. The temptress screamed in genuine terror as she attempted to
flee the carnage, wrapping her arms around the drooping breasts
that she had just displayed so freely.

It was too much for Tavaner to endure. Throwing down his beer
glass, he leaped into action. His first target was the Turk who was
still pounding the belly of Roberts. Unseen, Tavaner drove an upper
cut hard into the man's chin, jarring his teeth into his tongue. Blood
spurted from the Turk's mouth, adding to that which was already
covering Roberts's shirt. As the man fell, Tavaner quickly followed
the blow with a bone-jerking thud from his knee which caught the
stunned figure hard in the groin. Roberts, at last able to free himself
from the grip of the man holding him, reached forward to smash a
chair into his face. Tavaner was laughing. He was enjoying himself
as he kicked viciously again and again at the body squirming at
his feet.

It was Scala who saw the knife first. Another Turk had emerged
from the shadows of the bar. He saw the giant Tavaner as the British
soldiers' leader. On he came, holding the six-inch blade close to
his body. Scala watched him as if in slow motion, then took him
low, heaving the man sideways into the bar with the weight of his
sideways charge. The suddenness of the move startled Tavaner,
who saw the blade fall to the floor with a clatter.

The deafening music still blasted in the background as the Turk
regained his senses after Scala's charge. He reached to grab the
knife again, but Scala was on him. The Welshman's knee came up
to meet the man in the groin, and at the same time he drove the
ball of his hand upwards to take the man squarely in the face. He
felt the crunch of the man's nose breaking as he followed through

with a short, stabbing rabbit chop to the throat which caught the Turk as he fell. The man lay gasping for breath as bright red blood oozed from his shattered nose.

Tavaner grinned at the sight. 'That's my boy, Jim . . . that's my boy . . . let the black bastards have it!' he shouted.

Scala was stunned by the ferocity he had just exhibited. He turned in time to see Tavaner head butt a scrawny attacker who was attempting to tackle him from behind.

'Good sport, eh, Jim?' yelled Tavaner.

As Scala attempted to catch his breath they heard the sound of police sirens. It was Skinner who gave the order to evacuate, screaming above the din of breaking furniture and glass. C Company ran, leaving the Turkish mob sprawling, bleeding and moaning on the floor of the bar. Tavaner and Scala were the last to go, after first ensuring that all their charges had left the scene. They acted in unison, following the instincts of the veteran soldier. Then, comrades in arms, they dived through the shattered glass door in their wake.

A sudden movement caught Scala's eye: a flash of light on blonde hair. He stopped in his tracks like an animal alert to danger, and signalled for Tavaner to go on . . . he would catch him later.

As Scala searched for the slightest sign or movement the light from the bar momentarily caught the camera lens. A moment later the neon lights caught her hair. Scala saw the face, and the startled look, as the girl headed into the darkness of the small park behind her. Instinctively he shot off into the darkness in pursuit of the figure he had seen for only a split second.

The girl slipped as she ran into the darkness of the park, her boots sliding in the thick mud that the weeks of snow had left behind. Fear overtook her as she saw the man chasing her. She had seen him in the bar, and witnessed his savagery. Terror rose within her. On she ran, stumbling, but still clutching the camera that had captured the events in the bar. She could hear nothing now except the pumping of her own blood in her ears. She was running from the men she had watched for weeks since Peter Macabe's death. Now she feared those men were after her.

Sliding in the mud, Scala took the running girl at waist height, bowling her to the ground. She screamed and fought like a wildcat, recalling the way her man had fought before they threw him on to the track under the wheels of the approaching train. She kicked, catching Scala hard in the groin. He groaned in pain and grasped the girl harder as they rolled in the mud. She aimed another frantic kick, this time more wildly, which Scala parried and in return unleashed a backhand slap which caught the girl squarely on the jaw, knocking her head into the mud. Dizzily she fought for breath, giving Scala time to pin her flailing arms to the ground.

'For Christ's sake, give it up, woman!' Scala growled. 'Believe it or not, I'm not going to harm you. For pity's sake give it up!' He raised his arm again as if to strike a blow, and the anticipation of it stilled her. Now he was astride her, gripping her arms to the ground. Both figures were gasping for breath. 'That's better, for God's sake,' he gasped. 'Please believe me, I'm not here to hurt you – whoever you are . . .' He looked down at the pale face with its angry, frightened eyes blazing at him, and felt the hardness of her writhing body beneath him. 'Please believe me,' he repeated. 'I'm not here to hurt you, to hurt anyone . . .'

In the slight glow from the far-off street lights she saw the scar that ran the length of his cheek. In the light it made him appear ferocious. Her teeth clenched in anger, she hissed, 'Tell that to the poor bugger I saw you lay out in the bar . . . Tell him you're not out to hurt anyone.'

Scala relaxed his grip. 'He did have a knife that he was about to use,' he said defensively. The girl had not seen the knife as she snapped through the lens. 'I didn't cause the fight . . . I didn't want the fight,' he found himself muttering.

Her body relaxed beneath him.

'I'll let you up, if you promise not to bloody well kick. A deal?' Scala attempted a half smile. 'Now tell me . . . what are you doing here? Why the pictures?' he quizzed. He knew that he could allow no photographs of himself to be taken by anyone – just one picture that might appear anywhere would blow his supposed secret life sky-high.

'It's my job . . . what's yours? Beating the shit out of some poor kid cos he put his hands on your bird's tit? Isn't that what our brave lads do?' the girl whipped back defiantly.

'I think you have me wrong. I went to the bar for a drink,' Scala defended himself again. Furious at the realisation that he was doing so, he countered. 'What do you mean, it's your job? What job? Sneaking pictures . . . what kind of job is that?'

Slowly the truth dawned on Scala. He raised himself and offered a hand to help her to her feet. The girl attempted to wipe some of the filthy mud from her caked jeans and leather jacket.

'So what's a British hack doing here?' the question came softly.

'I'm not a hack. I take photographs.'

'It's the same thing.'

'You try telling that to my boyfriend,' she snapped. 'Or at least, my late boyfriend – the one that you bastards killed!'

Unaware of what she was talking about, Scala had no response. He watched as the girl attempted to stem the flood of tears. 'I don't know who or what you think I am, but I feel we need to talk.' He offered his hand to the girl. Through misty eyes she looked uncertainly into his, and found kindness. She took his hand.

There was only the man who served the coffee to look at the mud-splattered pair. They sat engrossed over the steaming mugs, deep in conversation. To the man who served the coffee, they were obviously lovers.

Scala listened. The girl was composed now, her fear gone. After days of talking to no one, she found herself wanting to unburden herself and reveal everything to the stranger with the scarred face. But to protect herself she began with an inquisition. How many times had he visited Poppa's Bar? Did he know the man Hearn? Had he been in Germany long?

After listening carefully to his answers she was convinced that he was a newcomer to Germany and the bar, and it put her at ease. Her instincts told her she was safe with this man.

Janine told Scala how she had hoped to prove to the scoffers in the newspaper office back home that they had been wrong. She had wanted to show that Peter Macabe had a nose for a good story and could bring it in; and, if possible, she had wanted to do it for the memory of the man whom she had loved. But time and a wall of silence had not helped her. The police would not even investigate Macabe's death, let alone assist her in the investigation. She feared she had failed him, and the arseholes who ran the newspaper would think themselves right.

'What have you got?' Scala asked seriously. 'Do you have concrete facts?'

'I have Peter's story, his words – and I do have some pictures that I snatched at Poppa's, that showed the man you were with tonight, with Hearn and this other guy . . . Peter told me his name – it was Brusse,' recalled Janine. 'It meant nothing to me then, and not much more now, but Peter reckoned that the guy was a bigwig Nazi-lover. He reckoned there was a link between the British soldiers and these Nazis – it says so in his copy,' blurted the exhausted girl.

'Where's the copy now?' asked Scala eagerly.

'At our apartment, safe . . .'

Scala sat silently, thinking. 'What would happen if I could get you proof that would support your man's story?' he said.

'We could plaster it all over the newspapers back home,' Janine replied.

'Hmmm. It wouldn't look too good, you know, if there was a headline that said: "BRIT SOLDIERS BY DAY: NAZIS BY NIGHT!" Would it?'

CHAPTER SEVENTEEN

Her tears had been shed. She had wept at the airport as she watched the plane carrying the coffin of the man she had loved take off for Britain. Now she wanted the bitter taste of revenge.

Scala understood those things. How many times had he wanted to exact revenge on those responsible for the deaths of men he had called 'friend' and 'comrade', men who had died in a score of battles in a score of conflicts? He knew her need to get even with the men who had killed Peter Macabe.

He had read Macabe's unfinished account of the meeting between Hearn and Tavaner and the other man. Scala had no knowledge of him, but, unknowingly, Scala and Macabe had trodden the same path. Scala saw the photograph of the group that had been taken by the girl in Hearn's bar. She had told him of the original tip that Macabe had been given by the soldiers in the dreary pub in Aldershot that had first alerted him to the story, and of how the newspaper had scorned the story. Now, as he sat on the polished floor of the apartment in Mommsenstrasse, sifting through the photographs and papers that Janine was producing, an idea was taking root in Scala's mind.

He sipped the steaming mug of coffee that Janine had given him before she went to shower away the caked mud. She continued the conversation through the open doorway of the bathroom down the hall. While she was gone Scala noticed the camera that the girl had carried as he had chased her in the park. It took just a second for him to reach out discreetly for it, unfasten the back of the camera and rip out the film. Now there would be no evidence of his having been at the bar.

A slight movement from the bathroom attracted his attention as he glanced upwards from the pile of papers to which he had speedily returned, and Scala caught a glimpse of the naked girl as she stepped from the shower to reach for the towel that hung on the door. Janine saw his admiring looks in the mirror and quickly pulled the towel around her before closing the door. Seconds later she stepped from the bathroom, hair still wet, face purged of make-up, in a towelling robe that ended halfway down her long, elegant thighs. Scala thought her a beautiful woman, but returned his gaze to the papers.

Her dignity restored, the girl went on with her story: 'No one wanted to know about Peter's death. The police were next to useless – to them he was just another foreigner who'd got himself into trouble with a gang of yobs. If *they* can't catch those who were responsible, then I want to get them my way – you know, the power of the press and all that crap. So I went back to the bar, and I've been going back to the bar for the last week, just door-stepping the place. Then tonight along came the big guy whom Peter had spoken with, the guy whose picture I took – and along came you, whoever you are!'

'It's not important who I am, really. Trust me. All you need to know is that I think I can help you. You see, I have a strange dislike of people who go around murdering other people.'

She saw the back of the camera, lying open and empty, and frowned. 'Trust? Now there's a strange word – it's not something we got used to in Fleet Street. But shit, I don't appear to have any choice! If you reckon you can help, then I'm willing to take a chance – call it instinct if you like.' Janine sat back on the sofa, crossing her long legs. 'Basically, I'll pay you if you help me. Help me to nail these bastards,' Janine hissed between clenched teeth. 'I don't have a whole lot of money, but what I've got is yours if you can help me to finish this.'

The offer amused Scala, who sat brushing the mud from his jeans as it dried.

'It's not your money that I want . . . I actually need *your* help. Together, I think we might be able to work something out. You see, there's a girl who also needs help – and she could, I'm sure, help you too. I think the power of the press might just be a bloody good weapon!'

He outlined the scheme that he thought would benefit both of them, and possibly save the life of Lynn Anders too. It would be the girl's best form of protection. He imagined the shockwaves in the corridors of the Ministry of Defence when the story was told. Christ, he would give a ransom just to see their faces! Then, at last, justice would be seen to be done.

*   *   *

Tavaner paced the floor of the bar, cursing every passing minute.

The last customer had left Poppa's long ago, and now only a single lamp on the bar still burned as he and the Irishman waited for Scala. The rest of the excited men from Allenby had given in to sleep, stashed away in the bedrooms above the bar. Now only the two men waited.

'I told ye the fucker wouldn't show!' blurted Hearn. 'I told ye. There's something about the man – you should not have brought him . . . I have the feelin'.'

Tavaner spun round in angry protest. 'I tell you the man's okay. He saved my skin in the bar, I can tell you. Must everyone be damned on your say-so? He was with us when the queer got his deserts. He's one of us, I tell you – whether he likes it or not. But the man stuck his neck out for me, and could have got a knife in the belly for his trouble. I say the man's okay!'

'And about bloody time as well!'

Carter was not in one of his better moods. He had bored himself senseless waiting in his hotel room for Scala to contact him. Through the night he had flicked through the numerous television channels, all of which were in German, a language he had never understood, and had settled in the end for the channel that showed graphic pornographic movies or the continuous over-hyped news reports of the American CNN channel. He had trawled the levels of his mini-bar to near extinction before finally succumbing to a light sleep.

The sudden ringing of the telephone had woken him with a jolt. Calmer now, he took in Scala's lame excuses, which carefully omitted to mention the brawl in the bar that night. The sitrep took but a few minutes. Carter listened carefully. He knew well what he must do.

The belltower that stood at the end of the parade of shops chimed three o'clock. Tavaner knew the warning signs. Hearn was about to enter one of his dark rages. The spluttering Irishman spat out a string of curses, all with the absent Scala in mind.

The sudden rap on the glass door startled Tavaner at first, and sent Hearn into a nervous, violent spasm. The relief showed on Tavaner's face as he opened the door to the grinning Scala. The smile appeared to exaggerate the scar on his face in the dim light from the bar.

'Thought we'd lost you!' smirked Tavaner.

'Got myself right bloody lost, I can tell you. Took me soddin' ages to work out where I was and to find the bar.'

Hearn was sweating profusely by now, his eyes bright red with excessive drink. He was hardly able to stand and looked as though he might pass out at any moment.

'Don't worry about him – he'll be okay in the morning!' remarked Tavaner. He and Scala sat down and relaxed in each other's company. 'I didn't get the opportunity to thank you for saving me from that bastard with the knife. So a big thanks! Sneaky little bugger would have carved me, for sure. But I liked the way you handled yourself . . . quick and clean . . . looks like you've done that kind of thing before.'

Scala smiled modestly. 'I've had my moments. If you'd ever seen some of the rough-arsed pubs back in Merthyr then you'd know – you get a good training in the art of keeping your nose in one piece.'

Hearn shuffled through the door behind the bar, leaving the two men alone. Tavaner left an appropriate pause before making his play. 'What are your plans?' he said eventually.

Scala was confused at the question, and looked perplexed.

'I mean, what plans have you for yourself? Do you have a game plan for your life?'

Scala shrugged. He conceded that he had not paid much attention to the future.

'No, neither did I,' Tavaner went on. 'I thought of nothing but the Army – thought that was where my whole life was mapped out. I'd always thought that "duty" was the keyword in life. When they barked I jumped, and off went Michael Tavaner to do his bit all over again for Queen and Country. I didn't give any thought to the future. Then, like all of us, I got older, and started to look around a bit, and I suddenly realised that I had sod-all in life – except the Army, and that life was rapidly coming to an end. There I was, forty-two years old, all dressed up and nowhere to go, no kids, no family. I'd always reckoned it was better to be single in the Army. The only responsibility I had was to the boys under my command, and if I wanted a screw then I'd go out and get one.'

Scala thought he saw a look of remorse on Tavaner's face at the thought of missing out on family life. He wondered how he would fare himself, now that Angie had decided to leave him. In his mind he saw himself in a year's time sitting alone in his small, dismal bedroom at the Union Jack Club, still trying to attract the young girls who worked behind the bar. It was not an image he cherished.

'It's not too late for family and all that stuff,' suggested Scala.

'It is for me, Jim. Anyway, my "boys" have always been my family. It's them, and all the others like them, that I care about. That's what pisses me off when I see the way they get treated. Look at Baker, for example.' He raised his eyes towards the soldier who he knew was sleeping above the bar. 'Only a young lad, but as good as they get when it comes to throwing a bloody Warrior around the place. He's a good soldier . . . but he'll be lucky if he can get a job as a bloody bus driver when he gets out . . . And you, Jim, look at you. Judging by what I've seen, the Army's finished with you. You're just seeing out your time. Let's face it, you've been passed over for promotion more times than the collection plate in church. The Army's washed its hands of you!'

Scala wondered if Tavaner realised just how close to the truth the man was. Scala had just been at that point before Matherson had emerged as his 'saviour'. 'The boys look up to you, don't they?' said Scala.

'They trust me,' Tavaner went on. 'I'd rather have their trust than their adoration. They know I won't let them down while I can do anything about it. I love them, Jim, it's as simple as that, and I can't stand to see them destroyed. You can't just throw away a man's life because society reckons it's got no further use for it. These lads can do only one thing in their lives – they know how to be soldiers, good ones too. They kill and they've been killed . . . I've seen them die . . . but I don't know what for any more.' Tavaner was speaking with a renewed sense of passion now. 'But what happens to soldiers when the Army doesn't want them any more? They're classed as "trouble" back in civvy street, that's what. We're a myth to the people back home – they all like to see us as heroes on *News at Ten*. But ask any bugger to give a lad a job afterwards, and they don't want to know.'

Scala imagined that Tavaner had pledged himself to a new role as 'saviour' for his young soldiers, and that through it he could give meaning to his own life. Without his soldiers and their love, Tavaner was a walking dead man. That had been the reason he had sought the friendship of others such as Hearn, and now, he presumed, Scala himself. Tavaner and those like him needed to remain soldiers, but, unlike mercenaries, they would have to be soldiers for a cause that they believed in. Scala now saw how Tavaner had been a choice target to be recruited by whatever faction whose spell he had fallen under. Tavaner and the 'boys' who followed him had found their new cause.

And now Tavaner was inviting Scala to join that cause, for the company sergeant major had recognised Scala's own need to be involved in a just crusade. He had judged that, like himself, Scala would never be tempted to sell himself as a mercenary. Scala, too, lived for his recognition of duty and a cause to fight for.

Nor would Scala disappoint Tavaner. When the group left for their unknown destination tomorrow, Scala would be with them. He had told Tavaner so.

'But be warned,' said Tavaner severely. 'Once in, there can be no turning back. It's a lifetime commitment and your life, from this moment on, will belong to the "movement".'

Scala thought the sinister warning equal to that which his own 'saviour' Matherson had spelt out for him after his first mission. And it was Matherson who held first claim on Scala's life.

The troops stood in neat rows offering their prayers to heaven as they did each Sunday. The regimental chaplain delivered the same sober sermon that he did each week. As one the men's voices rose in prayer echoing around the bright whitewashed interior of the chapel where generations before other young soldiers had offered their prayers for their own salvation in the struggles that were to come.

As he did each week, Lieutenant Colonel Cochrane stood at the front of the parade, heeding each solemn utterance that emanated from the pulpit. RSM Kendrick took his place in the row behind, flanked by Sergeants Hasker and Hibbs. Each offered his own prayer for salvation. But no troubled soul prayed harder than that of Lynn Anders. She craved divine guidance to ease her mind, but she feared it would not be forthcoming.

As the prayers rebounded around the packed assembly, she searched the congregation for the man who she believed would lead to her salvation. But the tall, angry policeman with the moustache was nowhere to be seen.

They rose early and, as Tavaner had forecast, Hearn showed not the slightest symptom of his alcoholic stupor of a few hours before. In their well-drilled fashion the men got ready, thrusting their few belongings into their overnight bags.

Scala had grown to know them all well. Tavaner had been correct; Scala too considered them good soldiers. He worked hard to envisage men such as Skinner and Roberts, as well as the younger soldiers Turner and Rogers who had been among Jarvis's tormentors, being allowed the opportunity of proving themselves in civilian life. It would have taken little persuasion by the big sergeant to get them to follow his cause.

All were casually dressed either in denims or in loose-fitting tracksuits. Tavaner strode purposefully among the bleary-eyed men who had accompanied him to Berlin and were now swilling mugs of steaming tea and stuffing thick sandwiches of hard crisp bacon into their mouths.

The entire group was ready and on the minibus within twenty minutes. This time, Tavaner insisted on driving. They bade farewell to the red-faced Hearn who stood outside the door grinning, hands thrust deep into the pockets of his smart gold corduroy trousers. No one in the bus spoke. To Scala, his mind fogged by the events of the night, the routine was being carried out as a military exercise. He sat himself at the rear of the bus, uncertain of its final destination.

As the bus pulled away, heading west out of the city, he scoured the scene from the rear window. He just hoped the girl would carry out her role.

Sergeant Ray Matthews was nowhere to be found on the camp. Lynn had toured the entire barracks in search of the man who would be her confessor. She jogged through the camp, clad in a black tracksuit, a familiar figure carrying out her familiar routine. As she neared the exit she saw the oversize figure of Hasker chatting to the soldier who guarded the barrier, and caught sight of Hibbs sitting behind the wheel of his pale blue Ford. In seconds the barrier was raised and the two sergeants sped through the wooded road and into the distance.

They travelled through the shadows that the millions of pine trees that made up the Grünewald forests on the western edge of Berlin cast over the narrow tracks. The thick, dark cloak of the forest appeared never-ending as the minibus ploughed onwards, past thick patches of frozen snow that still patterned the ground where the sun had been unable to penetrate.

He looked at the road behind. No one was following.

It took more than an hour for the bus to break through into the flat northern European plain which stretches from Warsaw to the Netherlands. On the horizon Scala caught sight of the Teufelsberg or Devil's Mountain, painstakingly created from the piles of rubble that remained after the bombardments of the Second World War, where now children skied in winter and families walked in the summer.

A further twenty minutes' drive saw them enter the valley that remained unseen by the naked eye, yet which housed the small, picturesque hamlet of which children's fairy tales were made. On through the town and into the dense wooded hillside that overshadowed the buildings the minibus climbed, eventually coming to a halt in a small clearing on the slope. Scala took stock of the scene. The men, the minibus, the valley and the village would be invisible from the plain. He thought it would be impossible for Janine to find them.

In silence the soldiers disembarked. Further into the woodland they went, surrounded by giant chestnut and oak trees. Tavaner led the way while the rest followed in single file, finishing with Scala.

His mind cleared in the clean air of the forest. Tavaner had promised that the day would provide the best possible introduction that he could hope for as he went in pursuit of his new cause. He would meet new people who would help forge a new beginning for himself. Scala remained lost in his thoughts as he brought up the rear of the little column that snaked through the trees.

The sudden sound was unmistakable to a veteran soldier such as himself. The crack of the AK-47 that echoed through the trees stopped him in his tracks.

Janine cursed. The road ahead was hardly visible as the mud continued to splatter the windscreen of the BMW. It had been a slow journey and keeping far enough behind the minibus to remain undetected had taken great skill. She was, she kept telling herself, no private detective – it had been difficult work. Many times she had feared that she was lost, but now, following the only road through the thick forest and on to the open plain that the bus could have travelled, she felt more confident.

A patch of snowdrops had begun to sprout where, a lifetime before, the young boys and old men had waged their war. They had all spoken different languages, from German and Dutch to Ukrainian and even English. But the men and boys who formed the Ninth International Kompanie of the Waffen-SS had fought as one for one cause. And here, on this spot in the closing stages of April 1945, they had died for that cause, attempting to thwart the overwhelming might of the Red Army. Almost to a man they had died; those who did not perish in the battle for this valley in the midst of the plain had met perhaps a worse fate in the Russian death camps.

The small concrete memorial at the heart of the clearing honoured the memory of the men who had fought here. To Scala it seemed fitting that other warriors, many of them sporting the same camouflage jackets as they had worn decades before, were gathering in this wood of death to carry on their work.

The sporadic crack of gunfire from the far end of the clearing snapped Scala from his thoughts and he surveyed the area, his heart racing at the images he observed. He estimated that there were some two hundred men engaged in a variety of tasks. Some were drilling in marching, while dozens more busied themselves erecting what seemed to be a makeshift arena in the centre of which a deep pit had been dug with a giant wooden stage in front of it. Elsewhere, groups of men were being instructed in the use of a vast array of weapons under the watchful eye of their instructors, all of whom he recognised as men from Allenby, now dressed in an assortment of combat fatigues and forage caps.

The smoke from two giant stoves sent the smells of mass cooking across the clearing, while above the entire scene a huge pennant bearing the emblem of a black rose entwined in barbed wire blew in the occasional gust of wind.

In the corner he recognised Hibbs and Hasker, now deep in conversation with a tall man with slicked back blond hair, a chiselled face and penetrating grey eyes. In his black roll-neck jumper, black loose-fitting jeans and heavy combat boots he stood out in contrast to the others. Oddly, thought Scala, the man wore a brightly coloured football supporters' scarf at his neck too.

'Impressed?' Tavaner's voice came from behind him, making Scala spin round to meet him. 'They're just like us, Jim – they're all soldiers just like you and me. And, like you and me, they're willing to fight for a cause they believe in, and the person who can lead that cause.'

'What's with the flag?' Scala pointed to the pennant.

'You mean our battle flag, don't you,' Tavaner went on. 'Simple, Jim. Look around you, and meet the men of the brethren of the Black Rose.'

'Who or what the hell is the Black Rose?'

'I am – and you are, Jim, now that you're one of us. What you see here is the tip of the iceberg, Jim. There are camps like this all over Europe – there's even one in Yorkshire somewhere. They used to be all different groups, most of which had the same aim but hadn't got a clue how to go about things. We had the BNP at home, for instance, and the Germans had their own outfits. They were all talking with different voices until recently. Then one man had the right ideas and brought them under one umbrella. Pretty clever, eh? It was his idea about the name, too. He thought it would be a good piss-take on an outfit of youngsters, mostly students, who tried to resist Hitler. They called themselves the White Rose. Got topped, most of them. Hence the Black Rose. It beats calling yourself Blood and Honour like the play actors back home, doesn't it?'

Scala would have thought it was a crazy dream or the plot from some Hollywood film if he had not been staring the reality in the face. 'Who's the bloke who got them all together?' he asked in amazement.

'You'll see him soon. A bloody genius, I can tell you. He's only young, but got to be quite a big mover in the various movements. I heard he was actually groomed by one of the old Nazis himself. But he has the right ideas, Jim, I tell you – and we have to start somewhere.'

The thought of the girl returned to Scala. He had not considered the scale of what he might be walking into. Now he wanted Janine to fail, and stay away from this place.

CHAPTER EIGHTEEN

It was better than he could ever have expected. He had almost given up hope of reaching the truth, especially after all this time. But now it was a different ball game. Now, he just listened. That was all he had to do. And he listened hard.

'If you think it's been easy living with this, think again. But God help me that's what happened, and I've seen those images every day since. I'll have to live with the memory of that night for the rest of my life, won't I?' Lynn Anders pleaded for absolution with every word, and with every upward glance into his eyes. But none came.

The girl had searched hard, and begged telephone numbers, and it had been mid-afternoon before she had finally made contact with the man from the Special Investigation Branch. She had wanted to confess, and he was only too willing to play the role of her confessor. Now as they sat in Lynn's cramped room the story of the night when she had witnessed Adebeyo's death spilled out, and the terror that followed at the hands of the sergeants, and her fear that history had repeated itself with Jarvis's death.

'What about the man Scala? Your fancy man – was he there? What did he say to you when you told him about everything?' Matthews demanded.

'He told me to say nothing . . . that I should trust him. I don't know if he knew anything about Jarvis's death. God help me, that's the truth!' she replied. 'I thought he was different – he was kinder, and he understood. That's why I . . . why I . . .'

'Screwed him!' Matthews finished for her. 'I think that's the word you're looking for.'

The girl flushed. 'But I swear I knew nothing about his past. I believed – and might still believe – in him. I honestly don't know any more. I've just been trapped in this God-awful nightmare. I had to speak to someone . . . I really didn't know who to speak to, you see. That's why I came to you . . . like I should have done a long time ago.'

Matthews revelled in holding the upper hand now. The girl was vulnerable. He felt she would swear to almost anything. He would destroy the inner sanctum that had been formed by the sergeants. He had always had a dislike for the goings on in these famous regiments who presumed that they were a law unto themselves. Now, he was in a position to destroy that myth.

Night came early to the woods, but the 'army' worked on. Still they trained and talked and planned. Through the early evening haze that covered the clearing, Scala watched the man he had been told was called Peter Coetzee. The South African was squatting by a fallen log next to one of the small tents that had been erected as overnight shelter for the men.

Scala observed as the South African stripped and cleaned the tiny sub-machine gun that he knew to be an American Ingram Mac10, capable of firing over a thousand rounds a minute. Ideal for close quarter combat and perfect for easy concealment, it was a weapon once favoured by the American Special Forces in Vietnam. Scala watched as Coetzee worked quickly and professionally before placing the weapon in a light green holdall which he slung at his shoulder and then disappeared into the darkness of the trees.

'I see you study our comrade, Sergeant Scala. There is a man like yourself.' The voice came from the darkness behind him.

Scala could barely distinguish the figure dressed in black that walked towards him. He saw the reflection of the brightly coloured scarf at his neck first, and then the blond hair. Volker Reisz revealed his gleaming teeth as he laughed. But Scala thought there would be no laughter in his eyes to support this outward show of friendship. He nodded his acknowledgement as the tall German came forward and sat beside him on a felled tree that was being used as a bench.

'Peter, like yourself, was a man who believed in his country, until he and others like him were betrayed by those who sold out to the blacks. Now he wages his struggle where he can,' Reisz continued.

'You mean he's a mercenary,' responded Scala, grinning.

'Absolutely not!' Reisz was solemn now. 'Any fool can be a mercenary, but it takes a man with a strong heart to fight for a cause that he truly believes in.'

Scala felt he was being chastised.

'I understand from Herr Tavaner that you have decided to join our happy group. I bid you welcome.' The dead shark-like eyes were unblinking and Scala felt himself inexplicably drawn to the man's gaze. 'I am certain that you will find joining our group rewarding. We need people like yourself, good professional soldiers who are ready to take matters into their own hands. Let us face facts, *we* soldiers are the people who are the instruments of change when the politicians fail to agree.' Reisz's emphasis made it clear that he thought of himself too as a soldier.

'Its something of an International Brigade that you have here, Volker. Whose idea was that?' Scala made the question sound innocent.

'It was the germ of the idea of the man whom you will see tonight – a good man with vision. I presume you thought you would never see the day when your British soldiers would be working alongside our own storm troops,' Reisz said matter-of-factly.

'Well, I'd be a liar if I said I was expecting it,' replied Scala.

'We . . . how shall we put it? . . . we complement each other!' smiled Reisz. 'During the last conflict, it must surely have been an error of judgement on the part of your politicians that we should be on opposing sides. You British and ourselves have so much in common. We should have been allies, not enemies. If we had done so, then today we would not be suffering the plague of the black scum who take our jobs and ruin our countries, or have to contend with the Jewish vermin.'

Scala showed no emotion.

'By the nature of the job, the British soldier is a right-wing animal. It is natural that we should join forces. That is all we have tried to do here.' Reisz grinned again. 'Shall we say that we run an "exchange" scheme?'

Scala looked puzzled.

Reisz explained: 'By working together we can cover more territory, you see, Sergeant Scala. I have been instrumental in carrying out many tasks on your shores, for example. We have ready-made contacts in Britain, and occasionally I am called upon to channel their talents or even carry out some of the tasks myself. You will recall the troubles at several of your soccer games that the authorities held the idiots from the Combat 18 group responsible for?'

'You mean it was you and your people?' Scala answered the question.

'Certainly . . . And then I disappear, leaving no trace and no record. It is simple. And here, it is the same. Who would suspect your very own British troops of working alongside ourselves? But who better to recruit for our cause? Your British troops are so professional – indeed some of the best in the world – and yet treated very poorly. Our movement needs your expertise, and in return our movement, when it comes to power, will look after your expert people.'

'You're certain you'll come to power?'

'In one form or another, yes!' replied Reisz sternly. 'The appetite of our countrymen is ready, as it is in so many other countries that have been plundered and ruined by outsiders. It is only a matter of time before the political will of the people is recognised. That is why we train, to provide the support for that will.'

Scala looked around the camp. He saw the men from Allenby grouped together in consultation, as if drawing up plans. They were listening gravely to Tavaner. He was instructing and giving details – but for what, Scala did not know. Scala had not been included in the briefings. To Tavaner, it was sufficient for the time being that the new man observed the workings of the group from a distance. Scala saw Hasker and Hibbs distribute red baseball caps to each member of the group, some of whom, he noted, also wore soccer scarves. Laughter and hoots of derision erupted from the group as the men tried on their caps. Scala felt frustration growing. Reisz watched him.

It was the greatest satisfaction that Ray Matthews had enjoyed in years. He had savoured every moment of the confrontation with Cochrane. The colonel's expression of shock and bewilderment, when Matthews had told him of the girl's confession, was an image that would remain with him for many years to come.

He didn't bother to knock on the girl's door. It would be just too bad for her if she was in the buff. Besides, she had nothing that he hadn't seen before. He whistled in self-congratulation as he pressed his weight against the girl's door and burst into the room. But the whistling stopped as he took stock of the situation.

There was no sign of the girl. The doors to her wardrobe were flung open and the empty hangers signalled that much of her clothing had disappeared with her. Matthews felt his happiness turning to rage.

Michael Kinze sipped from his crystal glass of champagne. By his side the elegant woman in the tight-fitting evening gown glowed with the pride that she shared with her husband. He had met the President on numerous occasions before, the first when the man had taken the trouble personally to welcome Kinze to South Africa on taking up his position. Kinze had liked the President instantly. He had thought the black leader a man of vision and a man of peace, no longer a terrorist. He was, Kinze now understood, the kind of leader who was so important for the future of the world – a man who preached reconciliation.

Since that first meeting the President had been a great supporter of the team, especially since over two-thirds of Kinze's international side were, like the President himself, from the townships. But this occasion was special. It was the first time he had stood on his native German soil and stood shoulder to shoulder with the President at such a function presided over by the Chancellor of Germany.

Kinze, along with his team, was being honoured. He knew that. It felt different now. It was different from the days when he had represented his own country and won the World Cup. He had been honoured then too. But now he was helping to make a little piece of world history.

Certainly there had been critics. There always were. But the game was a graphic way of showing that the old ways of South Africa were dead. That was why the President would share the platform with the Chancellor as the two soccer sides confronted each other tomorrow for the first time in their history in the Olympiastadion.

Ray Matthews' eyes bulged with fury as he listened to the words that came over the telephone. It had been bad enough that the girl had disappeared. But now this was too much to contend with.

The bare office at Allenby had been a bleak place to spend this Sunday evening, and now Matthews sat alone with only his rage as a companion, listening to the 'instructions' that were being given by a man whom he had never met – the man who now possessed Matthews' prize witness, Lynn Anders. Spluttering his protestations about the handling of the whole affair, he found himself conceding to the man at the other end of the telephone. It would be as he wished.

At first there were only a few. Then, carrying burning torches that set fire to the stillness of the night, they came in their hundreds. Scala thought he must be observing a scene from some bizarre pagan ritual. But the people who came wore only their everyday clothes. They were, to all intent, ordinary people. They had come from the village below, hundreds of them, to be joined by those who had journeyed from as far afield as Berlin and Hamburg in the other direction.

Slowly the torches massed in the clearing in the wood on the hillside. They stood illuminated by the glow from a hundred torches behind the cordon formed by the men whom Scala had seen working throughout the day. The platform that had been erected was silhouetted by the orange radiance that was given off by the burning bonfire at the bottom of the specially dug pit.

He saw the men from Allenby interspersed among the cordon of men, all of whom now wore a uniform of some description, and he saw Tavaner and Reisz standing side by side at the end of the cordon, highlighted by the flames of the bonfire. A huge banner, the emblem of the entwined rose, had now been erected behind the platform, providing a shimmering red backcloth that danced with the colours of the flames.

Scala had not expected the arrival of the crowd, who had come like spirits summoned to an unholy meeting-place. He studied the sea of solemn faces now mustered. The crowd was drawn from every conceivable stratum of human life; the old mingled with the young and old women chattered with young men. The excited assembly jabbered and shuffled with anticipation, as if waiting for the curtain to rise in a theatre.

As if in response to an invisible signal, the commotion subsided and a curious stillness descended on the clearing. Only the cracking of the torches now challenged the silence as three men appeared from behind the banner. Even in the glow from the fire, Scala could identify the smallest of the three as the man alongside Hearn and Tavaner in Janine's photograph. Günter Brusse was beside himself with pleasure tonight. He took his place on the left-hand side of a man with a gentle face and neatly trimmed beard – Klaus Stein, though Scala did not know him – as the three climbed the platform.

Stein, wearing a black leather jacket that reflected the glow from the bonfire, beamed at the throng and clasped his hands above his head in welcome and triumph. The crowd responded with a rousing cheer as if to pay homage to their idol. Brusse could not hide the wide smile of delight that showed his uneven teeth. Now Reisz and Tavaner had also climbed the platform and taken their designated positions behind Stein.

Stein's words of welcome echoed around the clearing. He spoke easily, calmly, forcibly but with an almost gentle passion that silenced the crowd. As one they listened. He told them of his pride at seeing their numbers; of the fitting tribute that they were paying to those men of the Waffen-SS who had died at this spot generations before, and of the debt that he and the crowd owed to the memory of those men.

Tavaner and Reisz joined Brusse in leading the applause that followed each of Stein's sentences.

'Our forefathers waged a war to purge us of the evils of the Jew and of those not pure in blood,' he told them. 'Their efforts have since been squandered by the politicians that have followed . . . that have ruined our glorious countries by their pitiful policies of integration. That can no longer be allowed to continue . . .'

They cheered.

He told them how they would struggle to resurrect the doctrines for which their forefathers had paid the ultimate sacrifice, and how once again they would strive for power.

They cheered, and they believed.

He told them that this time they would not be alone in their struggle. They had strong allies, not only within Europe, but now also from across the Atlantic.

Scala was captured by the calmness of the man as he spoke. There was no ranting such as he had envisaged. The man spoke directly and coolly to reach the heart of every person in the clearing. Stein was in full flow now. He quietly cursed those who promoted integration, and deplored those who practised it. Those who soiled their own blood with mixed race marriages should be hunted out and banished from the future pure race, and those who betrayed their country by working for immigrants or blacks should be made to pay the price. With each day that passed, he told them, the very fibre of their country and other countries like theirs was being undermined. Such a curse had come to Germany and would be played out in the full glare of the world spotlight the very next day, when the weakling government had given permission to allow the vermin that was the black race to insult the memory of their saviour Adolf Hitler by allowing the soccer match to be played at the ground that was as his shrine. It could not be tolerated.

The mob went wild with anger. To allow the game to be played at the stadium was an insult to the man who had been their God.

Then Stein gave them the man who stood to his right on the platform, the ally from America who spoke for the hundreds of thousands who believed as they did, and who, in the not too distant future, would challenge the very constitution of the United States.

*   *   *

The stained glass from Chartres set in the walls of moulded concrete radiates a ghostly bluish glow that illuminates the Kaiser-Wilhem Memorial Church. The broken church which has remained unbuilt following the bombing of 1943 and the later artillery bombardment of the city stands as a memorial to the futility of war. Thrusting skywards from the busy pavements of the heart of Berlin, its ruined stump of a tower dominates the eastern end of the Kurfürstendamm.

The place held an air of mystery on this cold, drizzly night. But Alex Carter had chosen it as a suitable spot at which to meet Ray Matthews. Here, in the shadows of the church where the mosaics of Christ the King blended with friezes of the great Prussian monarchs, Carter waited.

Inside the church the noises of sleepless Berlin were locked out, leaving the tower that Berliners nicknamed 'the broken tooth' as a sanctuary against the outside world. Carter stood in the shadows of the chapel, alone with only the sound of his own breathing. He glanced at his watch as he heard the sound of approaching footsteps. His man was on time.

The whole episode had seemed to Matthews to possess the melodrama of a Hollywood movie, but he assumed that it was how the 'spook' world might work. That was fine; just so long as they didn't interfere with him. But his first impression of Alex Carter took the SIB man by surprise; the spook was bigger than he had envisaged, with a personality that commanded respect. The man would not be crossed easily.

Carter outlined the basic details of the operation to the reluctant Matthews, who openly voiced his disapproval of the scheme. Matthews was still gripped by resentment that his case and his witness had been taken from him with such ease. Matthews had been otherwise occupied with flaunting his success before Cochrane when the girl had been shepherded away by the man who had proved his authority to the inexperienced young soldiers at the barrier. The girl had gone freely, believing her exit to have been arranged by Matthews. It had not been until the pair were safely on the return trip to Berlin that Carter had offered a full explanation.

'The girl's safe,' said Carter now in a hushed voice. 'Basically, I have the authority to make certain she stays with me. I can request your help, but if you refuse I do have the power to order your cooperation – though I'm sure it won't come to that,' smiled Carter in a quiet but commanding voice. 'Believe me, I appreciate how you must feel – I'd be resentful towards me too if I were in your shoes.'

'What about the other bugger, then? Scala – what's he about?' grimaced Matthews.

'Let's just say that we're on the same side. Now, I'm assuming you're with us . . . because in order to make this work, I'm going to need your help.'

He was perfect for the part, and he was giving one of his best performances that night. As he held the platform, Scala thought that Guy Rockwell must have rehearsed his speech a hundred times before – so much so, that some of the lines could have come straight from one of his movies.

'The Zionists have exerted a stranglehold on my country for too long . . . Every section of our society walks in the shadow of the Jew that seeks to undermine it . . .' The rhetoric was delivered with gusto and just enough sincerity to stir the crowd.

Scala watched with admiration from the side of the clearing, from where he could see both the 'show' and the approving crowd that buzzed with agreement.

'Together we can destroy the Zionists . . . whether it be at the ballot box or by the bullet . . .'

Rockwell's passion was infectious. The sound of loud, uncontrolled applause at his side made Scala turn to see Hasker. 'Bloody good, eh?' came the harsh Mancunian voice.

'Oh, yes! Most uplifting!' replied Scala.

The grand finale to the speeches began at the far end of the clearing. The sound of drumbeats echoed from the crowd which parted to allow the four ranks of drummers through. The crowd dispersed to form into immaculate ranks of four people who began a slow, regimented march past the platform. Each section of the parade that slowly snaked through the trees and the clearing was led by a handful of square-jawed 'troopers' in pristine blue uniforms. The 'troopers' – each of whom, guessed Scala, had not yet seen his thirtieth birthday – strode in ramrod fashion, their clean, handsome and determined faces staring straight ahead.

'Christ, I always thought these mobs were made up of skinheads and thugs . . . but these all look like good middle-class youths. Not a bloody skin amongst them,' Scala commented to Hasker.

'Bollocks, mate! The skins are only good for cannon fodder . . . it's the ones with brains we need.'

On they marched, like a ghost army from a generation before, thought Scala – an army of demons caught in the red glow of the torches and the bonfire, paying homage to the stone memorial to the dead and the enthusiastic group on the platform. Scala estimated that the rally had swelled to over a thousand people. He saw Tavaner and Reisz share a joke. Rockwell bounced on his toes with enthusiasm, while Stein saluted his followers by placing his hand over his heart.

It was all a bad dream, thought Scala. He had seen the newsreels of Hitler's Reich shown repeatedly on his television screen. Now he felt himself trapped in a repeat screening of the birth of the movement that had brought the world to the brink of destruction.

Janine's fingers trembled at the images that she saw through the viewfinder. She had not bargained for anything as crazy as this. How the hell had she been so stupid as to get involved in this, and follow this crazy guy with a scarred face into the middle of nowhere? But still she pressed the camera button.

She had lain in wait and approached the clearing on the tail end of the crowds that had gathered to hear the speeches. Then she had lost herself in the cold wet undergrowth of the wood, out of sight from those who watched from the platform. She had focused on the men on the platform – the men from Hearn's bar and the men who had ranted. What she saw through the viewfinder intoxicated her, banishing every other thought from her mind. She moved involuntarily, seeking a better angle. So intent was she that she did not notice Tavaner looking straight towards her; now he was pointing, shouting instructions and gesturing frantically. Finally the realisation came.

She looked up from the camera to see the men in combat jackets who had formed the cordon coming towards her, slowly at first, then quickening their pace to a run. One last frame . . . then she too turned to run.

Fear surged through her body: the adrenalin pumped and brought an energy and speed that she had never known. An image of a misty night on a lonely railway station and the death of Peter Macabe flashed through her mind as she ran. Her tight-fitting jeans were wet from the undergrowth, restricting her long stride, but terror at the thought of capture spurred her on. A tree branch whipped into her face, stinging her eye and knocking the breath from her body; she turned and saw the shadowy figures still chasing her. Once again she began to sprint, the camera swinging wildly and smashing into her chest as she ran, searching for a landmark that would give her a clue to the whereabouts of the BMW.

Scala had not seen the girl. It was Hasker who alerted him as the bulky sergeant bolted through the grass. Scala thought of attempting to stop him. 'Shit!' he spat. He stood frozen with indecision, uncertain whether to attempt to protect the girl and destroy his cover, or to leave her to her fate at the hands of those who pursued her and must surely catch her.

The gathering was in uproar now. What the fuck had the girl done to get herself spotted? How had he been so stupid as to persuade her to help? Now in his mind he saw her body, lying battered and lifeless at the hands of the grinning sergeant. He tried to push the image away.

The swinging camera smashed into her chin, forcing her bottom teeth deep into her top lip. She tasted blood and spat. The lights of the village further down the hillside were visible now and Janine's heart soared. The car must be nearby, she prayed.

At the edge of the trees she paused for a second, still hearing the crashing of the heavy-booted men somewhere behind her. She saw the track that had been the entrance to the wood and guessed her position. The car should be nearby, shielded from view by a wall of foliage amongst the thick pine trees. The crashing of the undergrowth behind her grew louder.

She gulped for air and started for the clearing that she thought she recognised, but was sent sprawling as her foot caught a hidden rock. She floundered in the mud and bracken of the undergrowth as the force of the fall knocked all the breath from her body. Her head swirled with dizziness at the shock.

The figure in faded combat jacket and forage cap stood over her, smirking in anticipation and cursing in German. Younger and fitter than the rest of the pack, he was on Janine before she could recover her wind. He reached for her mane of hair and yanked her to her feet. She yelled in pain.

The first blow took him in the back of the neck, sending him sinking to his knees. As he gasped, the second blow with the heavy boot crashed into his temple and bowled him sideways. Then Scala was on him, taking him in a vice-like grip from behind. The crack of the German's neck snapping seemed to Janine to echo in the silence of the night; her eyes stared wildly in dismay as the man died before her. So close to the German was she that she could smell his breath; she froze in horror as Scala tossed aside the corpse.

The crashing of the rest of the pursuers could be heard now. Scala grabbed the terrified girl by the sleeve and dragged her after him. Adrenalin took over as the pair careered through the undergrowth as they headed for the clearing where the girl hoped she had hidden the car. She had guessed correctly.

'I'll drive. Give me the bloody keys, woman!' commanded Scala. Janine was too frightened to question. Scala prayed silently, and his entreaties were answered by the sound of the engine starting at the first attempt. He rammed it into gear and crashed through the trees and on to the track that led from the hillside.

Neither Janine nor Scala spoke. Only the sound of their panting filled the car as the BMW slid and squirmed its way through the thick mud road that led to the village. Still no one followed, yet neither dared relax. Scala fought to control the sliding car as they drove on, the engine rebelling against its rough handling. His gaze was fixed on the rear view mirror as in the distance he saw the first signs of headlights emerging from the darkness of the hillside in pursuit.

CHAPTER NINETEEN

Dawn was showing over the rooftops of Charlottenburg as the small convoy of cars made its way slowly down the narrow back streets that led to Poppa's Bar. Without making a sound to waken the sleeping street, the twelve members of the Special Investigation Branch and military police, all in civilian clothing, leaped from the three cars and took up their positions. In his bed above the bar Paddy Hearn slept his usual deep sleep, encouraged by an excess of drink the night before.

The sound of the door being rammed and glass shattering echoed like the explosion of a small bomb as it travelled upstairs. The sudden noise shocked Hearn from sleep and sent him diving into the corner of the room where, with arms raised and fists clenched, he stood to meet the would-be attackers.

He conjured up an image of bastard IRA gunmen who would now, he thought, be pounding up the stairs to take their revenge. Seconds later the door to his room was sent crashing from its hinges with an ear-shattering sound of splintering wood. A moustached figure with a bull-like physique stood clutching a hammer as a second man appeared, holding an automatic pistol.

'Morning! Time for your early morning knock!' said Matthews, grinning.

Hearn lunged at his potential assassins. His first wild punch missed the mark, but his follow-through kick hit the man with the pistol hard between the legs, sending him to his knees. Again Hearn launched a frenzied attack, but this time Matthews parried the blow with his left arm and continued with a lightning upper cut thrust that took Hearn hard beneath the chin, sending him sprawling. As Hearn struggled to regain his wits the man was on him and wrenching his arm high up his back, forcing him face down on the bed.

'Patrick John Hearn, I am arresting you on charges of conspiracy and possession of illegal firearms ...' The voice of command barked from the man pinning down Hearn. 'I am Sergeant

Matthews of the Special Investigation Branch, and I caution you . . .'

The words swirled in Hearn's mind. His attackers were not IRA but police officers . . . worse than that . . . military police.

'Take yer fuckin' hands off me . . . who the hell do ye think yer dealing with here? There's no bloody cause for this . . .'

The tall man who spoke in a Scots accent entered the room and interrupted Hearn's torrent of insults. Alex Carter broke in with an air of authority: 'We have reason to believe that you are in possession of firearms, some of which may have been the property of Her Majesty's Forces, on these premises. We therefore intend to conduct a complete search of the building.'

Hearn knew the man from what seemed like a hundred years before. He had seen the face in Hereford, and Paddy Hearn never forgot a face. Rage took hold of him as he struggled against Matthews and one of the other officers, spitting his anger as venom at the man who he knew had come from the Regiment. A lifetime ago, the two men could have been friends and comrades. Now, only hatred existed between them.

The sound of the heavy pounding of feet thundered through the building as the raiders began the painstaking task of searching for the cache that Scala had reported. Hearn, now restrained and handcuffed to one of the officers, was left behind as Matthews and Carter paired off and headed for the cellar, where Scala had told them of the arsenal of weapons stored beneath the bar. Both men were expectant, revelling in the excitement of the occasion. They approached the entrance to the cellar with the anticipation of a child on Christmas morning.

The smell of dampness greeted them as they pulled open the door and descended into the darkness. Finding the light switch, they blinked in the new-found brightness that filled the cellar. They had expected much, but their anticipation ebbed as they surveyed the empty room before them. A rat, concerned at the intrusion into its home, scurried about. Nothing was to be found: the promised discovery of crates of explosives and racks of guns was not to be. They felt cheated by the wily Irishman.

Dejected, Matthews and Carter left the cellar to be confronted by the sneering face of Hearn. 'Looking for something, ye bastards? Fancy a drink, then? You might as well have something while you're here – no point in going away empty-handed.'

The ridicule burned deep in the two men. Matthews turned away, refusing to reveal his frustration, and disappeared into the room where Hearn had slept. The thrashing as the room was turned over could be heard downstairs where Poppa and the other men waited. Hearn was confident that no matter how hard the tall policeman searched, he would find nothing incriminating. He had made certain of that – his instinct had alerted him.

'Satisfied now, are ye?' he mocked the returning Matthews.

'Absolutely!' replied the policeman with a broad beam on his face. 'Just look what we found hidden beneath the mattress!' He stretched out his arm to reveal the magazine of a British Army SA 80 rifle, complete with rounds of ammunition. 'It would appear that you've been holding out on us, you crafty Mick sod, wouldn't it?'

Fury pulsed through Hearn as he realised that the magazine which the policeman held before him was one that Matthews had brought with him.

'You bastard,' screamed Hearn, struggling with the two officers who held him. 'You've fitted me up, you cop bastard! You know there was no soddin' magazine or a rifle in that bedroom.' Hearn's face was crimson now. 'You're a dead man! You're a dead fuckin' man, I tell ye!'

Carter whistled softly to himself.

Janine saw it first. The screaming engine of the car was unable to take more punishment, and the dial on the fascia showed that it was on the point of boiling. She watched it anxiously, unwilling to speak her fears. The bloody engine had been failing for some while, but Macabe had done nothing about getting it repaired. Now the girl who had loved him mentally cursed him.

Scala had hammered the car unmercifully, and now it was in its last throes of life. He kept watching for the headlights of the vehicles that he knew were pursuing them.

The lights still burned bright over Canary Wharf as Colonel David Matherson looked out from his office window. He thought the tranquil scene, still free of the usual daytime noise and traffic, held a serene beauty at this early hour.

Matherson had been at his desk for almost two hours now. A nagging pain behind his eyes had rendered him sleepless for the few hours during which he had attempted to get some rest. Now his mouth was thick and his stubble was already growing to a deep shadow.

The message from Carter had prompted his immediate attention, and it had taken only twenty minutes for him to reach the office from his Barbican apartment. The men at the Ministry would have his report waiting for them on their desk when they arrived that morning. It was a rare occurrence, but today Matherson prepared his own report without the assistance of his treasured secretary. He wanted no time to be lost on this one. As he read through the report he admitted to himself that, whilst he was not the quickest of typists, the job was satisfactory.

STRICTLY CONFIDENTIAL

FOR THE URGENT ATTENTION OF: Minister of Defence/Commander Colin Jacobson: Chief of Intelligence Services.
REFERENCE: 'Operation Phoenix':

SUBJECT: With reference to ongoing investigation into circumstances surrounding deaths of Private John Adebeyo and Private Christopher Jarvis, Royal Kent Rangers; confirmed that elements of RKR involved in subversive activities including right-wing extremist group calling itself Brotherhood of the Black Rose.

Organisation led by one Klaus Stein, known sympathiser of neo-Nazi movement, with aims of spreading political influence in Europe/Germany through elections supported by use of armed resistance.

Further inquiries from undercover operator suggest British troops involved in military operations against targets unknown. Situation ongoing.

Reliable witness being extricated from Germany today, and returned London.

Advise course of further action to be taken.

All things considered, Guy Rockwell decided that the night had gone well. He felt that he had given one of his better performances; he had not lost his old touch. Klans Stein had been good too; he held promise.

As he relaxed in the comparative comfort of his hotel room, he thought of ways in which he would be able to harness Stein's obvious charm and talents back home in the United States. He liked his ideas and approved of his methods. The boy had a bright future, that was certain. The two of them together would make a potent force to be reckoned with – an unholy alliance that would shake the world.

A strange tranquillity hung over the street as the battered BMW finally limped into the Mommsenstrasse and came to a gentle halt outside Janine's apartment. The first signs of life began to show themselves on the street as the pavements slowly filled with people on their way to work.

To Janine, the journey had proved an eternity. Her body was running on a mixture of fear and pure adrenalin, and at the sight of the entrance to the apartment block she flung her arms wildly around Scala's neck in gratitude. He smelled her expensive perfume and its fragrance momentarily erased the reality of their plight. Holding the girl brought a strange comfort to Scala; he decided he liked this girl who had not flinched from the challenges she had faced.

After scouring the street for signs of their pursuers, they entered the apartment. It took only a few minutes to gather the papers and photographs that Scala would need, and he packed them into Macabe's small briefcase along with the undeveloped film that Janine had taken that night. While the girl soothed herself under a hot shower, Scala left with the briefcase.

She would travel light, taking only the bare minimum that she had brought from the camp. The night alone in the strange hotel room had been sleepless and endless. The slightest noise had sounded to Lynn Anders like gunfire.

She was too nervous to eat the breakfast that was brought to her room. She waited for the knock that would tell her that Alex Carter had returned and that she was once again safe. With each minute that passed her fear increased.

When it came, the tap on the door seemed like a clap of thunder. The Scottish voice that came from the corridor soothed her apprehensions. But the floodgates of her fear opened again as Carter stepped into the room: her eyes were fixed on the figure who stood in the shadows of the corridor behind him. She was unsure of her own reactions as Scala walked into the brightness of the room. Perhaps she had loved him; perhaps she had simply felt the need to place her trust in someone. She could not say what it was that assured her that it was right to trust her life to his hands.

The simple 'hello' seemed weak, but it was all she could muster for the man with the scarred face who was now stepping back

into her life – the man she felt she had betrayed to Matthews. She
wanted to apologise, to beg his forgiveness for doubting him, but
she did not have words. There were only tears now. Carter made
an excuse to leave, and the two were alone.

Scala held the girl tightly around the waist and kissed her gently
on the forehead, soothing away her fears.

'I didn't know what to think, Jim, I'm sorry – I thought you were
like them, and Matthews told me all about you. It was all there
in black and white,' she sobbed.

'It's all right. You were meant to think that – everyone was. God
knows, I even got to believe some of it myself!' A grin spread over
Scala's face as he stroked her thick red hair.

She had felt remorse that she had given herself to him once. But
now her remorse faded.

'You know what you must do,' said Scala, switching to a business-
like tone and handing her the briefcase. 'The names and everything
are there. It's all up to you now! Everything will be okay!' He wished
he could reassure the girl further. But there were no words for that.
In less than two hours she would be gone, and there was nothing
that Jim Scala could do to govern her fate.

The noise of the shower was deafening, and she was oblivious to
the outside world. The hot water had washed away her fear, and
the events of the night before were but a distant nightmare. She
had faced death, and on reflection had found a macabre attraction
in living life on a knife edge. The image of her attacker being
calculatingly killed with such ease by her champion had, she
admitted to herself, held a gruesome fascination for her. She felt
complete, as she studied her nakedness in the bathroom mirror.

Footsteps now. She assumed Scala must have returned sooner
than expected, though she did not hear him speak. She had no
fear; daylight made the world seem safer. Covering herself with
the towelling robe, she stepped into the living room.

At first she saw only his silhouette against the brightness of the
window: the tall, lean, muscular figure who turned slowly to greet
the speechless girl as she tiptoed into the room. Fear swallowed her
as the man's gaze seared deep into her eyes. For a fleeting moment
she froze to the spot, gripped by the terror of the man in black. She
attempted to run, but the black-clad figure reached out and took
her by the arm, pulling her to his body. His iron grip bit deep into
her flesh.

The blond giant stared down and spoke through gritted teeth

as he held back her hair, exposing the fine lines of her neck. He looked around for the photographs that she had taken that night, but they were not there. Frustrated, his anger burst out and the girl attempted to shield herself from the blows that he rained down on her. The bathrobe was ripped from her body as he pulled her to her knees. Janine pleaded in pain and terror, offered herself in exchange for life, but the eyes of her attacker showed no mercy.

It was a clear, bright morning as the daily flight to Heathrow left Berlin on schedule. Lynn Anders felt that she should feel relieved at the prospect of leaving Germany for safety. Instead, she carried a burden of guilt because she was leaving behind the man she thought she loved.

She tried to console herself with the knowledge that he had wanted her to leave; wanted her to be safe and free to tell her story. But as she looked at the briefcase that Scala had given her, that she had never let from her sight, she felt only shame that she was deserting the mysterious man who had come from England to uncover the truth of the past.

Alex Carter reached across from his seat and squeezed her hand in comfort. He too had felt that he should be at Scala's side during the events that he was certain were about to unfold. But he too, like Scala, was a prisoner to 'duty'. His duty now was for the safe return of the girl at his side.

The body sat propped upright against the sofa; her gaze, it seemed to Scala, fixed accusingly on him. He had not been there when the girl had needed him. Now nausea rose in him as he examined the pathetic heap that had once been Janine Letterman.

She had fought her attacker as the awareness of her imminent death came upon her. Her killer had left her like a broken doll, discarded in the ravaged apartment, her mouth open fighting for breath as the scarf had tightened around her slim neck.

Scala stared at the scarf. He had seen it before, and he knew who had worn it. The football scarf in its white, red, black and gold colours had last been seen around the neck of Volker Reisz.

Scala looked again at the pitiful sight of Janine's body. She had known the taste of revenge; now he would take the trail of vengeance for her.

CHAPTER TWENTY

He was hard to convince, for Matthews still disliked the man. But he knew he could ill afford to ignore Scala. It had been Scala who had called, in desperate need of an ally. If his guess was right, he had precious little time to convince disbelieving security chiefs or suffer the cross-examinations of dim-witted policemen intent on investigating the girl's death.

Matthews had grudgingly agreed to meet Scala outside the girl's apartment, where they sat in the SIB man's car watching the scurrying of the German police who were now infesting the apartment where Janine lay. Scala still clutched the scarf that he had taken from her body. His SAS veteran's sixth sense told him that his fears were correct.

Matthews, meanwhile, was still congratulating himself on placing Paddy Hearn safely behind bars. But Scala's plea for help had given him a glib sense of self-satisfaction. It appeared, he thought, that the 'spook brigade' needed his help after all, but what Scala told him called for all his imagination. Vague recollections of the day when Arab terrorists had struck at the Olympic village in Munich in 1972 visited Matthews' memory.

'If what you say is true, it'll make Black Sunday seem like a birthday party,' Matthews agreed. 'I just hope to Christ you're wrong.' He took up his radio and transmitted his instructions. 'If you're wrong, they'll bloody well hang me out to dry ... And believe me, if I go, then I'll take you with me,' he warned.

Scala was convinced he would do so.

The soccer match that would make history, between the world champions, Germany, and the new force of South Africa, would be played in the imposing arena that forms the modern stadium. Fittingly, that stadium borders the one built to spotlight the might of Nazism decades before, with its gladiatorial sculptures which look out on to the terrace where Hitler once ignited the German people.

The stadium dominated the entire city, and in the sunlight on that clear day it cast long shadows over the surrounding area. Lost in the crowd, the men from Allenby looked like any of the others who made up the throng – the human mass that slowly snaked its way towards the shrine to the man they had called the Führer. They mixed with those who came by car and coach and crammed the U-Bahn and S-Bahn that led to the Olympic Stadium. To the unknowing they were invisible, in their red baseball caps and the trappings that adorned every soccer fan around the world.

Like the thousands of others, they had begun their journey early. Already, as planned and ordered by Stein's lieutenants, the army of skins who would be the storm troopers of the plan had packed the stadium. The men in the red baseball caps would be the ones who would command them – the men from Allenby. Rehearsed and drilled, they were now awaiting the order to go into action.

Tavaner stood head and shoulders above most of the crowd as they shuffled slowly towards the stadium. The red caps stood out like beacons, and enabled Tavaner easily to distinguish his men from the mass. He saw them divide as planned. Tavaner himself was still in the grip of fury. One day, he had vowed, he would find the man whom he had brought into the movement and who had run away from the hillside with the girl. And when he did, he would make that man pay for his betrayal.

Michael Kinze stood in the centre of the dressing room deep in the bowels of the new Olympic bowl, the eyes of each player fixed on him. They were apprehensive. But he reminded them that this day was a special day, for they would be making history. To play in this stadium was special at any time, but they would be the first team from the townships to have the honour of displaying their talents to the world; and he, Michael Kinze, hero to so many, would be leading them.

Matthews gathered his ten men at the U-Bahn station at the Olympic stadium as arranged. He needed an army, but these would have to do. Each man knew his task; most thought it impossible, but they hid their private fears.

It was as Scala had feared. He and Matthews and the band of SIB men had stormed the small office of the Polizei within the vast stadium. He had been greeted with ridicule; the red-faced police inspector's mouth had dropped open and he had snorted in disbelief as Scala issued the warning; but he had conceded that, if what Scala claimed was true the outcome could be horrendous. Yet it was too late to alter the arrangements, even if he could make someone believe him simply on the say-so of a mad Briton. All he could do was pass news of a hastily concocted plan around the hundreds of police officers dispersed throughout the stadium.

The motorcade made its way slowly along the avenue, enabling the thousands of cheering fans who lined the streets to see the President for the first time. The procession of gleaming black limousines which carried the Chancellor trickled its way through the vast car park and through the massive iron structures of the Olympic Gates towards the stadium.

Everywhere thousands of football enthusiasts, some black, mostly white, of all ages and sections of the society but most bedecked in the national colours of their teams, wove their way through the maze of entrances. The roar from within the stadium was already deafening.

Scala was in the corridors that ringed the tiers of seats in the ground. The bulk of a 9mm automatic revealed itself under his zipped-up brown leather jacket. The band of SIB men followed him and Matthews, running through the stone corridors and jostling the fans. Each corridor formed a natural wind tunnel and the chill blasts bit hard against Scala's flesh, causing his injured leg to ache. Yet he ran, eyes straining into the vast assembly as he looked for the men from Allenby.

The corridors reached a natural break in the ground, leading to the platform which housed the memorial to the heroes of the 1936 Olympics. From this position he could look out to the deserted open spaces of the Olympic arena of Hitler's time, whilst in the opposite direction he gazed directly into the heart of the new arena, out over the pitch where the game would be played and towards the gigantic electric scoreboard that dominated the far end of the stadium. To his right he could see the dark-suited officials who would greet the President and the Chancellor down on the pitch. Above them, in the stand reserved for the important and famous, an army of plain clothes security men formed a human cordon. Unseen by Scala, the music of a hidden orchestra were playing the rhythms and chants of Africa.

Scala took Matthews' field glasses and painstakingly began to scour each section of the crowd.

*   *   *

They stood side by side in harmony, one black, the other white, sending the crowd wild with delight. The ovation was immediate and genuine as both men waved to the thousands expressing their adulation.

It was difficult for Klaus Stein to watch, even on television. As he sat, visibly shaking with fury, in the comfort of Guy Rockwell's hotel room, Stein considered the scene to be one of blasphemy. It was an insult to the shrine of the man who had been the mastermind of the nation. Rockwell ignored the fondlings of the nubile girl curled at his feet and attempted to console his comrade. But Stein would have none of it. Both men watched the hands of the clock.

The red baseball caps had been intended to help identify the leaders of the men who would begin the action. But they also proved a homing device for Scala. As he surveyed the crowd through the glasses, with each second seeming like an hour, he suddenly stopped in his tracks.

'Got you, you bastards!' he grinned.

Matthews was startled, and looked out forlornly in the direction that he saw Scala was concentrating on. Scala pointed to a section of the crowd beneath the electric scoreboard, to the right of where the players would leave their dressing rooms and spill on to the pitch from the tunnel. Matthews saw the flash of red and identified the men in the vivid headgear. They were in two groups, one at either end of the crowd. Below them, were hundreds of youths who used their skinhead haircuts as a kind of uniform. They, he assumed, would be the ones who made up Klaus Stein's 'cannon fodder'.

A cordon of green-uniformed police officers were now taking up positions around the ground, each man facing into the crowd. Matthews and his men set off at a sprint along the stone corridor that would take them to the other end of the stadium. Scala followed.

Michael Kinze led his team from the dressing room and into the brightly lit tunnel. The sound of the players' boots reverberated as he walked slowly towards the daylight and stopped, allowing the world champions – the host nation – to milk the ecstatic applause of the crowd before he displayed his own team.

Kinze had stood on this spot on many occasions before, but today he was filled with a new pride for his team of foreigners whom he had nurtured. Lost in emotion, he paid little attention to the tall grey-haired figure with a moustache who wore an official steward's smock and carried a light green holdall. He spoke in a South African accent and stood with him now at the mouth of the tunnel.

Matthews and his men were almost engulfed as the crowd rose to cheer the South African side that emerged on to the pitch. But still the SIB men fought their way deep into the section of the crowd where their attention was concentrated.

There were still minutes to go before the first signal for action would come, at the closing of the playing of the South African national anthem, but already some of the skinheads' crowd were growing restless. In each section the men behind them in the red baseball caps barked commands aimed at controlling the mad dogs in the crowd, who were intent on causing mayhem. In some cases it was already too late. Minor scuffles, not visible to the police below, were breaking out. The skins earmarked the coloured supporters first. It began with a push or a slap; those who defended themselves stood no chance. They stumbled, waving their arms, some under the boots of the skins who sought them out. And still the men in caps barked commands which held the mass of the skinhead horde in check.

The music played, and the two men walked together, slowly, with dignity, along the line of the heroes of the German World Cup team. The President shook hands first and joked, followed by the Chancellor.

Scala was oblivious to the playing of the German national anthem. He could see the faces of the men he hunted now. They stood almost in line within the crowd – a thin red line, he thought. He saw the bulk of Hasker first, accompanied by Roberts and the boy Rogers. Further along, the angry face of Hibbs was lined up with Baker, whom Scala had liked, and Skinner as well as Turner. Only the face of Tavaner was missing from the members of the 'jury' who had passed sentence on Christopher Jarvis, he thought. There was no sign of the mammoth company sergeant major.

As one he saw the SIB men reach their targets and take up positions directly behind each of the figures in red caps. On a signal from Matthews, the men moved in on their individual targets. The section of the crowd that they commanded were now growing increasingly more violent.

Matthews was the first to move on Hasker. 'Don't move!' Matthews bellowed against the noise of the crowd. 'Armed military police. I am empowered to shoot and will do unless you obey . . .'

As each of the policemen followed suit, Scala saw the frozen, confused and angry looks that raged across the faces of the men from Allenby.

The anthem of South Africa was playing now. Both Chancellor and President stood on the terrace, motionless in honour; Kinze on the pitch by the side of his players. The last notes of the anthem finished and the human wave of violence was on the move. Smoking flares were hurled high above the heads of the crowds below, lobbed by the squadrons of skinheads who surged headlong into the peaceful terraces around them. Those supporters, black or white, who carried a South African flag were the first targets. The tide of brutality came kicking and punching and stabbing, tearing out seats to be used as weapons on the heads of those who dared oppose them as they came forward. As terrified sections of the vast crowd fled, a wave of green-uniformed police officers, carrying batons and shields, moved forward to clash head-on.

The 'disciples' who had followed Tavaner were held in check by the SIB men behind. For one brief moment of frenzy, Hasker attempted to break free of Matthews and disappear into the crowd. A discreet knee jerked upwards from Matthews, aimed at the man's abdomen, sent him crumpled to the ground. A look of satisfaction was spreading over Matthews' face.

Now would be the moment when Scala would expect the unthinkable to happen – in the midst of the chaos. He looked towards the stand to where the President stood, a sad and anguished expression gripping his face. His bodyguards were around him, tight. Now would be the time for it to happen – but where would the attack come from?

Scala felt powerless, like an observer on a battlefield, as he pushed against the fleeing, shrieking bodies. A woman fell screaming at his feet as she ran. The players milled on the pitch, uncertain what to do. Kinze was with them, staring around at the mayhem that was robbing him of his moment of glory.

The floodlights that illuminated the bowl of the stadium were on full, bringing an extra vividness to the erupting savagery. Suddenly the brightness of the coloured bag attracted Scala as he peered across the pitch. He saw Coetzee at the entrance to the tunnel, still carrying the bag, and suddenly he knew what he carried in the bag that he had watched him pack the previous evening on the hillside. Coetzee turned and scurried into the tunnel, towards the dressing room, unseen in the chaos. Scala yelled for Matthews.

The L96A1 sniper rifle was deadly accurate at a range of 600 yards; its 7.62mm cartridge would also stop a man at 1000 yards. The bolt action rifle was the favoured sniper weapon of the British Army, and it was also Volker Reisz's. He was at maximum distance to obtain an accurate shot, but he was confident. The vantage point was good, with a clear view deep into the bowl and the stand where the President and the Chancellor stood. Through the scope of the rifle he had followed the events that unfolded within the stadium, and smiled. Despite the uproar, he had a clear shot.

His finger squeezed tight on the trigger.

There was a clearing through the crowd from which Matthews and Scala hurdled the barrier fences on to the pitch, leaving the battles on the terraces behind them still raging. The two men ran for the mouth of the tunnel as the players of both sides began to flee the pitch to the dressing rooms where Scala figured Peter Coetzee was lying in wait.

A bead of sweat trickled from his temple as he waited alone. The sounds of the chaos outside were magnified as they boomed down the tunnel to the dressing room.

His heart was pounding; it was the same surge of excitement that had taken hold of him as he waited for countless attacks during his days in the bush war when he had killed so many of the ANC 'kaffirs'. Then they had called him a hero; and now he thought of himself as a patriot, still working for those who loved his country.

Gripping the handle of the Ingram, he pressed home a magazine. He waited behind the door that he knew would burst open as the 'kaffirs' fled the football pitch. They would not see him behind them as they rushed in, and he would have the element of surprise. He could take them before they knew what had hit them, and in the general noise and disturbance he would calmly make his escape.

The sound of studded boots running down the tunnel came nearer and nearer. He breathed deeply, controlling his senses. Still the sound of the boots approached. In his mind he could see them, the 'kaffirs' in their green strip running towards him.

The door to the dressing room thundered open. Matthews and

Scala came in low, rolling on the ground, sensing the danger from behind. Too late, Coetzee adjusted the level of his gaze and looked down, raising the Ingram. As one, the two men who rolled on the floor fired their pistols: Scala's shot struck home in the gut, whilst Matthews' killing shot took Coetzee in the throat. The South African slid slowly against the wall and folded on the floor, his eyes ablaze with anger and surprise. A final gasp of breath gurgled in his throat as he collapsed in death.

The SIB men were already bundling the soldiers from Allenby off the terraces and away from the fighting when Scala and Matthews emerged from the tunnel. Michael Kinze flashed the unknown pair who had saved his team from extinction a knowing look of gratitude as he stood alone at the edge of the pitch, watching the horror of the riot that was being played out on the terraces.

Scala, adrenalin pumping through his veins, looked up to see the President being shepherded out of the ground by his security men, and breathed a sigh of relief. He and Matthews shot a glance of mutual admiration to each other, and allowed a smile of self-congratulation to show itself.

It was a difficult shot at this range; but satisfying. Volker Reisz had trained well, and had been afforded ample opportunities to practise his skills as a sniper in the trenches of Croatia. His view had been hindered by the man who stood in front of the target, but now his finger tightened once again.

The report of the shot went unheard in the noise of the battle within the stadium. The impact lifted Michael Kinze from his feet, hitting him in the temple and shattering the right side of his skull as the bullet exited, killing him before his body had landed spread-eagled on the ground.

Scala saw the man's death as if in slow motion as he stood at the entrance to the tunnel. He stared in fascination at the gory mess that had once been Michael Kinze's head, and cursed himself for his short-sightedness. He saw it now. He had believed that the target had been the President, when all the time it had been the man whom they had branded a 'traitor' to his country.

Senses regained, Scala estimated the direction and angle of the shot. He had the place, and without thinking he ran, alone, to the rear of the now empty terrace where the President and the Chancellor had been standing, into the long, dark corridors that would take him to the open end of the stadium that looked over the old Olympic arena. On he ran, through the corridor, certain of where the shot had come from. He had been there, and gazed out over the site himself: it was the perfect spot.

The corridors were devoid of people now as the police gradually took control of the riot. The sound of his running feet echoed until he entered the open area of the stadium, from where he could see directly into the belltower that he had climbed with Tavaner. He stood for a moment by the roll of honour, beneath the names of the heroes of 1936, then leaped the railings that provided protection from the fifteen-foot drop below and landed like a cat. A deep breath, and then he ran across the empty stadium to the terrace where Hitler and the hierarchy of the Nazi Party had once stood. His leg hurt like hell, but still he ran forward to gain the protection of the empty buildings ahead. He zigzagged to make himself a harder target should the sniper be already focusing on him.

Breathlessly he reached the empty terraces on the far side. He saw the thin rope that led from the top of the tower to the ground, and the black shape of the tall figure that now stood at the top of the tower, intending to escape by abseiling down the wall rather than risking the lift. Scala recognised the blond hair of Reisz. Waiting in the shadow of the empty terrace, hidden from view, he watched as the black-clad figure reached the ground, leaving the rifle behind in the belltower. Scala raised his 9mm pistol, clutching it in his right hand and steadying it with the other. He steadied his feet in firing position.

'Halt!' he yelled. 'Stop or I fire. No more warnings, you bastard. Give yourself up.'

Reisz stopped in his tracks and turned slowly to meet his attacker, eyes burning with anger. A grin came to the square jaw as he recognised that the man pointing the gun was Scala.

'I am unarmed, Sergeant Scala, so I do not think you will fire, I do not think you will kill me. I believe you are a man of ethics,' Reisz taunted.

Scala's hands were still steady. He saw the image of Janine in his mind's eye – the broken discarded body that had once been beautiful, the dead eyes looking at him accusingly.

'You killed the girl, you bastard! You killed her like an animal!' he heard himself screaming. He had promised revenge.

Reisz slowly walked towards Scala, down the stone steps that formed the corridor in the terrace. 'Ah, the girl. I presume you mean the bitch with the camera. She was enjoyable, Sergeant

Scala. She pleaded and offered . . . I was severely tempted. She was very nice, very soft, very white . . . she squealed like a pig, Sergeant Scala, did you know?' Reisz was openly laughing now as he continued to walk towards Scala. 'Come, come, Sergeant Scala or whoever you are, did I not say that we were men alike?'

Still the images flashed in front of Scala – first the girl, then Michael Kinze. 'No closer, I said!' he shouted. 'I'll have no qualms about blowing your fucking head off . . . all legal like!'

'But Sergeant Scala, we are both warriors – warriors for a cause. We should not fight each other.'

Scala sighed. 'Well, I've got news for you. My cause is somewhat different to any shit thing that you'll ever be involved with – so all I say to you is "Fuck you!"'

The single shot hit Reisz squarely in the forehead and the back of his head erupted as the bullet exited. He fell on the concrete steps. Scala stood over the body, staring at the blond hair that was now saturated with crimson. In true SAS fashion he fired one more shot directly into the head, then casually walked away from the corpse.

He stood alone beneath the terrace where Adolf Hitler had once addressed his own disciples. Scala thought it fitting that one of his new generation of disciples should meet his end in this place. The sun was setting now, bringing a fluorescent glow to the early evening sky and lengthening the shadows of the old stadium. After the turmoil of the riot Scala wanted to walk alone in the shadows of the stadium, his mind filled with thoughts of Lynn, and of Janine and Jarvis as well as the coloured soldier he had never known called John Adebeyo. He would like to tell them all that justice was being meted out to those responsible for bringing terror to their lives. That had been his cause.

The sixth sense reactivated. He was not alone in the shadows that were cast over the stadium. He could not see another presence, but his senses told him of it. The charge came from the darkness beneath the stone terraces. The bear-shaped bulk of Tavaner ran at him; for a moment Scala thought he saw a flash, a glint of metal, and he felt a burning, searing pain deep within him. For a moment the two men met eye to eye, Scala flailing to reach the pistol holstered at his waist but caught in the spasm of pain that rocked his body. Then Tavaner was gone, vanished like a spirit in the shadows of the stadium.

Scala was on his knees now, feeling the warm, sticky dark blood that came from a lung wound. Head whirling, he collapsed, lying staring at the darkening sky as images from the past flooded his brain: the face of Angie standing at the door barring him from her life, and the images of Sean and Gemma at play. He heard himself whispering their names as he sank into oblivion.

EPILOGUE

The fax machine in Matherson's office chattered. Impatiently he thought the bloody men at the Ministry had taken their own sweet time about replying. He read the words on the paper in disbelief.

URGENT

ATTENTION: COL. DAVID MATHERSON.

FROM: SIR HARVEY MANTLE; M.O.D. LIAISON COMMITTEE/COM-MANDER JACOBSON.

SUBJECT: REFERENCE, EARLIER COMMUNIQUÉ RE POSSIBLE EXTREMIST ACTIVITIES BY ELEMENTS OF ROYAL KENT RANGERS. FOLLOWING CONSIDERATION, IT IS DECIDED THAT NO FUR-THER INVESTIGATIONS BE UNDERTAKEN IN THIS MATTER DUE TO PECULIAR AND UNCERTAIN CIRCUMSTANCES WHICH PREVAIL; PUBLICITY OF SUCH ALLEGATIONS FELT TO BE PREJUDICIAL TO GOOD NAME OF THE REGIMENT AND BRITISH STANDING WITH EUROPEAN PARTNERS.

COMPANY SERGEANT MAJOR MICHAEL TAVANER NOW OFFI-CIALLY LISTED AWOL.

PUBLICITY BLACKOUT ALREADY IN FORCE.

Matherson sank back behind his desk, head in hands.

Lynn Anders emerged from the darkness of the Underground station at Tower Hill and blinked in the spring sunshine. It was only a fifteen-minute stroll to the newspaper offices of Paula Ryan from where she stood, still clutching the briefcase that Jim Scala had given her in Berlin.

Paula Ryan had been keen to speak to Lynn Anders; her army husband had told her of rumblings within the ranks, and the mention of Peter Macabe had clinched her interest. The memory of the man justified her interest in what this girl had to say.

*   *   *

It had been a victory, and Klaus Stein was celebrating in style. Guy Rockwell had seen to that. At Rockwell's beloved ranch hideaway in the heart of the Californian mountains the two men toasted the future and the beginning of what Rockwell had hailed as a 'crusade for mankind'. There had been no one to point accusing fingers at the work of Klaus Stein or his associates. He had been careful to show no links between himself and the extreme elements of the British forces who had attempted to carry out mob rule. He sipped the deep red local wine and for a moment showed remorse at the loss of the comrade Reisz and his accomplice, who had been accused of assassination attempts at the Olympic stadium on the instructions of South Africa's hard-line nationalist groups.

They were true allies now. Guy Rockwell and Klaus Stein knew that there was much to be done.

She said nothing, but her smile warmed him. There were looks of uncertainty mixed with affection as she leaned forward and kissed him gently on the forehead, her red hair falling over his face.

He looked drawn and pale from loss of blood, but Jim Scala had been told he was on the mend. It had been a close call – the knife intended for his heart had glanced off a rib and punctured a lung. If it had not been for his quick discovery by the sergeant from the Special Investigation Branch, Jim Scala knew he would have been mere memory today. He sat propped on the pillows of his hospital bed and studied Lynn Anders' face. She looked fresh and inviting.

They exchanged the small talk that takes place between two distant lovers before the girl eventually plucked up courage to ask. 'Was it worth it? You nearly got yourself killed, and there was Janine and all the others. Yet the Army says it won't do anything.'

Scala shrugged. 'Who knows? It's all part of the job for me.'

A gentle smile sprang to her lips as she reached into her shopping bag and pulled out a newspaper which she held up for Scala to read. An instant beam came to his drawn cheeks as he perused the 'splash' story on the front page, led by the headline: 'BRIT TROOPS IN NAZI OUTRAGE; LINKED TO RACIST DEATHS!' The exclusive story and photographs went under the by-lines of Peter Macabe and Janine Letterman. The photographs which depicted serving soldiers sharing a platform with known neo-Nazis at secret hideaways were spread over the next two pages, while an eye-witness account from a serving female soldier told how she had witnessed the brutal 'execution' of a young coloured soldier at a British camp in Germany.

Scala chuckled. His heart leaped as he considered what the men in suits who ran the Army would be saying today. 'It looks like Macabe got his story after all!' he grinned.